Sudden Impulse

LIBBY R. KLEIN

Printed in the United States of America

ISBN-13: 978-1505205541
ISBN-10: 1505205549

DEDICATION

In Memory Of Jonathan Kessner

TABLE OF CONTENTS

ACKNOWLEDGMENTS

With the publication of this debut novel, I would like to thank the special people in my life who helped me journey into the world of writing.

My dear friend Barbara Rosen, who helped me work through the editing. I am indebted to her talent and intelligence.

To my editors, Elaine Deering and Rich Gold; your talent and inspiration will always be remembered.

Thanks to my valued friends Rose and Saul Minc, who inspired me.

My two grandsons, Joshua and Jeremy Klein, who both helped overcome my computer difficulties.

Adam Kotkin, my computer genius, was always at my side when I needed him.

My husband Seymour, never refused to listen to my rewrites. He deserves an award after years of putting up with me as I wrote this novel.

Thanks to my loving family for their encouragement: My children, Cheryl and Steve, Risa, Neil and Susanne.

My wonderful grandchildren, Adam, Andrea, Michael, Rachel, Richard, Eve, Robert, Andrea, Jonathan, Dariana, Jeremy, and Joshua.

Our nine great-grandchildren, who bring special joy: Ashley, Jake, Alexis, Justin, Avital, Bar, Brooke, Amanda, Shia. We are so blessed!

To my dear niece and nephew, Helene and Marvin Gurgold. Thank you for taking the time to help me with your suggestions.

To Jay Blotcher, a creative thinker and good friend.

This story could never have been written without Eve Bromberg, my creative writing teacher, who inspired me to write this manuscript.

To Stephane Mazade and Jeffrey Smith, thanks for your help.

"Loving anyone, anywhere, at any time, leaves you infinitely vulnerable at every single moment."

Keith Ablow

CHAPTER 1

Managing an active New York City real estate firm, "Field Realty," was not an easy task. In a city full of rude taxi drivers, screaming sirens, flashing lights, conniving agents, random shootings, and everyone looking to get rich quick along with meeting their one true love, Rose Field wondered how she had managed to become a successful real estate broker.

Before she opened her own firm, Rose dreamed about working for a larger company. Her difficulty in finding a new job left her feeling insecure. She thought to herself, "Why wouldn't anyone employ me? Was I fat and ugly?" No, she knew that wasn't true. Her figure is great for a tall 40-year-old, and her short, dark-brown hair frames her face well. She can surely compete with the younger agents in this business. Rose was eventually hired by Broad Realty, a large firm in New York City.

For several years Rose worked hard to make a living. As a struggling agent she found most of her bosses quite heartless. But she was determined to study for the Broker Real Estate licensing exam and make it on her own. Rose opened her own office on March 12th, 1985 and decided to use her family name, "Field." She became an expert, well respected by many of her peers. The astute sales agents she engaged helped her run a respectable business.

Two years passed quickly. The real estate market was booming. Ads for new employees brought excitement to the office. The previous year's hiring session was special because Rose met one of her best agents. She never dreamed a delightful, extraordinary sales person like Alana Stone would join her staff. Alana never missed a day of work from the day she was hired. Her slim figure and long dark hair made heads turn and her blue eyes twinkled when she spoke.

It was unusual for Alana not to show up at the office without a word. Rose and the members of her staff worried even more when Alana didn't answer her phone. Rose said, "In the year Alana has been here, she always called to connect with me in an emergency. Something must be wrong!" Tony, one of the sales agents, added, "It doesn't sound good to me. I would call the cops."

Rose continued, "Let's not be hasty." She called both Alana's home and cell phone again, but there was still no answer. Her anxiety mounted. "I'm calling the police!" She dialed the local police precinct, and was transferred to the detective division. Rose waited until someone answered.

"Detective Pezello here"

"I'm Rose Field, a realtor with Field Realty. One of my agents didn't show up today. No one has heard from her in more than 24 hours and we're concerned. She always phones when she cannot make it. I've been trying both her home and cell numbers, but no answer and no return of my messages."

The detective said, "Could you give me the missing person's name, address, and any immediate relatives you may know."

"Of course. Her name is Alana Stone, 5355 Second Ave., Apartment 4. She has an elderly mother who lives in New Jersey. Please call me as soon as you have any information. My cell phone number is 212-555-2121. It doesn't matter how late it is. I'm very worried." Pezello said, "We'll look into it and get back to you."

He hung up the phone and called his partner, Detective Mike Green. "Hey Mike, Pezello here. We have a missing person's report. Are you available? I'll fill you in on the details later."

"Sure, he replied."

"Good, meet me in an hour at 5355 Second Ave., Apartment 4.

The detectives arrived at the building and walked up to the second floor. Green rang the bell and knocked at the door. When there was no response, Pezello said, "Let's check to see if any of the neighbors have seen her." Pezello started toward another apartment. Just as Green was about to follow, he stopped and sniffed, "Wait! What's that smell?"

Pezello sniffed and shook his head, "I don't smell anything."

2

Green motioned him to return to Alana's apartment door and told his partner, "It's faint, but it's coming from inside."

Pezello stepped close to the door, sniffed and then looked up.

"Shit! Are you thinking the same thing I am?"

Green nodded and said, "The hell with the neighbors. We'd better get the super to let us in."

*

It was about 5 p.m. as Detectives Pezello and Green stood in the apartment in front of a shattered glass door leading out to a balcony. Alana was lying on the apartment floor, groceries scattered, hair matted with blood. The crimson bloody liquid surrounded her lifeless body.

Detective Pezello pointed to the sliding door and Officers Brown and Stern nodded. Officer Stern said, "Looks like the killer entered through this doorway, and smashed the glass when he couldn't open the slider. He grabbed his victim from behind, and stabbed her before she could yell for help!"

As members of the CSI unit arrived, Green and Pezello followed the officers into the crime scene. The detectives approached the body and watched as they secured the scene. They put on plastic gloves before touching anything that could damage the evidence. Stern said, "The murderer must have been on drugs; she was cut so many times. The Medical Examiner and Forensics will be here soon; they'll take care of details."

Green called for an ambulance as the medical examiner walked in and examined the body. After checking her pressure point, he turned and said, "Looks like she's been dead for at least 16 hours. That would make the time of death sometime after one in the morning."

Green absorbed the information and turned to Pezello.

"We need more information on her whereabouts after she left work yesterday. Maybe she was at a club last night and someone followed her home."

Pezello nodded.

"When we speak to the broker, we'll get the details. First we ought to see if we can find a phone number for the victim's mother. The broker said she lives in New Jersey."

The detectives continued the investigation. "It doesn't look like a robbery; nothing is moved. There's her handbag, untouched." Pezello, with latex gloves on, opened her purse, looked inside, and found her wallet.

"Hey, Mike, money untouched in her wallet, bills folded like they should be. I see a real estate card as well. She has a telephone book... Here's her mother's phone number." He made the call to Alana's mother. "I hate giving the family bad news, but someone has to bury the victim."

After the call, Pezello turned to Green and said, "There'll be a funeral service as soon as the body is released."

As Detective Green put the handbag down on a table, he looked up at the wall next to the victim and saw a splattering of blood spots. He brought it to the attention of the CSI. Officer Stern pulled a chip of paint off the wall, and put it in a plastic evidence bag, placing the real estate card in a separate bag as well.

The detectives were ready to leave the crime scene. Green said, "Give us a call when you have the report so we can continue our investigation." They waved goodbye and left the apartment.

Pezello suggested, "Mike, could you call the broker and give her the bad news."

"Sure. Got the number?"

Pezello handed his partner a slip of paper.

Green reached for his cell phone. He thought these are the worst calls to make.

*

Rose was at her desk by 8:30 a.m. She couldn't sleep after receiving the call about Alana's murder. The killer must be apprehended, she thought. I was reading about a serial killer leaving his deadly mark on victims. How can I connect what I read to Alana's death? I must be losing my mind. The call from Detective Green ruined my day, and I'm certain the news will wreck everyone's day in the office. It's impossible to work or concentrate, so why not remember the events that took place when Alana met the other agents? They all liked her, which made me happy, but some were a bit envious as well.

Rose thought, Alana learned fast and after one month won the office award for best agent. I knew when I heard her voice on the phone she would excel in phone canvassing. Again, her success did not make some of the other salespeople happy. Before I met Alana, I hired Tony Vincenzo. His jealousy was obvious when he saw how competent Alana was. "Ms. F.," he demanded, "why should Alana get the best times for calling new clients? I deserve that time of the day!" Alana paid no attention to Tony's words. She was happy to meet the other agents in the office, especially Claire, whom she connected with immediately. Soon they became somewhat unlikely good friends. Claire was a little rough around the edges, Rose recalled, but she helped show Alana the ropes, and she and Alana often went to lunch and shopping trips together. Alana became her fashion advisor.

Rose recalled that Tony was beginning to annoy her from the first day she hired him. His references were good, he had a great track record for renting apartments, but he became a nuisance. Arriving late the first day of work was his first mistake.

"Tony, I don't like tardiness. It's a poor beginning."

"Sorry Ms. Field, I overslept."

Rose remembered… I had a feeling I never should have hired him last year. He seemed arrogant and stuck on himself, and I saw the way he flirted with me and every other female in the office. Her gut told her he's a little too slick to be trusted. I thought maybe I was being too judgmental and should give him a chance. A few months later I hired Alana and never had a bad experience. How could I compare her to Tony? There never was a comparison. Now she's gone, and Tony is here, a thorn in my side. Nobody said life was fair.

Reminiscing, she had said, "Okay, Tony, please take the desk next to the window. When you're settled, come into my office, and I'll review the rules of this agency."

CHAPTER 2

Rose phoned the police department and inquired about Alana's murder.

"I'm Rose Field calling about the Stone case. Do you have any news for us?"

"Wish I did," Detective Green answered. "It takes time. Evidence was collected, but we won't know the results for a while. When I know more I'll call you. We want to resolve this case as fast as possible. Sorry I can't help you further."

"I understand, but please don't forget about us. We're all anxious about this case too. I'll be waiting for your call, Detective."

Rose hung up the phone as she thought, I'll feel better knowing the police are trying to solve Alana's murder. I hope they succeed. In her reverie Rose did not hear Tony walk into her office.

"Hello Ms. F., am I disturbing you?"

"No, no," Rose said. "I was just on the phone with the police."

"Is something happening with Alana's case?"

"We all need patience. Meanwhile, we have some new office rules you should know." She handed Tony a binder. "Take this paperwork. It will explain our latest office policies and splits in commissions."

"Oh," Rose continued, "I believe Alana's funeral will be delayed until her body is released. I'll put a notice on the bulletin board and you may tell the agents about the delay. The funeral will take place at The Shaker Funeral Parlor.

"Fine, I don't mind," Tony replied.

"Thank you, good luck on any deals in progress. Make me proud!"

"I guarantee you'll be proud of me sooner than you think." Tony said in a confident voice.

"A successful agent can make a fabulous salary," Rose continued.

"Not when my ex-wife is on my back continuously. She's costing me a fortune."

"Tony, I'm really sorry to hear about your marital problems. I hope those problems won't affect your work."

"Just watch me move and shake in this business. The sky's the limit." Tony was turning red in the face as he continued his dialogue with Rose.

"Tony, I'd really like to see you close many deals in this office. Right now I must take care of some chores, so goodbye for today. I'll see you in the morning."

Tony left the office impressed with Rose Field. I know I'm a great salesman, he thought. Now I have to prove it to her. Rose is an attractive woman. I wouldn't mind getting her in the sack. Let's see how far I could go! He walked back to his desk with many new ideas cluttering his mind.

Rose couldn't forget the entire Alana Stone experience. She reflected... Alana's life and death would always be remembered by those who knew her. Will I ever be able to find someone with such class, dedication, and a great work ethic to replace her? Who knows?

The realtor stopped working and thought about the time she discovered Alana. If I hadn't placed an ad in the New York Times, I never would have met her. Many agents answered my ad.

Rose remembered exactly how it all happened. Yes, she thought, I had just returned to my desk and began reviewing the sales job applications. Alana Stone's paperwork was first. After reading her resumé, I was quite impressed with her background. She had been an office manager and also rented apartments. Rose remembered her calling about the job.

"Thanks for calling," Alana had responded. "I hope the position is still open."

Rose thought her voice sounded articulate and soothing on the phone. She promised herself, I must meet her!

They scheduled an interview for Monday morning at 11:00 a.m.

On Monday morning, Alana walked into Rose's office promptly at 11:00. She was a sight to behold in her stunning outfit and long brown hair cascading down her shoulders. She was wearing a beige and white striped suit, white blouse, beige pumps, and was carrying a beige and white leather handbag. Everyone turned their heads to watch her.

Rose recalled saying, "Nice to meet you. Please sit down and make yourself comfortable."

"Thank you," Alana answered.

Rose smiled, thinking she seemed so sweet. She asked, "Do you think you can be a real estate tycoon?"

"I don't know about real estate tycoon, but I've always worked hard and will continue the same work ethic. I've always wanted to learn how to close deals like a whiz. If you could help me realize my dream, it would make me happy. I promise you won't be sorry you hired me."

Rose sighed as she relived the interview.

"I noticed on your resumé that you were an office manager and rented apartments for the agency."

"Yes, I worked for the company two years, but after awhile I wasn't happy because I wanted to learn more than they were willing to teach."

Instinctively Rose knew she had to hire Alana. She was quick in her responses and very bright.

"Okay, Alana, I think you have great potential. You can start working immediately if you wish."

"Thank you, Ms. Field. I'll be happy to start now, but where do I sit?"

Rose accompanied her to a desk next to Claire's. "This will be fine. After you settle yourself, please come back to my office and we'll have a meeting." She smiled and returned to her desk.

Alana settled in and finally returned to Rose's office, where they discussed office procedure and closing real estate deals.

Rose turned to Alana and said, "I'll teach you everything I know about this business." She handed the young woman a handful of paperwork and suggested she read through the rules.

"Enough talk for today. Why don't you go home and relax? I'll see you tomorrow morning and introduce you to the other agents."

As Alana walked out of the office, Rose thought, she seemed so eager and paid strict attention as I read the simple rules of the office.

Rose's personality, good looks, and ability to close deals were well known in the real estate community since the 90s. Any time she met with new clients or salespeople, they were impressed with her real estate knowledge and patience. She was the peacemaker in the office, making certain there was always a positive attitude among the staff. If any problems surfaced, Rose would fix them.

She never disappointed anyone. Now that Alana was part of the staff, Rose was determined to make them like her as much as she did. Little did she realize she wouldn't succeed with some of her sales agents.

A few weeks after Rose hired Alana, her mind filled with thoughts of Tony. How much do I know about him? Tony is the type who will make trouble in my office. He's not closing enough deals. I may have to fire him.

Rose arrived at the office at 9:00 a.m. and couldn't believe her eyes. For once, Tony was already at his desk making phone calls to potential customers. Rose thought it was good to see an improvement in his work

He answered, "The early bird gets the worm, Ms F."

He looks good today, she thought, quite attractive. His brown hair was combed back neatly and he wore a short-sleeved print shirt, perfect for the warm weather. His eyebrows were neatly groomed, and his nails were manicured. In this occupation it's important to look professional, Rose thought. No shaggy hair or rumpled shirts.

As the weeks progressed, the crisp autumn weather took hold. Rose watched Tony's production for a month. He wasn't closing enough deals to warrant him a job at Field Realty. At one point her attorney composed a letter firing him, but Rose never gave the letter to Tony since he was making an effort to turn things around.

His work habits improved significantly. The ads he placed in the *New York Times* brought many buyers to the office. Suddenly Tony began closing ten deals a week. He won the award for best agent of the month, but he was never satisfied. His hyperactivity caused him to work harder and close more deals. It worked well for Field Realty, but Rose still had bad feelings about him and a negative premonition.

Claire Smith, a full-time sales agent with Field Realty, loved to work at home, but came to the office regularly to update her listings and to add new properties to her records. She was 30 years old, had a good figure, but little taste in fashion or color coordination.

One day Claire came to the office in a hot pink stretch pants outfit. Alana saw her walk in and knew immediately that comments would be passed. She tried to warn Claire, but she was already walking through the office without a clue. The color looked fine, but every curve showed clearly. Tony and Harry, the other broker, made snide comments and whistled when Claire passed Tony's desk.

Rose thought it was cruel to humiliate Claire. "Hey guys, knock it off. Give the lady a break," she said. "You two are getting to be like two peas in a pod."

She knew Harry Thompson was a busy real estate broker. He did well building up his business. Now he leases the space to Field Realty while maintaining a separate office on the floor for himself. Where did he get the time to be so friendly with Tony? I have no right to be suspicious of their developing relationship, she thought, as long as Tony is loyal to Field Realty. It's hard to imagine a nice cordial guy like him would do anything to hurt my business. Rose briefly wondered if Tony and Harry could be gay. That would explain their disrespectful attitude toward women. Tony's flirtations were just a cover-up, Rose thought. For that matter, his marriage was probably a sham. That's why his ex-wife is giving him such a hard time.

One morning Rose arrived at the office and found Claire sitting at her desk, crying. "Claire, what's wrong?"

"Ms. Field, Tony and Harry keep insulting me. I can't stand it anymore. If they don't apologize, I'm quitting! I'm also thinking about reporting them to the authorities for sexual harassment if they don't stop."

"Please, Claire. They're jerks and don't know what they're talking about." She promised, "I'll talk to both of them on your behalf." Rose did not want to think about the possibility of a lawsuit being filed against the agency.

Ms. Field, I have to tell you something important," Claire said as she dried her eyes. "Tony and Harry are not your friends. I overheard them talking to each other about you."

"Claire, are you trying to get back at them for making your life miserable?"

"No, it's the honest to goodness truth. I think Tony must be doing private deals with Harry."

"That's very bad news, since Tony is supposed to be working for me. Please don't say a word to anyone. I have to speak to them. We'll see whether it's true."

"Don't say I didn't warn you! I've been overhearing all kinds of collaboration between the two of them." Claire continued, "I happened to pass Harry's office the other day and heard Tony's voice. I stopped for a few seconds and overheard both of them talk about a closing date coming up. I couldn't hear which deal they were talking about, but I heard Tony laugh about screwing around with the gross figures. That should make your ears perk up." Claire doodled on a pad, fidgety as she told her story.

Rose tried to be reasonable and said, "Look, they could be talking about a deal out of our office. It doesn't mean Tony is betraying me." She thought... who knows? maybe Claire is trying to get revenge. I always thought of her as a little gossip. This accusation puts me in a bad position. Tony is turning into one of my best agents, and Harry is my landlord. She thought again about the phrases Claire had repeated, "screwing around" and "gross figures," and wondered if they were really talking about an encounter in a gay bar.

Rose remembered all the negative events Tony had instigated. With Alana gone, they seemed so insignificant. What was important? Live and let others live in peace. What could we have done? All my agents helped create the dynamics in my office. Most of the time, it was Tony picking on Claire. It must have given him a feeling of power to humiliate his fellow worker. I despised him for doing it.

There were always uncomfortable issues to deal with in this business. I loathe accusing a salesperson of unethical tactics, especially when there is absolutely no proof of Claire's charges.

Tony and Harry returned to the office, and Rose promptly took the opportunity to confront them.

"Hi," she said nervously. "May we talk in your office, Harry?"

"Sure. Is something on your mind, Rose?" he calmly replied. "You look upset."

Tony smugly said, "Ms. F., you look like you have the problems of the world on your shoulders."

"Look, don't act so innocent. You and Harry are creating trouble in my office."

"What are you talking about?" Tony responded.

Harry didn't answer. He sat in his chair with a long cigar hanging from his lips.

I always hated the smell of his horrible cigars, Rose thought. She looked at both men and braced herself for what she must say. "Are you both executing real estate deals without Field Realty?"

Harry sat in his chair, puffing on the cigar dangling from his lips, circles of smoke filling his office, not saying a word.

"Who started these lies, Claire? I knew she was a lousy bitch when I first laid eyes on her." Tony raised his voice to a screechy pitch and yelled, "I can't stand women like her. She came on to me a few months ago, and I'm ashamed to tell you I slept with her."

Rose couldn't believe his words. She coughed from the smoke in the office and ran her hands through her hair. The news that Tony and Claire had been lovers caught her off guard. I don't know whom to believe, she thought. Maybe they're both lying to me. After a moment Rose turned to Tony and said, "She may be trying to get revenge, but Claire wouldn't accuse you of unethical business behavior if it weren't true, would she?"

Tony turned to Harry and asked, "Didn't Claire come on to me? You were in the office at the time the affair began, right? When I ended it she was devastated. Now she wants to get revenge." He turned to Rose and said, "That's why she's telling you lies about us."

Harry took the cigar out of his mouth and answered, "Yes, Rose, I heard everything. Tony and Claire were a hot item for a while. I saw the beginning and end of the romance."

Rose thought, the old story, everyone knew but me. I wonder how I missed all the action in my office.

"Tony, I can understand Claire's accusation. Maybe you broke her heart and that was her way of getting revenge. You better not lie to me!"

"Ms. F., I've been working for you for a year. I thought by this time you could trust me. Would I do anything behind your back? Of course not! I respect you too much, and so does Harry. Right, Harry?"

Tony turned to Harry and winked.

While Rose tried to concentrate on Claire's accusation, her mind became cluttered with negative thoughts. Why must I have aggravation now? So much on my mind, chores to complete and my instinct tells me Tony and Harry could be lying. It's all too much!

A dull headache caused pain and some dizziness. Rose grabbed the edge of Harry's desk for support.

"Rose, come sit down and relax, you'll feel better," Harry suggested, as he poured her a glass of water from the pitcher on his desk.

Tony moved closer and said, "Claire is the one to watch out for, not us. We respect and admire you as a business woman."

Rose almost believed them, as she took a sip of the water. She said, "Tony, I want to trust you. Since you've worked for this firm we've improved financially. Thanks for the water. I'm feeling better now. I hope the focus of your energy continues to help our firm."

"Ms. F.," Tony smiled, "we want to be your allies. Are we friends again?"

"Yes," Rose responded.

Harry added, "I never want to spoil our professional relationship, Rose. I was happy the day you rented space in my office. It's a pleasure to have you and your staff here."

The meeting ended, and they all left the office for lunch. Rose walked back to her desk thinking about the conversation she just had with both men.

What am I to think? Who do I believe? The realtor scratched her head and took a deep breath. Will I ever survive this business?

Claire was getting ready to leave for an appointment with a client.

When she saw Rose walking toward her desk, she confronted her.

"Ms. Field, did Tony confess?"

Rose replied, "Look Claire, there's no proof of your complaint, so let's just cool it."

"So you want evidence?" she answered. "I'll find proof, then you'll finally see they're conning you. Tony and Harry are the biggest liars in the world. I overheard what they said to you. You can't believe they're your friends."

Rose raised her voice in anger. "How dare you eavesdrop on my conference with other agents? You're becoming a sneak, Claire! Watch your step or you'll get in trouble."

"I'm not a sneak. I couldn't help overhearing all your voices. I must leave now for an appointment or I'll be late."

"Where are you going?"

"I'm showing a loft down in the SoHo area."

"How did you get the listing?"

"I put an ad in *The Village Voice* over the weekend and received eight replies. Not bad, right?"

Rose calmed down and smiled. "Claire, please write down the address and your client's name. I need a record in the office for security reasons. I hope you have a flashlight in your case. I always worry about showing property late in the day."

"Ms. Field, I never worry about meeting new clients any time of the day. Please don't worry about me. Wish me luck; maybe I'll put a deal together."

"Good luck, Claire. You look great in your outfit. Please be careful and alert at your showing."

"Thanks," Claire replied. "I just bought this suit. I appreciate the compliment."

Claire walked out of the office at 3:30 p.m. The days were getting shorter since the fall season took hold.

Thinking back, Rose had an uneasy feeling in her stomach. I should have stopped her from showing property so late in the day. No, she was so determined that I couldn't have anyway. Maybe I was too over-anxious and she needed to show me that a deal was possible.

After what had happened to Alana, Rose couldn't help worrying about Claire. The best medicine for my nerves is to work hard on office chores. Maybe she'll call and check in. Enough fretting – there's too much to accomplish.

Thank goodness Alana's body was released, she thought, and we were all able to pay our respects. Funerals are not my favorite way of spending my time, but Alana's internment was special. I'll always remember her. Meeting her mother gave me the opportunity to express my condolences. But now that the funeral is over, Rose thought, I must get back to business.

Rose spent the next several minutes calling potential clients, and was about to give up when one woman yelled at her. Rose screamed back, "Why am I wasting my time? Haven't you seen "Field Realty" ads in the *New York Times*?"

"Well" --- Rose noticed a change in the tone of her voice. "Maybe I did see your ads listed. Sorry I shouted at you. So many brokers call and annoy me. You sound like someone I'd like to deal with."

Rose was relieved and grateful for her change of heart. She gave Mrs. Cohen her number, as the other phone rang. "Have to say goodbye. Hope to hear from you soon."

Rose picked up the phone, hoping it was Claire.

"Field Realty, may I help you?"

"It's Claire. I need some information."

Her confident calm voice relieved Rose's mind completely.

"Sure, I'll be happy to help you. What's the problem?"

"I think I wrote the wrong listing price on the property I'm showing. Could you check the computer and give me the exact gross price?"

"What's the address?"

"251 West Broadway, New York City."

"Hang on while I check the computer. By the way, I'm so happy you called. I was worried about you."

"Thanks for your concern, but I'm fine. Please, my client is waiting for the numbers."

Rose checked the computer and smiled when she saw a listing price of $2,000,000. She returned to the phone and quoted the figure to

Claire.

"I wrote the wrong price on my listing, Claire noted. My figures have the loft listed at $2,100,000!"

"Remember," Rose said, "you must include the commission in the price. Does your client seem interested?"

"Yes, the Goldmans are artists. They say the openness of the loft suits them."

"Don't get too excited; stay cool. Make certain you give him a listing form with all the information about the building. See how he responds to the price, taxes and financing. You can tell him we deal with banks that help us close our deals fast."

"Okay, wish me luck; I'm ecstatic right now." Rose suggested, "Call me after your appointment and let me know how things progressed."

"Fine, I'll talk to you later." Claire gathered her notes and got ready to return to the Goldmans.

With her worries put to rest, Rose sat back in her chair, much more satisfied after Claire called about the potential deal.

CHAPTER 3

Claire thought of the potential transaction. If this comes through, she could have the freedom she always craved. Memories of neediness always plagued her.

Her mom had said, "You're always spending too much money. We can't afford to buy all the clothing you want. Go to work and earn money! When I was your age I gave my salary to my parents."

She criticized, "Don't gain weight! If you do, you'll have to spend more money on new clothing."

It was difficult growing up in a home like that, Claire recalled. Her mother was always comparing her to her younger sister Joy, who was taller, thinner, and prettier. Claire made raising her esteem and self-confidence her priority. Adding those qualities would come later when she entered the field of real estate. Lynn, a realtor and good friend, had said that she would excel in sales. She was good for Claire's ego, as she remembered Lynn once said, "Claire, you have the personality and looks that will take you far in the real estate field."

Claire answered, "Lynn, it's your faith in my ability that will take me over the top. I hope you won't be disappointed."

"I've never been wrong in my perception. Why should I change now?" Lynn smiled as she hugged Claire.

Claire never forgot Lynn's supportive words as she hurried back to her clients and handed the new information to Mr. Goldman.

"Thanks, Claire. My wife and I really appreciate the time and effort you've given us. I'll study the listing information at home and call you after I confer with my investors."

Claire smiled, hoping her deal would move forward. "I'll be looking forward to your call, Mr. Goldman."

He turned to Claire and said, "It's getting late; why don't we leave together? My wife and I will accompany you to the train."

"You don't have to walk me to the subway, I'm fine. Would you both like to join me for dinner?"

"We would love to have dinner with you, but we're meeting some friends. Thanks again for the invite."

Claire turned off the lights, locked the entry door and then she and the Goldmans said their goodbyes.

Claire raised the collar of her light jacket as the autumn wind chilled the air. Her body trembled as the brisk temperature dropped. She knew she was not dressed properly and wished she had worn her lined raincoat instead.

As she continued walking toward the train station, Claire realized Rose was waiting for a call, but her decision to have dinner seemed like a better idea at the moment. She walked into a small Italian café. The waiter seated her in the middle of the restaurant. She skimmed through the menu and waited for him to return.

"May I have veal marsala, pasta, and a glass of red wine?"

"Would you like a salad, Miss?" the waiter asked.

"Yes, with Italian dressing. It sounds perfect."

"No problem," the waiter responded, as he went to the computer and put in the order.

While waiting for her food, Claire tried to figure out her share of the commission. The amount made her smile. This would be her biggest deal since she started in the business. She thought, she could go on a trip to Europe, if the deal doesn't fall apart. She put the pen and pad back in her case and ate her food hungrily.

When she finished her dinner, she was about to call Rose, but the waiter returned to her table with the bill. Claire put her credit card and bill on the tray, and waited. She checked the time; it was 8:00 o'clock and already dark out. She wondered where the time went.

At first Claire was oblivious to a man at a nearby table watching her. Then she suddenly locked eyes with him for a fleeting moment. He looked about 30 years old, with blond hair slicked back on his head. Except for the piercing icy blue eyes, one would consider him attractive.

He kept staring at her, making Claire feel uncomfortable, as the last thing she needed was a stranger eyeing her.

She gathered her things to leave, still nervous about the guy staring at her. As she left the café, she realized that she forgot to phone Rose.

The stranger paid his bill and watched her leave. He cracked his knuckles, buttoned his coat, and followed Claire. He pursued her like a leopard stalking his prey.

He wasn't about to let this one get away from him like the others did, he thought. He was going to wait for the right time and then get her good.

All he could think of were the beatings and abuse he suffered as a child. His sisters Joan and Jean were never touched; they were his father's angels.

He could hear his dad yelling, "Billy, you'll never be any good!"

All Billy wanted was his attention, but nothing he ever did was good enough. His father told everyone how rotten he was; how one bad apple in a family is enough.

He was going to make them all pay for his misery, he thought. Killing the whore would set him free. She could be the sacrifice for his wasted life.

After getting the creeps from the man watching her in the restaurant, Claire made a mental note never to make late appointments again. She walked quickly toward the subway station, anxious to get home. The wind picked up strength, and newspapers flew everywhere. Strange noises frightened her and the darkness limited her vision. Her body stiffened when noises close by sounded like footsteps in the leaves. Claire relaxed when a young couple holding hands dashed past her.

The cold air chilled her body and triggered Claire to run. Speeding through the city streets would get her to the train faster. She longed to get back home to the safety of her apartment. Her tense muscles relaxed somewhat when she approached the stairway of Broadway Station. Thank goodness, she thought, drawing a deep breath. She figured that she'd phone Rose, who would be worrying that she didn't report back yet.

She tapped in Rose's cell phone number. "Hi, Rose, it's me."

"I almost gave up on you. It's past 8:30. I waited for your call and finally left the office. Are you all right?"

"Just walked down the steps of Broadway Station and have lots to tell you."

"Was the showing successful?"

"Yes, Mr. Goldman has all the information and will call me after he checks with his investors. Oh my God! There he is! Rose, a man followed me from the restaurant. I'm so scared!"

"What are you talking about?"

"No time to explain. He's chasing me down the steps. Help me, Rose. Help me!" She dropped the phone, looked at her attacker in terror, and yelled, "Who are you? Why are you doing this?"

Those were the last chilling words Rose heard, followed by a piercing scream.

"Claire, Claire, answer me! What's happening to you?" But there was no response. Although she was trembling and frantic with fear, she dialed 911. At that same moment, Rose heard someone unlock the front office door.

"Who's there?" she yelled. Her heart was palpitating, and she started to feel faint.

"Don't get nervous, Rose. It's me, Tony. I forgot my business cards and stopped by to pick them up. What's the matter?" he asked, "You look like you've seen a ghost."

Fighting back tears, Rose said, "Tony, thank goodness you came. It's Claire! She was attacked while she was talking to me. I lost the signal; I have to call the police... The phone was finally picked up.

"This is Detective Shaw. State your name, nature of the emergency, and location, please."

Still nervous from her ordeal she answered, "Rose Field. One of my salespeople needs help. She was just attacked on the stairs of Broadway Station as we spoke on the phone."

"We need your phone number for our records."

"212-555-2121. Is there anything we can do?" Rose asked.

"No." The phone went dead.

Why am I falling apart? Rose thought. How can I run a business, hire competent salespeople and have everything turn upside-down? Alana's murder was never solved. Every time I called the police, they had the same response, "No positive evidence yet." Time passed and her murder went cold. Losing Alana was a great loss.

Now another wonderful agent, Claire … attacked! What's going on in this city? A person can't go to work without worrying about being assaulted. Now I have to deal with the police again. What if Claire doesn't make it? What will her family do?

The 911 operator informed Beth David Hospital of Claire's attack. An ambulance was sent immediately to rescue the victim.

The paramedics found Claire bleeding profusely. One of the EMTs bent down to examine her. He yelled, "She's bleeding from stab wounds and will go into shock if we don't move fast. While I'm examining her, one of you attend to her wounds!"

The medical team finished their job, put Claire on a stretcher, and lifted her into the ambulance. She was having breathing difficulties. One of the paramedics gave her oxygen as the ambulance driver called the emergency room, informing them the patient would arrive in ten minutes.

Detective Green decided to call Rose and tell her the bad news. He tapped in her phone number and waited.

"Rose Field," she said.

"Ms. Field, this is Detective Green. I told you I would call about Claire Smith."

"Yes!" Rose murmured. "Is she all right?"

"Yes, for the moment. She was stabbed several times and is being transported to Beth David Hospital. I called her family and they're probably at the hospital by now."

"Detective, may we see the patient? We're just like family."

"When I spoke to the ER doctor, he said family could see her any time. We'll have to ask you some questions later."

Rose put the phone down and suddenly broke down from the calamity. She couldn't stop crying. Then Tony came back to her desk and tried to comfort her.

"Look, at least we know she's okay!" he said. "Everything will fall into place. Let's settle down and get ourselves ready to see Claire."

The crowd thinned down after the ambulance left the scene of the crime. Somewhere in the shadows of a tree-lined street, Billy watched. He saw the ambulance leave with Claire, but did not know if she was alive or dead.

Billy had been a medical assistant at Beth David Hospital for five years and was astute in medical knowledge. He had to find out if she survived. If she lives, he thought, all my plans were for nothin. I'll have to figure out a way to make sure the whore dies.

He watched until the ambulance disappeared. Then Billy headed home to figure out a new plan of attack. Returning to a dirty, cluttered studio apartment was not what he looked forward to. Living next to the noisy train station kept him from sleeping nights. Maybe one day he would live in a new updated environment. When he got home, Billy was feeling completely frustrated. All he thought of was the possibility of this victim living. There has to be a way he could see her again in the hospital. If she's alive I'll kill her! Since Billy worked at the hospital, it would be easy for him to find her room. He decided to immediately leave his apartment and carry out his new plan.

"You won't get away from me again!" the aide yelled, as he locked his door and ran down the steps of his three-story walk-up. He ran past smelly garbage pails and the noisy train, until he finally reached the hospital; his body drenched in sweat.

Rose and Tony arrived at the emergency room and requested information from the nurse. Rose asked, "Would you direct us to Claire Smith? She was admitted earlier this evening."

"I was told the patient should not have visitors," the nurse answered.

"We have authorization to visit her from the doctor in E.R.," Rose continued.

Tony added, "If you want to verify what we said, you can call him any time."

"Rose was fidgeting and said, "Tony, I have no patience for all this nonsense. We came to see Claire, and I'll do what I have to do to see her!"

The nurse left the desk to verify what they said. Moments later, she returned and granted them permission to see Claire. "She was just brought up to her room. Go to room 225. Don't stay too long."

Rose and Tony left the emergency room and made their way up to Claire's room. They were almost at Claire's door when Nurse Rena Schmidt, stopped them. She was a pleasant woman with a lovely smile and twinkling blue eyes. Her short blond hair was neatly combed and her slender figure was outstanding in a clinging white uniform. She said, "Please wait here, the patient is unavailable at this time. Sit down and relax." She returned to her desk while Tony and Rose sat, quite annoyed at the delay. They had no choice.

After waiting half an hour, Tony approached the nurse. She smiled and said, "The doctor left the room. You can visit the patient now."

They quietly walked in and found Claire sedated and half asleep.

Tony said, "We should leave and return tomorrow."

"Yes, I agree with you. Let's just go."

Claire fell into a deep sleep while Rose and Tony left the room. They continued down the hallway to the elevator and finally reached the entrance leading them out. As they walked out of the hospital, Billy walked in.

He looked quite ordinary dressed in his work clothes. Blue jeans, a sweater and white jacket with an I.D. badge on the left upper pocket. Since his job required him to assist doctors and nurses, Billy was free to roam through the hospital unnoticed. He reported to Ms. Gayte for the evening's schedule.

"Hi, Penny, who do I work with tonight?"

"Billy! We've been looking for you. You're late! You could have helped out with our last patient. She was stabbed; we don't know how serious."

"I'm only 10 minutes late. Sorry, the traffic was unusually heavy on Second Avenue. Can I go back now?"

"No, we need help with a gunshot victim, Juan Perez. Dr. Wang is with him now. Go to the E.R. and assist him."

"Okay, so I get this Perez kid. Fine, I'm on it."

Billy walked to the back of the emergency room, but instead of helping Dr. Wang, he walked to the nurses' desk to find out any information he could about Claire.

"Shit! If only I wasn't late, I cudda killed the whore. What the hell can I do now?"

He needed to work off his emotions, but time was against him. If he took more time, he would be late for his assignment. He bit the bullet and restrained his rage. The tension buildup in his body and triggered him to crack his knuckles for relief.

Rose and Tony returned to the hospital the next day, hoping to see Claire awake. "May we have two visitors passes to see Claire Smith?" Rose asked.

The receptionist answered, "Yes," as she handed Tony two passes. They proceeded to walk toward Claire's room. As they entered the hospital room they saw her mother, Betty and sister, Joy.

Rose smiled as she walked toward them.

Betty said, "We came early this morning. Family is allowed any time to visit a patient."

"Do you have any information about her prognosis?"

The nurse covering Claire turned when she heard Rose's question.

"Dr. Roth should be giving us the results of the patient's x-ray soon. He'll answer any questions you have. If you're wondering why I covered her with two blankets, it's to help her body temperature rise. She was cold and agitated; now she'll feel warmer and the sedation should quiet her down. That's all I know for now."

"Thank you so much for your input," Betty said.

"Claire is a lucky gal; the fact that she's alive is a miracle," Tony added.

"Are you a medical doctor?" Betty snapped. "What do you know about stab wounds and whatever else is medically wrong with her? My daughter is a fragile person. This attack could ruin her mentally and physically for the rest of her life." She started to cry hysterically. Joy tried to comfort her without success, then said, "Please, sit down and try to relax. If Claire opens her eyes, we don't want her to see you crying, right?"

"I'm sorry," Tony said, as he tried to change the subject. "Just thought I'd mention, we've enjoyed working with your daughter and hope she has a speedy recovery."

"Claire was extremely happy working in real estate," Mrs. Smith mumbled as she wiped a tear away with a tissue. "She said you were a motherly type of person, Ms. Field. I'm guilty of not mothering Claire enough." Joy grabbed her mother's hand and squeezed tightly.

Everyone in the room turned toward the bed as they heard Claire moan.

She opened her eyes, blinked, and looked around the room. Her smile lit up the room when she saw her family, Rose, and Tony. "Come closer to my bed," she whispered. Instantly, they rallied around her.

Dr. Roth walked in and greeted everyone. He examined Claire thoroughly, turned to her visitors and said, "Are you all the patient's immediate family?"

"Claire is my daughter! My name is Betty Smith, and this is my younger daughter, Joy." She lifted her hands to her mouth and winced, afraid to hear what the doctor would say. "How is she, doctor?"

Doctor Roth turned to Rose and Tony, "Would you mind stepping out of the room for a few moments?"

Rose and Tony nodded and went into the hall.

The doctor turned to Betty and said, "Our privacy regulation forbids me to talk about the patient in front of anyone without proper authorization." Addressing Claire, Betty, and Joy, the doctor continued, "There's good and bad news. The good news, Claire, is that you're going to be fine. Unfortunately the knife punctured your spleen and you're having some internal bleeding. We need to perform immediate surgery to prevent you from going into shock."

Betty was visibly agitated after hearing the test results, as Rose and Tony returned. Silence permeated, but suddenly a loud wailing cry from Claire's room caused the nurses and aides to come running. Betty Smith couldn't face the reality of her daughter's ordeal. It was easier to lose control than to discuss surgery with Doctor Roth. Joy hugged her mother, trying to soothe her with calming words.

"Mom, everything will work out for the best."

Betty answered. "I think I can control myself now. I have to, for the benefit of my daughter." She was much more relaxed and ready to move forward.

"Is there anything we can do to help?" Tony asked.

"Well, we haven't eaten for hours. Would you mind bringing us sandwiches and coffee?"

"Of course we will," Tony answered.

Rose and Tony welcomed the opportunity to leave the family alone. Tony said, "I think all of us need a break." Rose and Tony left the room and made their way to the cafeteria. They stopped at the rest rooms and never noticed Billy coming down the hallway with the same thought.

How the hell am I gonna find her? Billy anticipated. The growling in his stomach told him to eat first and figure it out later. He always thought better on a full stomach. Dressed in his hospital scrubs, the aide blended in with the rest of the staff. The one thing that set him apart was his evil, scheming mind planning to hurt Claire.

Billy watched Tony and Rose walk into the cafeteria. They were oblivious to his presence at a nearby table. He rushed eating his food so he could get back to the emergency room. Tony and Rose ate their dinner, unaware Claire's attacker sat a few tables away from them.

"Rose, I think we should bring their food back and then head home. There's nothing more we can do tonight."

"You're right. I'm getting very tired. This was an unbelievable night." They cleaned their trays, picked up sandwiches and coffee for the Smiths, and returned to Claire's room.

When they returned, the room was empty. Rose asked an aide, "Where did they transfer the patient?"

"Why don't you check with the nurses?"

Tony put the food down and walked to the nurses' station. He questioned the first nurse who looked up to acknowledge his presence. It happened to be Nurse Rena Schmidt.

"Do you know what room Claire Smith is in?"

Rena answered, "Yes, she was transferred to Room 232 about 20 minutes ago. She needs to get prepped for surgery tomorrow morning."

"Where did her family go?" Tony asked, thinking of all the food they had bought.

"Why don't you go home? I'll be happy to deliver the food to the patient's family. I know they'll appreciate your thoughtfulness."

They thanked the nurse and went home.

As Rose and Tony walked toward the exit of the emergency room, they saw Billy wheeling a patient toward the x-ray room. He walked past them looking like any other aide on staff, dedicated to his job. Nothing about his demeanor suggested a hint of wrongdoing. He flashed them a friendly smile as they crossed paths. "Have a pleasant night," he said.

Innocently they smiled back and Rose said, "The same to you."

Billy finally brought his patient to the x-ray department, and released him to a technician.

On the way back to the emergency room he overheard two nurses talking about a patient's surgery the following morning. He quickly approached them, and in his charming manner asked, "What type of operation is the doctor performing?"

"Dr. Roth is scheduled to do spleen surgery on a patient who was stabbed."

Billy felt a rush of excitement and began cracking his knuckles again. The nurse noticed his quirky behavior and said, "What's your problem? Why do you have to know about this particular patient?" Without waiting for an answer she turned to leave and said, "Look, I need to deliver this food, so please excuse me."

Billy's heart was pounding. He suddenly hoped Claire was the patient they were talking about. "Let me deliver the food for you. I'll be more than happy to save you the trip."

"No, thanks. I promised I would bring the food up to the family." She turned back, looked at Billy sharply, and asked, "What are you so anxious about?"

Billy, realizing the nurse's suspicion, reversed his plan. He said, "Look, Dr. Wang is expecting me. Forget my offer. I didn't realize how late it is. Sorry!"

He thought … I'll figure out another way to get her. At least now I know she's close. If I could find out what room she's in from the nurse, I could carry out my plan. It can't hurt to ask.

"I was wondering … what room are you taking the food to?"

"I'm not at liberty to tell you. I don't even know who you are," the nurse answered.

"My name is Billy. What's yours?" Billy craned his neck to get a look at Nurse Schmidt's ID badge, which was obscured.

"Maybe the next time I see you around I'll tell you my name," she said, her voice laced with suspicion and sarcasm. She walked away and left Billy shocked at her bluntness. He was almost ready to follow her, when he heard his name being paged on the loud speaker.

"William Reilly, please report to the Emergency Room."

Nurse Schmidt entered Room 232 holding a bag of food and drinks, and placed the bag down on the table. "Mrs. Smith, your friends sent sandwiches and drinks. I promised to deliver everything so they could go home and get some sleep. How is our patient tonight?"

Claire was still drowsy from the sedative. She looked up at the nurse,

Rena answered, "Everything will be fine. You're lucky to have such a wonderful family around you." Joy opened the bag of sandwiches and brought the food and drinks to Betty. She turned to the nurse and said," My mother will feel stronger when she fills her stomach. All this waiting around … Do you have any ideas?"

"My suggestion is that you both go home and get some rest. The surgery will take place early in the morning. You'll need lots of energy and patience when your sister's operation is completed. She'll need your love and support."

"That's an excellent idea. I'm going to get my mom ready to leave. Who looks after Claire tonight?" she said, reaching for her mother's coat.

"The nurses will check on Claire," Rena replied.

Joy noticed the nurse's name on her tag and asked, "Rena, would it be possible for you to be my sister's private nurse on the night shift or should I call for one?" We want Claire to have constant attention."

"I'm assigned to this floor tonight along with two other nurses. We'll all look in on her. Don't worry!" She examined Claire's wounds, listened to her heart, and checked the intravenous bag. Then she said goodbye and left the room.

Joy watched as her mother dozed and Claire fell asleep. She looked at her watch and thought, it's almost 8:00 o'clock and we're still at the hospital. I'd better wake her.

Rena rushed back into the room with news about Billy. "I forgot to mention an aide seemed quite curious about Claire's health."

"Why should a hospital aide show any interest in my sister?" Joy said.

"The aide mentioned his name was Billy Reilly. He wanted to bring the food up to your sister's room. Do you know him?"

Joy thought awhile and answered, "No." She turned to Betty and said, "Are you awake? Do you know an aide named Billy Reilly?"

Betty was still exhausted and sleepy, but answered, "No, doesn't sound familiar."

While the Billy incident was being discussed, Detective Pezello entered the room sporting a wrinkled tan raincoat. His gray hair was tousled. As he approached Betty and Joy, the detective twisted the ring on his finger, then said, "Can I speak to someone who is a relative of this patient? We need more facts about her case." He kept twisting his ring, waiting for someone to respond. The belt attached to his raincoat was dangling down to the floor.

"Detective, I'm Claire's sister and this is my mother, Betty Smith. Excuse me, detective, you're losing the belt of your raincoat." She thought how untidy the cop looked.

"Didn't realize it, sorry!" Pezello said.

He probably had a bad night, Joy thought. "Detective, my sister is very sick and can't answer questions in her condition. Would you come back after the surgery tomorrow?"

"If possible, it would be more helpful if I can speak with her sooner. From experience, it's best for us to get a victim to provide a description as early as possible. Otherwise, facts start getting fuzzy. It will help us with the investigation.

Detective Pezello looked at Claire and shook his head in empathy. He was concerned for her safety, since he knew that attackers usually return to finish the job. I'm going to try and find a guard to protect her while she's so weak, he thought. A phone call will do it, I hope.

The cop wouldn't share such frightening information with the family yet. He thought ... first thing to do is call the command office. Sergeant Fox will cut through all the red tape and get this young lady the protection she needs.

"I hope your sister has a quick recovery, Ms. Smith. Maybe we'll get lucky and catch him." Pezello handed Joy two cards with his name and phone number. She slipped them into her purse, planning to give one card to Betty. She said, "Thanks for helping us resolve my sister's case."

He waved goodbye and left the room. As soon as the detective was able to use his cell, he called the command office. "Hello, Pezello here. Is Sergeant Fox around?"

"Sorry, he's out. Do you want to leave a message?" the receptionist said.

"Yes, please tell him to call me on my cell. Say it's important." Disappointed, the detective left with good intentions to follow up on this case.

I think I'll hire a private nurse anyway, Joy decided. She asked her mother to stay with Claire so she could attend to this chore. "I'll be back in about 20 minutes, then we'll go home," she promised her.

Joy left the room and hurried toward the elevator. When she landed on Level One, she asked directions to the nursing office. Joy finally found the office, but it was closed. A sign on the door said, "Will return in two hours." She was upset, but thought a supervising nurse would be on call. Well, thought Joy, I'll ask around the hospital for the head nurse, maybe someone can help me!

Joy questioned nurses and aides, hoping to connect with someone. Then a thought occurred to her. Maybe Detective Pezello could secure a guard for Claire? She opened her handbag, looking for the card he gave her. Joy looked through her purse for the cop's name and phone number without success. Where is it? I can't stand the clutter in this handbag. She accidentally dropped her purse, and everything landed on the floor of the hallway.

Joy was agitated and angry, but began picking up all the items.

Here I am, she thought. 20 minutes have passed and I'm on my knees picking up clutter. She continued tossing lipstick, powder, comb and brush into her handbag, so frustrating. My mother must be worrying about me by now.

"What happened to you?" he said with a smile. "May I help? It seems you had a little accident."

"Oh, thank you, it's not necessary. I'm so clumsy, always dropping things. If you want to help me it's all right," she answered. As they picked up each item, Joy looked up at the Good Samaritan. He was a nice looking young man dressed casually in white sneakers, jeans, blue sweater, and jacket. Her heart quivered as she noticed his blond hair and blue eyes. He looked so much like Jim, only more considerate. Feelings of tenderness overcame her.

Billy had a similar reaction. He thought it couldn't hurt to ask for her phone number. "Are you interested in seeing me again?"

Joy tried to control her excitement as she answered, "Yes." She found her sister's business card, scribbled her name and phone number, handed it to him, and asked, "What's your name?"

He smiled, pointed to his ID Badge, and said, "William Reilly, but everyone calls me Billy," as he quickly stuffed the card into the pocket of his jacket.

CHAPTER 4

Rose hardly slept a wink worrying about Claire. She had left Tony about 11:00 p.m., hoping a night's rest would prepare her for the next morning.

I hope Claire can take the trauma of surgery, she thought. If she does, I'll still have to help her with the Goldman deal. It will be too much for her to cope with, in her condition. She tossed and turned, unable to fall asleep. Thoughts of Tony's concern since Claire's attack lessened the stress. She was about to fall asleep when the sound of the telephone startled her.

Oh no! Something terrible must have happened! She heaved a sigh of relief when she heard Tony's voice.

"Please, don't be angry with me. I tried to sleep, but the excitement of the night made me hyperactive. I didn't know what else to do but call you." Tony sounded apologetic.

"I'm not annoyed. I'm having the same problem. Maybe talking to each other will calm us down."

"Rose, I can't stop thinking about some nut attacking Claire. It's spooking me out. I've got to get the image of her out of my brain. After all this is over I'll need a psychiatrist."

"Look, Tony, there's nothing we can do about Claire's attack, but we can try to be supportive."

"Both of us are exhausted and anxious. What if I come over and help calm you down; maybe we could calm each other down? What do you think?"

"At this hour of the night ... Are you insane?"

"Maybe I'm nuts, but we could be nuts together. Okay?"

Rose was surprised and shocked at Tony's proposal, but after what she had been through, found it tempting. Who would know or care about pursuing a personal relationship with him? A voice in her brain whispered, "Don't mix business and pleasure." She knew Tony had many affairs with other women, or at least bragged that he did, but told herself that this was different. This will be a friendly meeting. We're both suffering and could help each other through this crisis, she thought. Besides, he's probably gay, she reminded herself.

"Tony, be here in 20 minutes."

"I'm putting on my jacket and leaving the apartment now! You made the right decision." He closed his cell phone and dashed out of the apartment. My heart hasn't raced this fast in a long time, he thought.

It didn't take long for Tony to arrive at Rose's place. He rang the doorbell, and when she opened the door, they looked at each other and smiled.

"I never thought I'd invite you or anyone else to my home at this hour! Tomorrow we'll walk around like zombies."

"May I come in?" Tony said, looking awkward as he stood in the doorway.

"I couldn't stop you if I tried; come join me for a drink."

"A screwdriver is fine," he answered. "Rose, you have a charming apartment." Tony nodded as he admired her tastefully decorated home, with exquisite paintings by famous masters. "You never talked about your home."

"You never asked me. My husband was an art expert and loved beautiful things." He used to travel around the world looking for unusual artifacts, either sculpture or paintings. Museums bought many of his pieces. He had just opened an art gallery in downtown New York City, when he became severely ill. I tried to keep as many special art works as possible before I sold the gallery. My life was different then. It took time for me to make changes, but I did.

Tony felt relaxed, sitting on a beige club chair, enjoying his drink.

Rose continued, "Times change and we move forward. Let's toast to Claire's recovery."

Tony moved closer to Rose, and they clicked glasses on the toast.

They were both bleary-eyed, not having slept. Rose looked at her watch and couldn't believe it was 1:00 a.m.

"Don't keep looking at the time; it doesn't matter how late it is. I haven't felt this calm in a long time. I enjoy your company and think you're a wonderful woman. I would do anything for you -- just try me."

Rose listened to his compliments and felt a mixture of curiosity and tenderness toward him. Was he comforting or propositioning her? She said, "I may be able to do you a favor. We're all going through a rough time at the office because of Claire's accident. Would you like to assist us with the Goldman deal? I'll call him tomorrow and ask if he's serious about buying the loft building downtown."

"I would consider myself a lucky guy if I could help you with this deal, but Claire has to approve."

"What is Claire going to do? She's having surgery in the morning, and won't be in any condition to do any real estate for a long time. I'm sure she'll cooperate and let you handle the transaction, if there is a deal." That little voice in her head said, "Watch out. What are you doing, Rose?" She brushed the warning away, thinking only about this moment with him.

Rose and Tony had about three or four drinks and were feeling lightheaded and very cozy with each other. He longed to embrace her and put his arm around her shoulders. She leaned against him willingly, comforted by his touch. His heart pounded, and the arousal he felt needed to be consummated. He reached for Rose and kissed her hungrily on the lips. He crushed her in his arms, kissed her neck, eyes and slowly opened the buttons of her blouse. I was wrong about him, she thought, bemused. As he held her gently, Rose looked up into his eyes, her skin rosy red and desire inside her mounting. She could not speak, as his smell permeated her senses and she longed for more kisses. Rose was in ecstasy as she responded to Tony's lovemaking. She felt an explosion when he entered her and they became one.

They fell asleep in each other's arms, oblivious to the reality they would face tomorrow. Tonight they did not care.

CHAPTER 5

On the way back to Claire's room, Joy fantasized how the handsome Good Samaritan had impressed her. She reflected on how thoughtful and sensitive he was, when her handbag fell and everything scattered in the hospital hallway. "Billy Reilly," she whispered dreamily. "Will I ever see him again?"

Reality set in when she approached Claire's hospital room. Without a private nurse, accidents could happen. The possibility of her sister choking or in pain was frightening.

Joy entered the room and whispered, "Mom, what are we going to do? I'm worried. The office is closed. Claire will have to depend on the night nurses. Rena promised she would look in on her."

"Stop concerning yourself! Nothing is going to happen. I'm sure all Claire has to do for attention is push a buzzer. Rena Schmidt is on duty tonight. We have no reason to be apprehensive." Secretly, Betty's heart was racing, worrying about her sick daughter. She was a sorry sight, dark circles under her eyes, the stress causing exhaustion.

Joy looked at her mother and wondered … I don't know what I'm going to do if she gets sick. I'll be alone and miserable. Finally she said, "You're right, I think we should go home and get some rest. Claire is sleeping and needs all her strength for surgery tomorrow."

Betty said, "Okay, let's get going."

They kissed Claire goodnight and finally left the hospital room. Claire awakened, looked up at her family and said, "I love you both." Then she waved and blew a kiss.

Joy and Betty quietly entered the hallway and continued on toward the nurses' station and elevator. They entered an empty elevator and Betty pushed the down button to the lobby. The elevator started, then stopped at the next floor. As the door opened, a young aide entered, wheeling a patient on a gurney. Joy and Betty moved to make room for them. Suddenly Joy recognized Billy. He didn't realize it was her, since he was occupied with his patient. Then he looked at Joy a second time and remembered the pretty young lady he had helped in the hospital hallway.

He decided to ignore her. She's with someone, and I don't wanna get involved. We'll become acquainted another time. Billy looked straight ahead in the elevator, never acknowledging her.

Joy felt a pang of rejection. Why doesn't he recognize me? I'm standing one foot away from him. I'm going to forget about him! Who needs him, anyway? The elevator door opened and Billy walked out with his patient, disappearing into the crowd. He left Joy disillusioned as she remained on the elevator.

It wasn't until Betty grabbed her arm that she reacted.

"What's bothering you?" Betty asked, as they walked out of the hospital.

"Nothing," Joy answered. I know there's no reason to bring him up to my mother,

She thought. I'll never see him again anyway.

Betty accepted Joy's answer. She was so exhausted she had no energy left to question Joy any further. I want to go home and get the rest we need, so we can return in the morning and help get Claire through this ordeal.

Just after her family left, Claire's sedative had dissipated and her pain was more severe. Ouch, damn it!" Claire yelled. Every movement was agony and tears filled her eyes. She looked around the room; her body suddenly wet, heart pounding, hands trembling. Every shadow triggered an anxiety attack.

Nightmares of the accident continuously filled her dreams and plagued her constantly. "Enough of this," she thought, and then yelled, "I need help!" as she managed to press the nurses' intercom button with all her might.

The nurses were busy writing their reports, but Rena noticed Claire's light flickering.

"I'll attend to the patient in Room 232. She probably needs a sedative for her pain."

Rena entered Claire's room and saw how disturbed she was.

"Claire, what's wrong?"

"I'm feeling awful, and the pain is getting me down. Please give me something."

The nurse checked the chart attached to Claire's bed. "I'm sorry, but Dr. Roth's instructions are, no strong sedatives until after surgery tomorrow morning."

"I can give you two Tylenol tablets for the pain. That should help until you're prepped for the operation."

Claire looked so fragile and vulnerable. Rena moved close to the patient and tried to brighten her spirit. "Don't be frightened; in a few hours it will all be over. Try to stay calm. Take deep breaths and relax." She gave the patient Tylenol tablets with water and Claire swallowed the pills. "I don't want to be alone. Call my family and ask them to come and stay with me. I keep reliving my attack in my dreams. It's driving me insane and I'm scared. The pain I feel is not helping either! Do you understand?"

"Yes, I know what you're going through and would probably react the same."

Rena looked down at her watch. It was 4:30 a.m., an ungodly hour to call anyone.

"If I call your sister at this hour of the morning, she'll think the worst. What if we wait until 6 o'clock? She'll be expecting to hear from me. Doesn't that sound more acceptable? I'll stay with you awhile."

"You're right, I don't want to upset my family unnecessarily. I'll bite the bullet and try to think pleasant thoughts. I hope the Tylenol helps so maybe I can relax."

Rena waited a while longer and noticed Claire was more relaxed.

"Now that you feel a little better, I need to go back to my post. I'll check with you in about 20 minutes." She squeezed Claire's hand. "Don't fret, I'm a click away if you need me."

Rena left Claire in a more relaxed state and returned to the nurses' station to finish her work. When she recovers from this mess, she'll need psychiatric help and lots of tender loving care from the family, she thought. She continued walking to her desk, sat down, and checked her mail.

A skeleton group of three nurses were left on the early morning shift. It was very quiet, which was normal for that time of day. Rena checked up and down the corridor; everything seemed fine. She looked at her watch and saw that it was 5:00 a.m., time to check on Claire. She walked up the hallway and peeked into her room. She saw that the patient was asleep and seemed to be comfortable.

As Rena walked back to the nurses' station, she noticed someone walking from the north end of the corridor. She couldn't see who it was at that moment since he was too far away. The figure down the hallway became clearer as Rena noticed an aide wheeling a gurney. He was walking directly toward her station. She suddenly realized who he was: the young man who had offered to take food up to Claire's room. He had a horrible habit of cracking his knuckles. Well, she thought, I guess he's bringing a patient to one of the rooms on this floor. I'll find out soon enough.

Billy kept a slow pace as he walked down the hallway with a sedated patient in his charge. Where the hell is Room 232, he thought. I'm getting sick and tired of this job. Do I have to cover every floor to find that whore? He approached Rena's station and recognized her. Damn! There she is, the nurse with an attitude. If she's on this floor, I must not be far from my target.

They looked at each other cautiously. Billy, in his charming manner, smiled at Rena and said, "Hi, nice meeting you again. It's pretty quiet here, isn't it?"

Rena checked the time and looked up, wondering why the aide would be wheeling a patient around this early in the morning. She waited for him to get closer and asked, "What are you doing here at 5:00 in the morning? My schedule doesn't show any patient transfers at this hour.

"No, Dr. Wang instructed me to transfer her. You can check with him if you want."

"What room are you taking her to?"

"Room 262. I'm not familiar with the rooms on this floor. Do you know whether I turn right or left at the end of the hallway? Maybe I'll get there if I continue walking straight." He grinned at Rena as he held the gurney tightly with both hands.

Hmm, she thought. He's so-o-o weird. I was right about him the first time we met.

"The patient's name please, and may I see her chart?"

Billy gave her the chart. Rena skimmed the patient's chart, looked up at Billy, and said, "Just continue walking straight ahead. When you reach the end of this hallway turn right. The room is on the left, in the middle of the corridor."

"Thanks for your help. I hope I can return the favor one day."

Billy wheeled the patient away from the nurses' station. When he reached the end of the hallway, he moved the gurney next to the wall. I think I'm safe checking some of these rooms. It can't hurt, he thought. Maybe I'll get lucky.

Suddenly he heard her voice, "Why are you entering this room? I told you to go to the end of the hallway. This is not the end of the corridor!" Her tone was authoritative, hands on her hips. She startled him.

"Oh, it's you. I heard a patient in the room call for help. Thought you were back at your desk. How did you get here so fast?"

"I didn't hear any call for help, and I don't have to explain to you what my responsibilities are! If the patient needs assistance, nurses at my station will do their job. Your responsibility is to take your patient to her new room and not get distracted."

Billy wanted to strangle her, but he controlled himself. I don't like anyone coming up behind me like that, he thought. One day she's gonna make me so nuts, something bad will happen.

He continued on to the new room and didn't look back. After delivering the patient, he needed to calm down. Billy left his charge and walked toward the rest room. He looked at himself in the mirror and thought, not a bad looking guy! I'll wash my face and comb my hair. That should make me feel better. Now I'll go home and figure out a plan that makes sense. I could have accomplished so much if that bitch hadn't interfered.

I'm so tired, Billy thought. Can't wait to get home and sleep. That nurse better not cause any more trouble, or I'll make trouble for her!

Billy couldn't avoid Rena, since the only elevator open at this early hour was near her station. As he wheeled the empty gurney past the nurses' post, he waved.

"I'll see ya soon. Thanks for your help."

Rena looked up but didn't respond. She didn't like him and refused to acknowledge his greeting. She turned to her friend Gene, a male nurse on duty with her, and asked him, "Did you ever dislike anyone just because he irritated you?"

"So far I've been lucky. I like almost everyone and I hope they like me."

Gene had become a nurse recently. He was dependable, efficient, happy-go-lucky, and good-looking. She liked him because he had a heart of gold and would do anyone a favor.

Rena looked up at the clock, and saw that it was 6:15 a.m.

"Gene, I'm going to check the patient in Room 232. She's going down for surgery soon. I'll be back in five minutes."

"Don't worry, Gene is always here to help. Who's prepping her for the operation?"

"I'm not certain, one of the nurses' aides or me. See you soon."

Rena walked quickly down the hall to Claire's room. She was sleeping peacefully. Satisfied, she walked back to her desk to wait for the patient's pre-op orders.

Rena realized she had forgotten to call Joy about Claire's condition. She quickly picked up the phone and dialed her number.

"Good morning, this is Nurse Rena Schmidt. I said I would call."

Joy answered, "When I didn't hear from you, I was a little concerned."

"Sorry; the good news is your sister is doing fine. The last time I checked her, she was sleeping like a baby. When are you and your mother coming to visit her? She's asking for her family."

"Mother and I are ready to leave immediately. We were so edgy, couldn't sleep at all worrying about her. Can we see Claire now?"

"Yes, get to her room before 7:00 a.m. The doctor and aides are coming to prep her for surgery. I have to go now. Good luck to you. I wish your sister a quick recovery."

"Let's get ready to leave," Joy ordered her mother, as she grabbed her jacket from the closet.

Claire's attack caused stress in her family. Joy kept nagging her mother. Her authoritative behavior hurt Betty's feelings and made her nervous. She's not the only one concerned about Claire's surgery, Betty thought; I don't want us to quarrel all the time!

"Mom, what's taking you so long?" Joy turned to Betty, annoyed.

She's doing the same thing again, over and over. I can't take it! Betty steamed inside but controlled herself, looked at Joy and said, "I'm ready. Please don't yell at me!"

Joy looked at her mother and felt guilty. "Okay, I'm sorry for rushing you. It's just that we have to get to the hospital fast to see Claire before surgery." She walked over to Betty and hugged her. I'll try to be more patient from now on, she promised herself.

"Let's go, it's getting late."

They left the apartment as Joy turned off the light and locked the door. They continued on to the hospital in a Yellow Cab.

Betty and Joy arrived at 6:45 a.m. and rushed up to Claire's room. Nurse Rena Schmidt waved them on to save time. Quietly they entered her room. Happy to see Claire's smiling face and outstretched arms, they responded and walked toward her.

"My sweet Claire," Betty whispered as she kissed her daughter lightly on the cheek.

Joy hugged her sister and said, "Don't worry. The surgery will be over fast, like a dream."

"I hope it's not like my dreams. I'm constantly having visions of my attack," she winced as fear darkened her eyes.

Joy thought for a moment. How can I reassure my sister her nightmares will disappear?

"Claire, it's natural to have bad dreams. In time those visions will go away and you'll sleep peacefully again."

Betty listened to Claire. Her body stiffened as she remembered how much she hated the person who attacked her daughter. She turned away from her girls and began crying. She tried to control herself for Claire's sake. Joy turned to her mother and said,

"Mom, what are you doing? Your daughter is going to surgery soon, and you're crying. Go to Claire and smile. Give her your strength!"

Claire couldn't control herself. "Please, stop it, stop it!" she pleaded. "I'm not afraid. Don't worry about me!" Betty and Joy grabbed Claire's hands and held them tightly. It was an emotional moment.

As the family comforted Claire, Nurse Rena Schmidt and a technician walked into the room.

"Sorry," the nurse said. "The patient must be prepped for surgery now. You may rejoin her again in the pre-op waiting room. Betty and Joy kissed Claire and wished her good luck.

As they left the room, Rena prepared the patient for transport. She turned to Joe, the technician, and said, "Please call the office and ask them to send an aide up to Room 232. The patient will be ready for transport in five minutes."

A voice over the loudspeaker requested, "William Reilly, please report to Dr. Wang's office immediately."

Everyone heard but Billy. The noise of diners and clattering dishes drowned out the page in the café. Luckily one nurse saw him.

"Hey, Penny is looking all over for you. Dr. Wang has a transport for you. You better get going," she snapped, and waited for his reaction.

"Jesus! I didn't hear a freaken thing here, it's so damn noisy. Thanks for telling me," he responded.

The aide moved fast, arrived outside of Dr. Wang's office in minutes, where he was met by his supervisor, Penny.

"Sorry I'm late." He fidgeted as he waited.

"Reilly, Dr. Roth's patient in Room 232 is ready for transport. Get moving now!" Penny ordered.

"Sure, yes."

"Sign your name and the room number of the patient on this form," she continued.

He finished the paperwork and readied himself for the assignment. Billy went to the storage bin to find a gurney. He had no idea who the patient was, nor did he care. The aide had a few negative words with Dr. Wang once and didn't want to antagonize him again.

Screw this job, he thought. Can't even have a lousy cup of java this morning. Who the hell is in the mood to transport anyone at this hour? After this assignment I'm heading home. If I don't get some sleep, I won't be good for nothin'.

"Damn, damn, damn," he thought. "I can't stand any more of this place. No matter where the hell I look, I can't find the whore. Who knows if I'll even recognize her?" As he wheeled the gurney, Billy was so agitated, he said, "Screw it all." He cracked his knuckles from nerves, grabbed the gurney, and continued walking.

Remembering what she looked like was a new concern. He thought many patients looked alike in their hospital gowns and hairnets. Let's see if I can recall anything about her, he thought. The tart was slim, had long brown hair, and damn it, she looked like someone I once knew a long time ago. I can't remember another thing. He kept walking, oblivious to his surroundings, and strode almost past the nurses' station on the second floor. Billy recognized Gene working at his desk and asked for directions.

"Hi, could you direct me to Room 232?"

"You were just here a few hours ago, right?" Gene asked.

"Yes, this hallway looks familiar. I transferred a patient to a room on this floor. Wasn't a nurse with short blond hair working with you at this station?" Billy asked.

"Yes, she's prepping the patient you've been sent for. Walk to your left; go straight down the hallway to the end. The room is on the right."

"Thank you," the aide answered.

Billy followed Gene's instructions. When he walked into Room 232, Rena was still fussing over the patient. The technician told her an aide had arrived and transport was ready for Claire. The nurse moved aside and let Joe and Billy handle the transfer from bed to gurney. She still didn't realize that Billy was the aide assigned to move her patient.

"Who-o-o- a-r-r-e y-o-o-o t-w-o- people?" Claire slurred her words as the two men covered her with a blanket.

"Just relax," Joe whispered in her ear. "You're being transferred now. Good luck!"

Rena watched Billy wheel the patient out of the room, never realizing who he was. She removed her mask, cleaned up the mess, and said goodbye to Joe. Her shift was over.

Unaware Claire was the patient he was looking for, Billy pushed the gurney to the O.R. Can't wait to get to the patient's waiting area, he thought. I have so much to think about. So far, all my planning isn't worth shit. Need to take a day off and make a new plan. Who knows where that bitch is by now?

Claire was half asleep and not aware of her surroundings. She felt herself moving along a hospital hallway in a daze. Why can't I move? In her muddled mind she thought her hands were strapped to the gurney. She tried to open her eyes but couldn't. The terror and fright caused her heart to beat rapidly, and sweat filled every pore of her body. I'll count to one hundred to ease the panic I feel.

"One, two, three, four, five, six, seven," ------

This patient must be nuts, Billy thought. Why the hell is she counting? She's half out of it and don't know what she's saying!

The aide finally arrived at the O.R. and wheeled Claire into the holding room. He placed the gurney next to the wall, removed her chart and began reading the information regarding this patient. Just as he was turning the page with all her personal data, a nurse approached him.

"May I have the patient's chart, please?"

As Billy handed the chart to the nurse, Claire managed to turn her head toward him and opened her eyes. She felt dizzy, but vaguely thought she recognized the aide. In a state of confusion, Claire trembled; she couldn't utter a word or call for help. The sedative pulled her into a deep sleep.

As Rena left Claire's room, she heaved a sigh of relief. If only my feet and head didn't ache so much. God, you would think I had just finished prepping my first patient. I'll take some Advil for relief later, she said to herself. Rena continued to walk through the hallway toward her desk. She calmed down and straightened her hair. If the hospital wasn't so short on staff, I'd leave here in a minute. I'm annoyed they asked me to work overtime. Oh, good, there's Gene. A friendly face will lift my spirits. When she saw him she smiled and said, "Hi Gene, Anything unusual happen on the floor while I was attending Ms. Smith?" She took the Advil pills with a glass of water while waiting for him to answer.

"Nothing special, except for the aide they sent to transport Ms. Smith."

"What about the aide?"

"Well, he's the same guy that delivered a patient the other day. Remember you mentioned you didn't like him?"

"Was it Billy?"

"I think so. You really got upset with him. In fact you ran down the hallway to check up on what he was up to."

Rena said, "Gene, he certainly is a weird character, isn't he?"

"Rena, do me a favor. You look tired. Take a break now!" Gene knew she needed to rest.

"Good idea." She left her desk and went to the cafeteria for a cup of coffee and a muffin.

As she tried to relax and enjoy her food, a veil of fear enveloped her. What does this feeling mean? I've got to stop thinking of him. Claire is fine; there's no reason to worry. I don't know why I should think anything is wrong. She kept eating her food and drinking the coffee. It's no good, she thought. That awful feeling in the pit of my stomach is prompting me to check up on Claire.

Rena left the cafeteria and walked toward the operating room. She walked up the steps to the second floor, turned the corner near the O.R. and walked toward the nurses' station.

"Hi, I'd like to check on the status of Claire Smith, please. Is she in surgery yet?'

"Just a moment, please," the O.R. nurse replied. "Not yet. She should be going in next."

"May I see her?"

"No, that's highly irregular, don't you think? She's not supposed to have any visitors according to doctor's orders."

"I'm the nurse who prepped her for surgery. Does that make a difference?" Rena pleaded.

"Oh, well, yes, I guess that does make a difference," the nurse said hesitantly. "You can check her anytime. Why would you do that if you just finished tending her?"

"I'll feel much better."

Rena walked into the waiting room and approached the nurse on duty.

"Is Claire Smith fully sedated?"

"She's almost ready," The O.R. nurse answered. "Why are you so concerned about this patient?"

"Just a friendly interest so I can tell her family I saw the patient."

Rena stood over Claire, tested her pulse, and checked her heartbeat. She thought the patient looked fine. Why did I get so paranoid about her? She looked up and saw the O.R. nurse walking toward her.

"I'm sorry, she's ready to go. You'll have to leave, please." The nurse wheeled Claire into the operating room, and Rena left the waiting area feeling much better.

As Rena walked out through the doors of the O.R., the nurse saw an aide standing in the corner of the hallway. Her heart raced a little as she thought he looked like Billy. When she took a closer look she realized it wasn't the aide. The nurse continued up the corridor toward the waiting room. She knew the family would be waiting for Claire's progress report. Rena walked into the room. Directly in front, sitting on a leather sofa were Betty and Joy.

"I knew I'd find you here," Rena happily reported.

"Do you have information for us?" Betty requested, sitting at the edge of the sofa.

"I want to report Claire is doing well and is just about ready for surgery. It's going to take a few hours, so why don't you two take a break?"

"Thank you for the update on my daughter. We know you made a special effort to give us the news, and yes, we'll take a needed break now," Betty responded.

"I have to get back to my station. Good luck to you and your daughter."

Rena left the waiting room, relieved that Claire was fine, and hopeful that her surgery would be successful. She knew Gene must have been wondering why she was gone so long. Rena hurried back up to her station, and Gene greeted her with a smile.

On the operating table, Claire was half asleep, but still aware of her surroundings. As she looked up, the strong overhead lights in the O.R. hurt her eyes. When will this all end? Who was that face! He seemed familiar, but I can't remember where. She fell into a deep sleep, and the team of doctors got to work.

Under the anesthesia, Claire had a dream.

It's so dark here, I'm scared. No, I won't be afraid. I'm going to keep walking until I get to the subway. It's too cold; I'm not dressed warm enough! Why didn't I wear my winter coat? It's too late now. I've got to eat; my stomach aches for food. There's a café. Wonderful! While I eat I'll call Rose and tell her about my deal. She'll be happy for me.

"Bacon, eggs and coffee, Miss?" the waiter asked.

Suddenly, she was running through a tunnel. Someone is following me, but who? I can't stand it! He's going to kill me! I've got to get away! I'll never get away from him! Help me, Help me, PLEASE! He's going to stab me again and again and again! Please, Please!

Claire's dream ended and she was transferred to the recovery room.

After thoroughly examining the patient, Doctor Roth told the assisting nurse, "I'm going to see her family and tell them the operation was a success. I'll return to check on the patient in twenty minutes."

He removed his surgical gloves and mask, washed his hands, and left the operating area. The surgeon walked toward the waiting room, relieved that he had good news for the Smiths.

As he entered the waiting area, Betty greeted him.

"Dr. Roth, how is my daughter?" She asked in a worried tone.

"She came through the surgery like a soldier. It's over and she'll be fine. Give her time to come out of the anesthesia. She's in recovery now and will be taken back to her room shortly."

CHAPTER 6

The incredible aroma of coffee brewing and bacon sizzling on the stove awakened Tony. For a moment he forgot where he was and the fabulous night he had just experienced. Memories of lovemaking and closeness with Rose motivated him to rise.

"What do I smell?" He raised his voice so Rose could hear in the kitchen.

As he put his clothes on, he yelled again, "Do you hear me?"

"Yes, I do. Are you ready for a five course meal?" Rose said, as she turned on the coffeemaker.

Tony tiptoed behind her, wrapped his arms around her waist, kissed her on the cheek, and grinned. She continued to scramble the eggs and turn the bacon.

"What have I missed all these years?"

"Me," Rose responded. She remembered the amazing night with Tony and smiled with satisfaction. Who knew one of my best sexual experiences would be with this guy she thought might be gay?

"We should go to the hospital soon," Rose suggested, as she sat down for her meal.

"Yeah, You're right!" Tony responded as he joined her. He noticed the charming whimsical tablecloth covering a small round table and a setting for two.

"Where'd you learn to cook up a storm and set a beautiful table?"

"I've always loved to cook and serve with a flair. Glad you appreciate my talents."

They finished their breakfast. Tony helped Rose clear the dishes as she wiped the counters.

"Thanks for helping. We should leave for the hospital. I'm sure the surgery is over." They grabbed their jackets and left the apartment. Before departing, Rose called the answering service. "Please tell my clients I'll get back to them later in the day. If Mr. Goldman calls, give him my cell number. Thanks." Today Claire is my priority, she told herself.

Rose's apartment was three blocks from the hospital. Walking was the fastest route. They entered the lobby, as Tony guided Rose through the door and finally to the front desk.

"We'd like two visitor passes for Claire Smith." Rose requested.

The desk clerk checked her records and replied, "According to my records the patient is in the recovery room."

"Take the elevator up to the second floor; you'll see a waiting room. Families of surgery patients usually wait in that area.

"Thanks," Rose replied.

Rose and Tony left the desk and took the elevator up. They continued on to the waiting area, where they saw Betty and Joy sitting on a sofa. Both women stood up and greeted them. Betty said, "We're so happy to have company."

Everyone sat down. Then Tony asked, "Have you heard anything?"

Betty answered, "We were told that the surgery went well and Claire is in the recovery room." They sat for a while until Rose remembered to call her voicemail. "I'll be back in about ten minutes. Have to check my answering service. Never know what could happen in real estate." Rose walked out to the hallway to make her call. As she left the waiting area, an important thought entered her mind. She wondered how her new relationship with Tony would affect their business arrangement. Time will tell. She realized that she'd have to always keep her guard up, knowing about his past. There's still the question of Claire and the deal she's working on. Who knows what to expect? She thought about Alana's case going cold and the cops' dwindling calls. But she told herself she wouldn't give up. She decided to call again tomorrow and keep reminding them.

She retrieved her cell phone from her purse and dialed her office to check for messages. Rachel answered and informed her, "Mr. Goldman called in reference to the loft property downtown. He asked for Claire, but knew nothing about her accident. I told him you would get the message. His phone number is 555-2100."

"Thanks, Rachel."

When she ended the call, she felt encouraged. This means good news for Claire's deal, or why would he bother to call?

Rose returned the call. She listened to the phone ring four times and was about to hang up when she heard a voice.

"Hello, Goldman here."

"This is Rose Field, calling for Claire Smith. I'm a broker with Field Realty." She felt relieved when she heard his voice.

"Thanks for returning my call. What happened to Claire? She was the nicest agent to work with. My wife and I were impressed with her.

"I'm happy you were pleased with Claire. Unfortunately there was an accident. She was attacked the night she showed you the property."

"What! Oh my God! Ms. Field, we offered to walk her to the train, but she refused. Is she badly hurt?"

"Bad enough. She just got out of surgery and it looks as though she'll be okay"

"My wife and I wish her a speedy recovery and regret her decision that night."

"I agree with you," Rose continued, thinking the choices we make in our lives should be questioned before we make them.

"Mr. Goldman, I was wondering whether your call was about the loft in SoHo."

"Yes, we have investors ready to move on this deal. I wanted to let Claire know that I'll call again with an offer, but first there are details I must attend to."

"Fine, since Claire is unavailable, I'll follow up and help you." Rose was very cordial, but thought about the offer she had made to Tony. Why did I do it? She was beginning to get upset at the thought of Tony's involvement. She pushed him out of her mind for the present but knew she would have to face the issue in the future.

"Thank you for returning my call, Ms. Field. You'll be hearing from me in a few days."

"When Claire hears the good news she'll be happy. I'm certain her recovery will be faster because of you, Mr. Goldman."

Rose hung up the phone and suddenly felt a rush of heat, causing a flush in her cheeks. She found her way to a rest room and tried to calm down. Too much excitement is making me a wreck, she thought. Rose looked in the mirror and noticed her cheeks were tomato red. She grabbed the edge of the sink and looked closer, inspecting the rash on her face. It must be hives from my nerves, she thought.

What's the matter with me? I should be calm with the possibility of a fabulous deal on the horizon. I know what the problem is, she reflected. Many years in this business have taught me a deal could fall apart.

Rose combed her hair and freshened up. She felt better and returned to the waiting area. I'm nervous about the Goldman deal and don't think I should tell Tony anything yet.

As she walked back, she thought about the consequences. I could certainly use part of the commission to enhance my life. Think of what the money would mean to the Smith family. Why did I say anything to Tony? It may be a delicate situation, since we were so intimate that night. I would have promised him anything.

Rose entered the waiting room and approached Tony and Claire's family.

"We were ready to send a scout out, Tony said smiling. "Have you heard any news?"

"Tony, I must talk to you privately." Rose whispered.

"You seem excited Rose. What happened?"

"Betty and Joy, please excuse us. Some business matters have come to my attention."

"Don't worry, its fine with us," Betty answered.

Tony and Rose left the family and walked down the hallway until they found a quiet corner.

"Rose, what happened?"

Even though she knew waiting would have made sense, she couldn't help telling him about the call. "Mr. Goldman called to say Claire's deal would probably move forward. He's calling back with a bid on the SoHo property."

"I'm happy to hear the good news, Rose, and if you want me involved in any way just say the word."

Rose bit her lip, thinking, what the heck have I done?

*

Billy walked through the corridor on his way from the O.R. I can't stand this job, he thought. If I had the guts I would quit now! How long can I play this game? Damn, damn; too much time has passed and now I can't find her. Where the hell is that bitch? His anger triggered a panic attack; he couldn't breathe. What the hell is happening to me? He felt unsteady on his feet, fainted, and landed on the floor.

Ellen, a nurse walking by, tried to comfort Billy as she called for help.

"Coming," one of the doctors responded.

"I'll examine the aide if you move aside, please," Dr. Roth offered.

The doctor checked Billy's eyes, blood pressure, and heart.

"His vitals are within normal limits. He probably hyperventilated. He'll be fine, but he should be observed for a while. Oh, he's opening his eyes."

"Nurse, I have a patient waiting for me. Stay at his side. When he's fully awake, tell him to cool down. I'll be right down the hallway if you need me."

Finally, still in a daze, Billy asked, "Where am I?"

"You fainted, but you'll be fine. Can you get up yet, or are you still dizzy?"

"I'll be okay in a minute," he answered as he tried to stand up.

One of the nurses brought Billy a glass of water.

"No, I don't want water. I just want to get out of here," he said in an angry tone.

The nurse backed off as Billy stood up. Ellen thought a small thank you would have been in order. "Okay, okay," she said sharply. "I guess you're better and able to get around on your own." She couldn't believe how curt, abrupt, and nasty he had been.

Billy realized how rude he sounded. "Oh, I'm sorry that I caused a problem. Don't know what happened to me. I'm fine and really late for my next assignment. You know how annoyed the doctors get!" he mumbled.

The aide walked away, never looking back. He was fuming inside for having had that fainting episode and drawing attention to himself. Stupid, stupid, stupid me; when am I gonna learn to be invisible, he thought. He walked through the hallway confused, upset, and extremely cranky. His body trembled and sweat appeared on his face. Without realizing what he was doing, he cracked his knuckles. Shit, he thought, I haven't done that in a long time. I must be in bad shape! Better put my hands in my pockets!

He wanted to get back to the office for his next assignment, but as he approached the O.R. waiting area he decided to go inside, calm down, and relax. He walked into the room. Suddenly, directly in front of him, sitting on a leather sofa he recognized Joy. His mind started racing. Jesus! That's the girl who gave me her phone number! I can't bother with her now. I'm too upset. Wait! Didn't I ignore her in the elevator? Maybe I should say something.

He was about to sit down when he felt a tap on his shoulder. "Didn't you help me when I dropped my purse?" Joy asked, as she felt butterflies in her stomach.

There was no way to avoid the young lady. "Yes, it's you!" As he looked at Joy, a calm feeling overcame him. She's a real looker, he thought. Why did he hesitate?

"I'd like to thank you again for helping me." Joy's eyes sparkled.

Billy suddenly had an idea. He thought, this gal likes me, I can tell, and that's good for a change. I'd like to get involved with her. Never know how her friendship will help me in the future. He tried to make more conversation with her.

"Why are you hanging around here?" he said.

"My sister is in surgery, and my mom and I are waiting for her progress report."

"Would you like to join me for coffee?" Billy asked, "Maybe a break will take your mind off your sister."

"I'd like that, but I have to let my mother know. Maybe she and some friends want snacks. Wait here; I'll be right back." *I'm so happy he remembers me,* Joy thought.

As she walked away, he couldn't take his eyes off her body. *What a gorgeous figure, and her eyes are as blue as the sky. What the hell is going on? I was a nervous wreck fifteen minutes ago, and now I'm on cloud nine.*

Joy went to her mother and excitedly asked, "Is Claire out of surgery?"

"Yes," Betty answered, relieved. "She's in the recovery room and we'll be allowed to see her in one hour."

"You'll never believe who I met at the other end of the waiting area!"

"Are we playing guessing games? Who did you meet?"

Tony and Rose couldn't help but overhear the conversation and strained their ears to hear more.

"Mom, remember the night I tried to hire a nurse for Claire? I dropped my purse, and of course everything fell out."

"Sure, you met the King of England!" Betty finally laughed.

"He's like a king to me. Well, I recognized him earlier on the elevator, but he didn't say anything to me. That doesn't matter. What does matter is we talked just now and he invited me for coffee. I told him yes. Does anyone want snacks?"

"No thanks. It sounds like love at first sight; can we meet the young fellow?" Betty asked.

"I don't think he'll mind. Why don't you all come with me and I'll introduce you?"

"Great idea," Rose replied. "I'd like to meet the Good Samaritan."

"So would I," Tony added.

They followed Joy to the other end of the waiting area. Joy walked on ahead, trying to find Billy. She looked everywhere, but he had disappeared. She looked up at her mother, eyes filling with tears, "I guess he couldn't wait for me."

"Didn't you say he works here?" Betty said. "Maybe he got called away."

Joy didn't see Billy as he slipped away after seeing her talking to

Betty. Why the hell did she have to bring her freaky family with her, Billy wondered. Shit, I had everything planned. We were gonna go for coffee and sandwiches; maybe I would've asked her for a date … maybe! Can't stop thinking about her.

Billy checked his watch and realized it was time for him to go home. He walked quickly past the office and waved to Penny.

"I'm leaving," he said.

"So long, don't be late tomorrow! There's going to be lot's of action, as usual." Penny smiled.

He signed the clipboard and walked out of the hospital. On the way home, Billy passed a liquor store and decided to bring home a bottle of vodka. Just what the doctor ordered for my nerves, he thought. Another day of lunacy at that crummy hospital makes me crave a few drinks. Can't wait to go home and drink myself into a stupor. No one will give a damn anyway! He walked into the liquor store, "A bottle of Absolut, please." The clerk nodded, reached behind and grabbed the bottle.

The amount $20.95 flashed on the computer. The salesperson put the bottle in a brown paper bag. Billy paid the bill, picked up his purchase, and left the store.

He dragged himself down the street toward the train station. As he walked down the steps he almost fell, as he ran to catch the train.

There's a seat … great! The aide sat down and tucked the bag containing the liquor under his jacket. He sat for a while thinking about getting home to enjoy the vodka. Suddenly his eyes closed. He fell asleep and dreamt. He heard his father's ongoing complaints.

"Hey, Billy, just opened the envelope with your report card," the father nagged. "You failed two courses again! What the hell is wrong with you! Your sisters keep getting A's in all their subjects, but you haven't got the same brains as them, now, do you, boy?"

"I can't help it, dad. I'm not as smart as them," he mumbled, devastated at his father's comments.

"Billy failed his subjects, Billy failed his subjects," his sisters sang in unison. They taunted him until he couldn't stand it. He cracked his knuckles to release the tension in his body.

"Why are you all floating everywhere? I'm getting dizzy watching you. Stop saying those things!" He covered his ears with both hands. I hate them all. My mom is the only one who keeps her mouth shut.

Suddenly somewhere in the dream Billy heard a voice saying over and over, "Fourteenth Street, Fourteenth Street." His body quivered as he opened his eyes and heard his station being called on the loud speaker. He left the train and walked up the flight of steps toward the street. Billy raced down the avenue, anxious to get home as he held the bottle close. A little more patience and I'll feel better. I'd do anything to feel like a human being, anything!

The aide finally reached his apartment building and walked up the steps to his apartment, still clutching his bottle. He turned the key, opened the door, and walked into his dirty, messy studio. Who cares if my place is filthy, he thought. He took his jacket off, opened up the bottle and poured himself a drink. This is great. Finally I'm alone with my vodka. He sat down on his leather recliner and gulped down the first glass of liquor.

After the third drink he was feeling much better. He yelled out loud, "I knew a few drinks would cure what ails me! No, B-Billy, d-don't talk so loud because the neighbors will hear you," he whispered. "W-Wow, I'm a little drunk … I think."

He moved away from the recliner and headed toward the bathroom. I'm gonna take a dump, and then enjoy a few more drinks. Think I feel like throwing up. Shit, I feel lousy. Thought drinking made ya feel good!

He was inebriated but still awake, many thoughts racing through his head.

What will make me feel good? Maybe the girl I saw in the waiting room? I bet she could turn me on. Tomorrow I'm gonna call her and ask her out. Right now I gotta have another drink.

He could hardly walk, but zigzagged from the bathroom across to the table where the liquor bottle had been placed earlier.

Only a little left, he thought. I should have bought another bottle of booze. Stupid me, I'm not drunk enough.

He guzzled down the remaining vodka, and collapsed on his living room floor.

CHAPTER 7

Dr. Roth examined Claire thoroughly, turned to the nurse, and said,

"Please move Ms. Smith back to Room 232."

"Yes, doctor," she answered.

Finally Claire was alert and ready for transport. She thought. How lucky I am; someone's watching over me.

An aide arrived and transferred Claire on to the gurney, and moved her up to the room. After he carefully helped the patient into bed and made her comfortable, her family and friends encircled her.

"Oh, darling," said Betty. "We're so happy that you're done with the surgery. Now all you have to do is get well."

As everyone hovered around Claire, Rose said, "Tony, I think it's time to get back to work."

"I hear you," he answered.

Betty said, "Thank you for spending time with us. Your concern is appreciated."

"As they walked toward the door, Tony turned to Claire and said, "We'll call you about the deal when you feel better. Until then, don't concern yourself about a thing."

Claire answered softly, "Thanks for everything."

Tony and Rose made their way to the main level and exited the door leading to First Avenue.

"Rose, I hope we never have to come back to this hospital again. I'm sick of the waiting and antiseptic smell."

"I don't think so, Tony," she replied. "What if her surgery wasn't successful? What if the doctor decided to keep her in the hospital longer?"

"Guess I'm ready to get back to my life."

"Of course, I understand where you're coming from. You seem a little apprehensive. Would you like to stop at my place for a cup of coffee? We'll hang out awhile and then return to the office."

"I love your idea. Let's do it!" Tony responded, a grin on his face.

"Would you rather stop at Starbucks instead of bothering at home?" he added.

"No way, I hate their coffee. I'd rather be home with you. We have plenty of work waiting for us at the office. Let's grab the moment while we can." Rose took his hand as they left the hospital.

They continued walking north on First Avenue, and suddenly the sky turned black. Heavy rain and winds engulfed them both. Tony put his arm around Rose's shoulder and held her close. He turned to her and whispered in her ear, "Every day my feelings for you grow stronger." He kissed her cheek as the cold winds made them shiver. Rose looked up into his eyes and felt a hunger for his touch. "Tony, I have the same feelings for you." They looked into each other's eyes and knew they had to get home fast.

Rose's apartment was only a few blocks away, and they could either find a cab, take refuge in a coffee shop, or make a dash for it.

"It won't take long. Let's just run for it," Rose suggested.

"You're on!" Tony replied.

Rose dashed ahead with keys in her hand. She quickly walked up the steps, turned, and yelled, "Let's go Tony. Where are you?"

"I'm right behind you!"

He dashed behind Rose as she opened the door; grabbed her from behind and closed the door with his leg!

I feel like a teenager again, Rose thought, as she turned her face to Tony and kissed him hungrily. She pulled away for a moment and looked him in the eyes, smiling.

"What will the neighbors think? Every door will open when they hear the noise."

Rose didn't have a chance to finish her thought. Tony grabbed her arm and guided her to the couch, where they embraced passionately. He held her face in his hands and kissed her tenderly as his tongue found hers. Tony removed her blouse and skirt. As Rose helped him open the buttons, her fingers trembled. As their yearning became unbearable, she looked into his eyes and whispered, "I need you!" Rose took his hand and led him to her bed.

Tony's pants and underwear were scattered all over, as they continued their lovemaking. He mumbled holding her close, "I adore you."

I know, darling. I love you too with all my heart," she responded, as Tony continued to pleasure her. Rose moaned, unable to contain her ecstasy. They continued on and on until finally the volcano erupted and they fell into a deep sleep.

The loud ring of the phone awakened them, "Shit!" Tony yelled as he jumped up in bed and picked up the phone.

"Who's that?" Rose asked groggily as he answered the phone.

"It's your phone service. You have an important call. Are you okay to talk?"

"Yes," she said. He playfully pinched her bottom and Rose whispered, "Dirty old man!" He smiled, sat down, and listened.

"Hello, this is Rose Field."

"I have a message from Mr. Goldman. He wants to talk to you immediately. I wrote his number down if you need it."

"Thanks, I have his number. Talk to you later." She hung up the phone.

"Don't get too excited. Call him and see if he's ready to propose a bid on the property." Tony became all business.

Rose said, "I'm optimistic about the deal and the buyer." She walked to the bathroom to freshen up and yelled, "Tony, be a doll and make some coffee while I finish in here."

"Sure, I make the best coffee in town." He proceeded into the kitchen.

Rose went to her desk, where she had Goldman's card sitting on a folder. She dialed his number. No answer.

Rose heard his greeting and left a message for him to call back.

"Just the stress I need in my life. Why couldn't he be home?"

"Don't get upset. Come and join me for the prize-winning coffee of New York City. Did you know I won an award?" He laughed at his own humor.

"Tony, I think I need more than coffee. I'll make sandwiches."

"Put food in front of me and I'm ready to dine. Don't worry about Mr. Goldman. There's nothing we can do now, so let's eat and make love again."

"I won't forget tonight, our special time together." As Rose prepared ham and cheese sandwiches, Tony served the coffee.

She looked at the time and suggested, "Let's get back to the office! Maybe there's a message from Mr. Goldman. If not, I'll call him."

"Rose, think about the commission."

"I hear you. Let's not talk about it again until I talk to him. Who knows? Maybe it's all about nothing."

CHAPTER 8

In Billy's dream he saw a woman's image in the distance.

"Who are you?" he asked. He couldn't see her face in the haze.

"What do you want?" Billy mumbled, frightened at her presence.

"I'm your mother," she answered, her face becoming clearer.

"What are you doing here?"

"Billy, I have to talk to you before it's too late."

"I know I've done some mean things Mom, but I'm turning my life around. You'll see, one day I'll make you proud."

"I want you to lead an ordinary life. Get to know the nice young lady you met. She'll bring good luck into your messed up life."

"I know you're right. I'm gonna call her today and plan to meet her again. Stay and talk to me. Please, I need your good common sense!"

"Billy, I have to go. You have bad thoughts most of the time. Better get some help or your life won't be worth anything. Remember, I love you and always will!"

As he opened his eyes, the room spun out of control. Billy tried to lift himself up, but he was unable to. The dream was too much for him. His mother had died when he was a teenager. She was the only stable influence in his life, and since then his life wasn't the same.

God sent my mom to speak to me, he reflected. How is it possible that she knew so many things? It was only a dream, but she made sense.

Billy finally had the energy to pick himself up. He stretched his arms and took a deep breath. He dropped back to the ground and started doing some pushups.

I shouldn't allow myself to get drunk. It stinks, he thought. Guess while I was soused I must have loved it. I'm gonna call Joy.

He continued doing a few more pushups, as the more he exercised, the better he felt. He looked around the apartment, revolted by what he saw. I'm living like a bum! How can I ever invite anyone to this joint? After I make the call to Joy, I'll call a realtor and get a decent apartment.

He tried to find Joy's phone number, but couldn't. Everything is so messed up; I couldn't find anything if I tried. Getting more frustrated by the minute, Billy looked everywhere he could think of. Suddenly he remembered; I'm so dumb, so dumb. Dumb! Dumb! The night Joy dropped her handbag I was wearing my jacket. Her phone number is probably in the pocket.

Billy walked to the closet, opened the sliding door, and removed his hospital jacket. Her number had to be in one of the pockets. He checked the right pocket, nothing. Suddenly Lady Luck appeared. In the corner of the pocket his fingers touched a card. He quickly pulled it out and prayed it was Joy's. His heart beat faster when he saw Joy's phone number, name and address, written on the back of her sister Claire's real estate card. "Look," he mumbled. "The sister works for a realtor. She could be useful to me one day when I move."

As Billy dialed Joy's number, he thought about how happy she made him feel. It's a new experience for me to think in a positive way about anyone. Something about her triggers good in me for a change.

Her phone rang, but nobody answered. After the third ring Joy's recorded greeting came on.

"Shit!" he said. "Why couldn't she be home?" He hung up the phone. I'm not leaving any message, no way. I'll call her later.

Billy was suddenly thinking in a more positive way. If I wanna get involved with her, I gotta plan some new ways to deal with my life. That's a beginning. Maybe I'll call Claire's office. All I have to do is call the office number on her card. Maybe I should wait until I meet her. Then she'll help me.

He looked around his apartment for a newspaper, "Shit!" he yelled. "I can't find a damn thing in this fuckin' place!"

He gave up looking and went to buy a paper at the corner newsstand.

As he walked down the steps to the street, he looked at his watch and yelled out loud, "Jesus, I missed a day at work! They'll all think I died. Better call Penny and tell her I caught a bug." He made the call and waited for her to pick up. When her greeting clicked in, he left a message saying he was sick.

CHAPTER 9

The next morning Claire's family rallied around her hospital bed. They made plans for her return home. Betty hugged Claire, "Honey, Doctor Roth said you'll be going home in a few days. Bet you can't wait to sleep in your own bed!"

"You're right, there's no place like home, but I'm still in agony. Ask the nurse for a painkiller, please?"

"Of course, sweetheart. Is there anything else I can do to make you comfortable?"

"No, just get the nurse!" She continued holding her head with her hand.

Betty pushed the intercom button while they waited patiently. The nurse arrived and gave Claire a shot. When the nurse left, Betty said, "You look exhausted; get a good night's rest. We're leaving, but we'll be back early in the morning.

"Good idea," Joy uttered.

Claire's eyes fluttered in an attempt to stay open, but suddenly she was fast asleep. Betty and Joy left the room and went home.

As Betty and Joy left the hospital, Joy blurted, "Mom!"

Betty turned her head. "What's on your mind?"

"I can't get Billy out of my head. He was so handsome and helpful when I dropped my purse in the hallway. Why didn't he call? You'd think I would have forgotten about him by now, with all our problems. He probably didn't like me after all."

"Why are you so silly? How long have you known him, two days?"

"I know, you're probably right."

Betty put her arm around Joy's shoulders "Don't you worry for one minute. He's not the only young man around."

"I know, but there was something about him. Too bad." She sighed. "Mom, is it all right for me to sleep at your place tonight? I don't want to be alone."

"I was going to suggest that you spend the night with me." They continued on their way to Betty's apartment.

Joy and Betty entered the building and took the elevator up to the sixth floor.

Betty unlocked the door, and they went in. She put the keys on the end table and took her jacket off.

Joy walked directly to the phone and dialed her voicemail. "Hey, Mom, my friend Pearl called to ask about Claire. Someone else left a message. It was a guy, but he didn't leave his name. The voice was familiar. How am I supposed to know who it was?"

"If that person wants to speak to you, he'll call again. You left your robe and slippers in the front hall closet for emergencies. Why don't you change clothes and make yourself comfortable?"

"You're right, I'm tired. Think I'll take your advice."

"I'll make us some tea."

"Mom, you're a lifesaver. I could use some therapy now. I think all of us could, especially Claire. Imagine the adjustment when she comes home!"

"Now eat those delicious cookies and enjoy the tea."

After the relaxing interlude, Joy put her cup down, turned to her mother, and said, "I'm going to check my messages again. Maybe the mysterious caller left a name. I'll be back in a minute."

Joy listened to her messages. This time there was only one. She recognized the voice. When she realized Billy had called, her knees almost buckled. Slowly she put the phone down.

"You're kind of quiet. What's up?" Betty waited for her daughter's answer.

CHAPTER 10

The intimacy they had shared the night before faded as Rose and Tony returned to the reality of office procedure. They greeted the other broker Harry. He responded, "Hey, how are you both? I haven't seen you two in a few days. How's Claire?"

"The operation was successful and the patient should be coming home in a few days," Tony answered.

Harry's phone rang, and he returned to his office while Tony and Rose sat down at their desks preparing for the day's schedule.

"Wish me luck, Tony. I'm going to contact the client and see whether our deal is still on." Rose tapped in the number and waited a few seconds.

"Mr. Goldman please. Rose Field returning his call." She waited for the secretary to connect her. Then she heard his voice.

"I'm glad you called. I have some good news. My investors decided to go forward with the deal. They gave me permission to propose a bid on the property."

She looked up at Tony and smiled. He responded with a huge grin.

"Great, what's your offer?" Rose asked.

"Well, since the property needs substantial work, we suggest a bid of $1,500,000."

"I'll discuss this with the seller and get back to you." Rose hung up the phone and turned to Tony. "He bid $1,500,000."

"Good beginning; you have to get him higher," Tony said seriously.

"I'll suggest to the seller that we counter at $1,800,000."

"Sure, you can always negotiate. Give him the counter offer and see what happens." Tony waited, tapping his fingers on the desk.

"Good thinking," Rose said. "I'll ask him to send a written proposal for our file, but in the meantime I think I should be prepared to offer some additional perks in return. I'll run it by the seller, but first let's get the formal offer from Goldman."

She called Mr. Goldman back and waited impatiently until he picked up on his end. "Mr. Goldman, it's Rose Field."

"Yes," he answered. "What a quick response! How can I help you?"

Rose answered, "I would appreciate a written proposal faxed to my office for my records. It's office policy."

"No problem. I'll have my secretary do it now."

"Thanks. When I receive your offer, I'll call my client and get back to you."

"Fine," he responded.

As she completed the call, Rose looked at Tony and said, "If this deal materializes we'll have some happy campers in this office. I think we should call Claire. The news will cheer her up."

"Don't rush. Wait until the contracts are signed. I've gone to closings only to be let down when the buyer or seller walked out. Have patience and tell Claire later. You could jump the gun, and boom, no deal."

They were so involved, neither one heard the door open.

"Excuse me, I saw your Real Estate License outside and thought you could help me."

"Please sit down," she said, as she looked up at the nice looking young fellow, slim, with blond hair and blue eyes. "Are you interested in a rental or sale?"

"I'd like a one-bedroom rental," he answered.

Rose handed him her real estate card, along with an application. "We have some beautiful apartments to show. Please fill this form out and return it to me when you're finished."

The young man walked to an empty desk, sat down, and began filling out the paperwork.

Rose couldn't take her eyes off him. He looked familiar, but she couldn't seem to place him. Oh, well, what's the difference, anyway, she thought.

Jeez, the young man thought, why the hell do I have to give so much personal information? Screw them, I'll make some of the answers up. How will she know anyway? Holy hell, I have to give referrals. I'll give my stupid landlord's name. I never had trouble with him. I bet I'll never get an apartment anyway.

He finished the application, walked over to Rose's desk, and put the completed form down.

"I'll call you after I check your referrals. Hope you have some for me?" she said.

Billy answered, "Can't remember names and phone numbers now. I'll check my phone book at home and call you tomorrow."

Rose suggested, "My phone number is on the card I gave you. Call me as soon as you can. After we check your referrals, we'll show you the company's listings on the computer." Rose stood up, shook his hand, and watched as he walked out.

Rose and Tony looked at each other. "Tony, he looks so familiar, but I'm blocked. Can't remember where I saw him."

"You know, I had the same feeling." Tony added. There's just too much to do. I can't take the time to think about that guy. Look at his application. What's his name?"

Rose perused the information, checked his name, and turned to Tony. "It says Reilly."

Tony shrugged and said, "That doesn't mean a thing to me."

"Me neither," Rose answered.

CHAPTER 11

Billy couldn't forget the message from his dead mom. "She'll bring good luck into your messed up life, he thought. He walked through the halls of the hospital, consumed with thoughts of Joy. Wish I could leave now! Gotta hurry home and check my voice mail. I wanna see her, he thought. Don't have to invite her to my apartment yet. We'll just meet somewhere else, maybe a diner or an Italian restaurant. I love pasta, and I bet she does too. Mom thought Joy's love would add sunshine to my life and anchor me. I can't wait for the day I see her and hold her close.

He finally finished his workday, left the hospital, and walked toward the bus terminal, day-dreaming about Joy. When his bus arrived, Billy stepped up, paid his fare, and walked into a melting pot of people. The smell made him gag. Someone needs a bath; can't stand the odor, he thought. Maybe if I move toward the back I'll be able to breathe easier. Billy stopped halfway through the bus, looked around, and stood in front of a young dark-haired woman. Maybe she'll leave soon and I'll get her seat. As he settled into a tight spot in front of the lady, she informed him, "Mister, I'm getting off at 53rd Street, you can sit here when I leave."

Billy swayed back and forth, holding on to the pole to keep from falling. "Thanks," he said as he looked at the woman. Something about her triggered a memory.

Damn, who does she remind me of? The hair, her eyes ... can't take it! He cracked his knuckles nervously. The noise caused some of the passengers to look at him. Jesus! I'm sweating like a freak, must control myself, he thought. I can't get that feeling again, it's bad for me. Hurts too much!

The dark-haired young woman reached her stop, walked to the exit, and stepped off. At that moment instead of sitting down, Billy pushed through the crowd and made a dash for the door. He followed her from the moment she left the bus stop. She walked west on 53rd Street, unaware someone was behind her.

What the hell am I doing? Why did I get off the damn bus? Can't take my eyes off her; if I do I'll lose her. Too many trees, I can hardly see.

He couldn't control the overwhelming urge to punish her. She or someone like her had deceived him in the past. She would pay for the evil deed. Faster and faster he walked, eager to drag her into an alley. The trees were his cover, as he zigzagged back and forth. He saw her slow down at 9th Avenue and hurried to catch up.

Billy observed the buildings and alleys. Which one would make a better spot to attack his victim? Finally he walked right behind the woman. Sensing someone behind her, she stopped, turned, and stammered, "Oh it's you, I th-thought I left you behind on the b-bus."

Billy quickly moved toward her, his eyes glaring, and grabbed the woman by her hair. There wasn't a soul in sight to witness the crime as he dragged her into the alley of a vacant building.

"Help! Help!" she frantically yelled. "What are you doing? What are you doing? Stop! Stop!"

Nobody heard her cries.

"You whore! Shut your damn mouth!" he screamed, as the woman cried like a baby.

"Don't do it, don't do it! I have children. Have mercy, mercy ------!"

"I have to, so shut the hell up!" Billy put his hands around her throat and squeezed hard. She grabbed at his hair, pulling some strands out, but it was to no avail. He was squeezing so hard that her shouting stopped and she fell limp to the ground. "You got what you deserved!" he hissed, as he turned and left her lying in a heap.

Billy felt calm, relieved. Now I'll go home and attend to more important things. Maybe Joy called me back? He walked to the bus stop and waited patiently for the bus to come. When it arrived, he boarded and sat down comfortably in an empty seat.

Look at that, an empty bus just for me. No crowds or smells for me to worry about. As soon as he settled in the seat, Billy dozed off without a thought on his mind.

What did Billy Reilly know about mercy? His evil act of murder cast a dark shadow on the Moro family.

Maria, a fourteen-year-old with dark brown eyes and long black braids returned home after school. Everything seemed normal. Her ten-year-old brother Juan would be coming home from school soon. Maria knew she was responsible for him. Her mom worked and she had to help out.

Can't wait for her, she thought. When Juan gets home he's always a pain in the ass. Give me this or that! She removed her jacket and was ready to call her friend when she heard a knock on the door.

"It's me, Maria Open the door!" Juan yelled.

"Okay, I'm coming. Hold your horses!"

"What took you so long to answer?" Juan shrieked.

"Give me a break. Do I have to jump the minute you open your big mouth?"

Juan walked into the house upset. "I wish Mommy were home. You never treat me nice."

"What do you want from me? I just got home myself and I wish for the same thing too. Okay, do you want a glass of milk and cookies?" Maria felt guilty picking on her younger brother. It wasn't his fault that Dad left us all. Now Mom has to work to support us.

"Come on, Juan, let's drink the milk and eat the cookies. Do you have homework?"

"Yes, not too much today. I have a science project due next week. Would you help me get started?"

"What kind of project?"

"What is a volcano?"

"I had to do an assignment like that once. Sure, I'll help you."

Maria looked at the time and started to worry. It was six o'clock. Mom usually came home by five p.m.

"Why isn't Mommy home yet?" Juan said, as he continued to snack on a third cookie. Maria didn't want to frighten him, so she made up an excuse.

"She probably had to do some food shopping. We hardly have eggs and milk left."

"Maria, can I watch television, please?"

"I guess so. Remember you have homework."

Juan left the table, walked into the den, and turned the television on. Maria picked up the phone and called her girlfriend Jenny.

"Jenny, it's me, Maria."

"Is something wrong?"

"I'm not sure. My mother is late and I'm starting to get scared. She's usually home by 5:30 at the latest."

"Don't get crazy. Maybe she's shopping or she met someone she knows. You know how mothers can keep talking to each other, right?"

Maria's trembling voice asked, "Well, how long do I wait before I tell someone?"

"Look, I'm coming over. Don't over react yet. It's only six o'clock. Try not to show your brother how nervous you are. He'll drive you crazy! Want me to come over?"

"Thanks, Jen. I need the company."

"I'll be there in 10 minutes."

"Where's Mommy?" Juan yelled from the den. "She's never this late. I'm afraid!"

Maria went into the den to comfort her brother. "Just relax, if she doesn't come home soon, I'll call Auntie Sophia. Let's sit and watch more television. Jenny is coming over to keep us company.

The situation was deteriorating quickly, as Maria lost control of her brother Juanito. Frustrated and frightened, she finally called a relative.

Aunt Sophia notified the police about her missing sister, and then continued on to the Moro home. When she arrived, she found that the children were scared. She tried to calm them down, to no avail. No news is good news she thought, but her heart skipped a beat. I have to stay strong for the family, God forbid! She crossed her heart.

"Did you all eat? I stopped at the Chinese Restaurant and bought some food, just in case."

"No," whimpered Maria. "What happened to my mother?"

"We don't know. Maybe she'll walk in any minute. Let's eat now!"

"I'm hungry," Juanito yelled.

"Of course," Aunt Sophia responded. "Jen, would you like to join us for dinner?"

"I ate at home. Thanks anyway."

Sophia busied herself serving the children. She kept checking her watch. Eight o'clock already; where the hell is she?

"Maybe she's hurt," Juanito mumbled as he chewed on a dumpling.

"We don't know any such thing yet," Sophia said.

"Thanks for coming, Auntie." Maria hugged her aunt.

"Children, that's what we do for family. I love you!" Tears trickled down her cheeks. She turned and wiped them away with a tissue so they wouldn't see.

Sophia wrapped her arms around the youngsters. The warmth and closeness of their aunt felt good.

"Okay, let's finish dinner," she said. Suddenly Juanito banged on the table with his fist and yelled, "Where's my mom?" He was more frightened than ever. Sophia was just about to hug her nephew, when the doorbell rang.

"Don't open the door, Maria! Find out who's out there first," Auntie ordered.

"OK, who's there?" she yelled. "Oh! Who? Detective Pezello? Y-y-y-yes, my aunt is here." She opened the door and saw two men flashing their badges. Maria, shaken, ran to Jen crying hysterically, "Jen, Jen it's the police. I just know something happened to my mother!"

Jen hugged Maria and tried to comfort her.

"Did he say something happened to her? Jen asked, as she tried consoling her friend.

"Not yet. Why would the cops come if she's all right?" They waited while Sophia approached the two men.

"I'm Detective Pezello; This is Detective Green. We're following up on your call. We need some information!"

"Yes, I called you about my sister Lilly Moro. She never came home from work today. Do you know anything about a missing woman?" Sophia nervously asked.

"We can't be certain so quickly," the detective replied. "You said your sister never came home tonight? No calls either?"

No," Sophia answered, feeling light headed and faint, knowing this scene could only mean bad news.

"Do you have a picture of your sister?" the detective requested.

Sophia asked Maria, "Please bring a picture of your mother." She calmed Juanito, who was trembling in her arms. "I'll never see my mom again," he whimpered.

Sobbing, Maria left the room in search of a photograph.

"Please, we don't want your family to think the worst," Pezello said.

The two men sat down facing Sophia, while waiting for Maria to return.

"Here's a picture of my mom at Juanito's last birthday party," Maria said, as she handed Detective Pezello the photo.

"Thanks, it will surely help us," Green answered.

"I know my mother is hurt real bad! You guys wouldn't be here if she were okay," Juanito sobbed, as Sophia held him closer.

"Don't think bad thoughts yet." She smoothed his hair, trying to make him feel better.

"Think we have what we need for now, except for her age."

"She's 37."

"We'll call you when we know more," Detective Green said.

"Thanks for your help." The policemen left the apartment, and the family wondered what would happen next.

"I'm thirsty. Give me a glass of water!" Juanito cried. He grabbed his sister's hand.

The girls led him into the kitchen and gave him a cold drink.

Sophia knew she had to prepare the children for the worst. My hands are wet and clammy. Before I tell them, I'll go to the bathroom and freshen up. That should cool me off. She opened the bathroom door, sat down on the toilet seat, and sobbed uncontrollably, still wondering what could have happened to her sister.

"Auntie, Auntie where are you?" Maria yelled.

"I'm in the bathroom, I'll be right out."

Sophia composed herself, knowing that she would have a hard time explaining to the children. She looked at herself in the mirror, straightened her hair and mumbled, "Be an actress, be an actress! I must take care of these children no matter what happens."

In a nearby apartment, Ann Finn is hysterical as she is on the phone with the police.

"Now, lady, control yourself. You say your son was playing catch with his friends, and what?"

"Officer, my son ran to find the baseball. It rolled into an alley, and he found a dead lady!"

"Where are you? What's your name, phone number, and where is the body?"

"My name is Ann Finn, and my phone number is 555-4123. The building address is 734 West 53rd Street. What do I do now? My son is frightened!"

"Look, we have to talk to your son and his friend. Stay home and wait for me to call you!"

As he was walking out of the Moro's apartment building, Detective Pezello's cell phone rang. He picked it up, "Pezello here." After a pause, he continued, "Okay, we'll be right there." He turned to his partner and said, "We have a homicide a few blocks away." Call the coroner and tell him to meet us at 734 West 53rd Street, pronto!"

CHAPTER 12

"Hey Tony, could you get the phone, please? The damn telephone hasn't stopped ringing since I put the last ad in the *New York Times*."

"Sure, Rose," Tony said as he picked up the receiver. "Field Realty, how can I help you?"

"Rose Field, please. This is Mr. Goldman."

"She'll be with you in a minute." Tony turned to Rose and said, "Mr. Goldman on line 1."

"Thanks Tony, I have the call," she answered. "Hello, Mr. Goldman, thanks for signing our agreement and getting the paperwork back to our office so quickly."

"The faster we get started, the happier my investors will feel. Is Claire well enough to work on our deal?"

"She just got home from the hospital yesterday. I don't think she's ready to negotiate yet, but I'll meet with you as soon as possible. The owner counter offered $1,800.000, and I'm prepared to offer some concessions—refinish the floors, plant a window garden, work out some favorable financing."

"I'll get back to you as soon as I speak to my associates, but I can't promise you they'll be willing to go any higher than my last offer," Mr. Goldman answered.

Tony sat quietly at his desk listening to the conversation. He walked to Rose's desk and said, "Sounds like you might have a deal."

"I hope you're right. She gave him a meaningful look and said, "I think it'll take some work."

As they discussed the Goldman venture, Harry walked in from the adjoining office. "Hi, you two. Have you listened to the radio?"

"What are you talking about?" Rose answered.

"Some kids playing ball found a dead body in an alley on West 53rd Street."

"Another tragedy," Tony shook his head. "What happened?"

"The cops say the victim was female, about 35. She was strangled."

"You can't be too careful walking alone in New York City," Rose uttered.

"The police will catch the killer, you'll see," Harry responded. "Better get back to my office, the phone is ringing."

Rose and Tony looked at each other. Neither one said a word for a while. Finally Tony broke the silence.

"I hope this killer doesn't make a habit of choking people. Remember the Boston Strangler?"

"Tony, you're scaring me. Don't talk like that. Now I'm going to be afraid to go home."

"I didn't mean to frighten you, but you have to be careful walking in the city. Don't wander around at night alone."

"You don't know whether she was killed day or night, do you?"

"It's going to be in every newspaper and T.V. news channel. We'll know more details later."

CHAPTER 13

"Mom, I'm so excited. My legs feel weak and my hands are clammy. Does that mean I'm in love?"

"If I knew what you were talking about I could answer your question. Who are you supposed to be in love with?" Betty asked.

"Billy's message was on my voicemail. He said he would call me, and he kept his word. I'm calling him back."

"Joy, you're moving too fast! How do you know what he's like or what love really is?"

"If I don't find out soon, I'll never know. Be back in two minutes."

Joy walked quickly into the den and dialed Billy's number. The phone rang five times, and finally his greeting echoed in her ear.

She was disappointed. "This is Joy returning your call. You can reach me on my cell phone, 555-0655." She hung up and went back to her mother.

"Honey, get your mind off him. Since Claire is home now, let's do something worthwhile. She's probably anxious for us to visit and keep her company."

"Fine, let's do it!" Betty and Joy left the apartment and flagged a cab to Claire's place.

"It's difficult to hear with the radio blasting away." Joy spoke loudly so the cabbie would hear.

"Sorry, lady, I was listening to news about a murder in midtown."

"Please, I hate hearing such horrible news. Could you please lower the radio? I'm trying to call someone."

"Yeah, I'll turn the volume down."

Joy called Claire's house to check with the home health aide on her status.

"Hi, this is Claire's sister. Is everything all right? We'll be there in about 15 minutes. Are you okay with food and household goods?"

"Great," Joy exclaimed, after listening to her reply.

She turned to her mother and whispered, "The aide said all is well. The fridge is full. I'm so grateful Claire is home from the hospital. It could have been a tragic ending."

"Stop talking like that, Mom. Don't be morbid! Be happy that life is good and will continue to stay that way."

Betty paid the driver, and they walked to Claire's building. Joy's cell phone rang.

"Hey, this is Billy," he greeted her.

Betty watched her daughter with perceptive eyes, "Uh-huh, that has to be Billy!"

"We finally connected," Joy said.

"When are we getting together?" Billy asked. "Could I see you tomorrow night? Let's meet for a drink and dinner."

"What time?"

"Meet me 7:30 at Joey's Diner, York and 75th."

"Fine, see you then," Joy replied.

She closed the cell phone and looked up at her mother. "Mom, I knew he would call again! I'm going to meet him tomorrow for dinner. I'm so happy! He's an angel."

"Joy, your face is tomato red. Is that a fever coming on or are you blushing?" Betty teased.

"I'm wonderful. I feel like the sun is shining on my face, and the blood is tingling in my body. You can't tell me that isn't love."

"I'm not sure, my dear. Things never happen so fast, but I guess passion can grab hold of two people. Please be careful! Now let's go upstairs and visit with your sister."

After he got off the phone, Billy's thoughts traveled between the thrill of the murder he committed just hours ago and the anticipation of his upcoming date with Joy.

The next morning, Billy awakened, hair tousled and bleary-eyed. She deserved what she got, he thought. Now, what do I do first before I meet Joy? He jumped out of bed and walked quickly to the bathroom to relieve himself. As he dashed through the door he saw his reflection on the bathroom mirror. Jesus, I look like hell turned over twice. He washed his face and brushed his teeth, picked up the hairbrush, and combed his unruly hair. When finished, he looked admiringly at his reflection. Guess I can look good when I try.

He walked into the bedroom and dressed for work. Better take a change of clothing along. Who needs the stress of going home before I meet her? Billy felt a rush of adrenaline as he grabbed his jacket and left the apartment for his job. While he waited for the bus, he daydreamed about Joy holding his hand tightly, smiling at him.

"Mister, you better step up on the bus, so we can get on too." Billy jerked forward and moved quickly toward a seat.

He walked into the hospital and was immediately spotted by Penny.

"Hi Billy, you're early, something special today? Penny slyly asked. "You're usually late."

The aide looked at her with ice blue eyes. "Even if I had something special today, why would I tell you?"

Penny looked back at him, shocked at his cold reply. "Well, I didn't know you had a special secret!"

"I signed in. Can you tell me where I start work today?" He asked her in an annoyed voice.

"Dr. Wang needs a transfer from the O.R., so grab a gurney and get going. No hard feelings, I hope?"

Billy didn't answer. He lifted his assignment report and moved quickly out of the office. She's a bitch, he thought. One day I'll take care of her. He grabbed a gurney and headed toward the elevator.

When he arrived at the O.R. he checked the patient's report. "Donna Weintraub," he murmured as he scanned the room, looking for her chart. Because of the massive numbers of surgeries, it took time to find the patient. Billy walked up and down the room checking the charts. Suddenly Nurse Rena Schmidt approached him. At first, she didn't recognize him.

"I'm on duty this morning. May I help you?"

Billy knew her instantly and turned to walk away.

"Why are you in the O.R.?" The nurse raised her voice.

The aide knew he would have to calm down and face her. His heart raced as he put his hands behind his back and cracked his knuckles.

"Oh, y-yes. I'm supposed to transfer Donna Weintraub to her room."

"Why didn't you answer me? I don't bite."

"I don't know," Billy answered, "Guess I was a little frustrated not finding her."

"I know exactly where her bed is. Follow me, please."

The nurse helped Billy transfer the dazed patient onto the gurney.

"Thanks for helping me."

"It's okay," Rena replied.

As Billy walked away, the nurse remembered him. Didn't I find him sneaking around the patient's rooms? Maybe I'm paranoid, but there's something about him I still don't like. Oh well, better get back to work.

Billy transferred the patient to her room. He made her comfortable, and as he was ready to leave she opened her eyes and called to him. "Please, doctor, I'm in sooo much pain. Please help me!"

"I'm an aide, not a doctor," he whispered. "I'll ask Dr. Wang to give you something. Wait a minute, I'll be right back."

"Thank you for being so helpful." She closed her eyes and waited for the aide to help.

Billy walked down the hospital hallway and stopped Doctor Wang. "Doc, your patient, Miss Weintraub is asking for a painkiller."

"Thanks for telling me, Billy. Tell her I'll be right in to see her. You certainly know how to do your job well."

CHAPTER 14

On the way to Claire's apartment, Joy was dreamy-eyed about her date with Billy that evening. A minute later she was awakened from her reverie by her mother. "Open your eyes dear; we've arrived."

They stepped out of the taxi, walked into the lobby of the building, and continued up to the apartment. When Betty rang the doorbell, the aide greeted them.

"Hi, Susan. How is the patient?" Betty asked.

"Claire is resting and feeling fine. Can't believe how excited she was waiting for you."

They opened the door to Claire's bedroom. She was sitting in her bed, propped up on several pillows. Her dark brown hair was pulled back to one side with a stylish comb. The pink nightgown brought out the color in her cheeks as the sun's ray gave the room a golden glow.

"Gosh!" Joy observed, "You look beautiful." She walked to her sister's bed and kissed her on the cheek. Betty greeted her daughter with a hug. "How are you feeling, baby? You do look lovely today."

"Oh, I think both of you need new glasses. Nobody ever called me beautiful."

Joy turned to Betty and said, "Look Mom, she's blushing because we complimented her. Claire, we're speaking the truth. Anyway, how are you feeling?"

"I'm fine, but bored hanging out at home."

Betty said, "Don't you have to see your doctor soon?"

"Yes, in two days. If he gives me a good report, I'm going back to work. Do you guys want coffee or a cold drink?"

"No, thanks," Joy answered. "We're fine."

"What's going on with you, sis?"

"I met the love of my life."

"She hasn't gone out with him yet, and already she's in love!" Betty muttered, showing her disapproval.

"Who is he?" Claire asked.

"His name is Billy and he works as an aide at Beth David Hospital."

"This is getting interesting," Claire remarked. "Let's hear more about Billy."

"Well, I met him accidentally in the hospital hallway. He helped me when I dropped my purse and everything spilled all over the hallway."

"He certainly sounds like a doll. I wish you good luck on your first date. When are you seeing him?"

"We're going out tonight. I knew you would be happy for me. Mom thinks I'm rushing into this relationship too fast."

"No, honey," Betty said. "I just want you to be careful. You know I love you and want you to be happy."

"Thanks, Mom," Joy answered. "Think I'll take you up on a glass of Sprite, Claire."

"Sure! Susan, could I have two glasses of Sprite for my family, please."

"Of course," she answered.

While they discussed Joy's love life, the telephone rang, and Susan answered it.

"Yes, this is Susan. Claire is fine. Her family is visiting now. Who shall I say is calling? Rose? Okay."

Joy and Betty sat quietly near Claire as they waited for her to answer the call.

"Hi Rose," Claire said, smiling. "I'm glad you called. We were just talking about the office."

"Claire, it's so good to hear your voice. How are you feeling?"

"Better than you can imagine. In fact, I'm anxious to work again. Is my deal with Mr. Goldman still intact?"

"Yes, my dear. We have an exclusive agreement with him and his investors. When you return I'll give you all the information. Now I think you should rest and get your strength back."

"Rose, I must be getting better since all I think about is real estate and food. That's a good sign, isn't it?" She smiled and nodded to Joy and Betty. They both winked back, each giving the thumb's up sign. "I have an appointment with my doctor in a few days. If he gives his approval, I'm coming in on Monday. Thanks for calling."

"Get well fast. I'll talk to you at the end of the week. Goodbye."

Claire put the phone back in the cradle and turned to Betty and Joy.

"You sound wonderful, Claire," Betty smiled. "I have a feeling you'll be out and about very soon."

"Thanks for your vote of confidence."

As Rose hung up the phone, she looked over the two rental ads she recently put in the *New York Times*. Apartments were hard to find, so she knew the phones would ring.

Tony promised to come in and answer the phones over the weekend. Rose hoped he would keep his promise, as he hasn't called.

As she cleared her breakfast dishes and prepared to leave for the office her phone rang. She recognized the voice, "Tony, I was just thinking of you. Are you still coming in today?"

"I have to attend to some chores, but I'll be there."

"Fine. You'll be able to come in tomorrow as well, right?"

"Sure."

"Is there a problem? You don't sound like your old cheerful self."

"It's a family problem. I'll keep in touch with you. Take care."

Wow! He was definitely unfriendly, she thought. I didn't have a chance to tell him about Claire coming to work on Monday. Well, he'll find out soon enough.

She looked at the time. 8 o'clock, better get moving. I'm hooked on Tony, and now he's driving me crazy. Maybe he's getting back to his old ways. I hope I'm wrong.

The receptionist, Rachel, was sitting at her desk when Rose arrived.

"Good morning, any calls for me?"

"No, Ms. Field," she responded and returned to her work. As Rose walked to her office, the phone rang.

"Hi, my name is William Reilly. I registered with your company last week. Do you have any one-bedroom apartments to show me?"

Rose thought for a minute and then recalled the young man who had applied with her agency. She said, "Yes, I remember you. I do have a few apartments to show, but you never came in with referrals. We have a rule in our company to check the background of all the applicants. Do you have the referrals now?"

"I'm working on it. As soon as they arrive I'll bring them to your office."

"Is there anything else I can help you with?" Rose asked.

"No, I'll be in touch with you soon. Thanks." Billy hung up and grinned, wondering how the hell he was gonna get the referrals. That'll be the day, he told himself. Then suddenly he remembered, holy shit! I'm taking Joy out. Her sister works at that place, so I'll get her to help me. That's the best idea yet. Boy! Am I brilliant!

Rose stepped out for a while when Tony finally showed up. He was in a bad mood, as he sat at his desk waiting for the phones to ring. My weekend is ruined, but Rose can't say I'm unreliable. As he scanned the real estate section to check the ad, he thought about his marital problems and wondered how he would survive the agony.

Harry walked in and approached Tony's desk. "Hey, how are you doing?"

Grateful to have someone to talk to, he answered, "Lousy. My ex-wife is driving me nuts. I don't need Rose on my back!"

"Rose? What did she do to you?"

"Nothing yet. She acted like she was going to give me a piece of Claire's deal. So far she hasn't said one word about the transaction. What am I supposed to think? I have a feeling I'm screwed. I don't know when Claire is returning, nor do I care. I also admit I was intimate with Rose. Think I'd have learned a lesson not to get involved where you work, right?"

"Right, you must have led her on. When are you going to zip up your zipper? Your dick is getting you into more trouble than it's worth. Didn't you have an affair with Claire too?"

"Yeah, that was stupid! My marriage went on the rocks because I cheated on my wife. Guess I'll never change."

Suddenly they heard footsteps in the adjoining office.

"Is anyone here?" Rose yelled from the entry hall.

"She's here, Harry! Who the heck needs her in the office today? I told her I'd come in and handle everything. Look, do me a favor and keep everything quiet. I'm fed up with her. Maybe I can do some maneuvering to get the Goldman deal."

"That's a pretty cheap trick, Tony!"

"I don't care, so why should you?"

"You should care. We have a Code of Ethics to follow."

Harry couldn't get over the lack of integrity he had just witnessed. He shook his head, wondering about him, and then went back to his office.

Tony walked back into the main office in a huff, and saw Rose. "Oh, I didn't think you were coming in today. Don't you trust me by now? If I said I would cover, I meant it. You didn't have to check up on me!"

"I'm not checking up on you. I just wanted to discuss why you've disappeared from my life. I miss you and want to know what happened."

"Nothing happened. I'm having problems with my ex-wife. She wants more alimony and I can't afford it. Oh yes, one more thing. You told me I would get to help Claire with her deal, but you never followed through. That would have lined my pockets if it worked out the way you said."

The phone rang. Rose quickly picked up. "Field Realty, may I help you?"

"This is William Reilly. I'm following up on a visit I made to your office. Just wondering why I haven't heard from you since that day."

Rose hesitated for a brief moment, realizing that she just had this conversation with Reilly a couple of hours earlier. "Oh yes," she responded. "Were you able to get three referrals?"

"No problem. When can I see some rentals?"

"When we receive your referrals, one of our salespeople will call you."

"Please don't take your time. I have to move by next month."

"Get the paperwork to us and we'll get moving. I have to go now."

"Could you believe the nerve of that fellow? He never sent

referrals, but he keeps calling, expecting us to call him and show apartments. We'll see how long it takes him to get going. Sorry, Tony, getting back to Claire. She didn't want to share her deal. In fact that was the other subject I wanted to discuss. She's coming back to work tomorrow and I'm throwing a small welcome back party for her. Please join us, and if you can help me set the office up, I'd appreciate it."

"Things were going along fine without Claire. Why couldn't she break down and share her loft deal with me?"

"Tony, stop it! That's what life throws at us. We learn to take it! I never promised you a thing. It's her transaction to do with as she wishes. I have to leave now to shop for the party. Can I count on you for tomorrow?"

"Sure."

CHAPTER 15

It's amazing, thought Joy. A few days ago Claire was in the hospital, and now she's making a quick recovery. Visiting my sister made me happy. Guess I'm lucky she's on my side when it comes to Billy. Now I have to decide what to wear tonight.

She went to her closet and looked through her clothes. Okay, maybe the black dress? She put it on and looked at herself in the mirror, murmuring, "No, I hate the way I look; too drab." She threw it on the bed. "I think my green sweater and jeans may work." Joy tried again, pulling the sweater over her head and buttoning the tight jeans around her waist. "I look horrible," she commented, as she looked at herself in the full-length mirror. "Too chunky. What's wrong with me? Nothing fits right. Am I getting fat?" She peeled off the sweater, tossed it on the bed along with the pants and dress, and tried again. She moved through every piece of clothing on their hangers and almost gave up.

"There's nothing in this closet I like enough to wear tonight," she said. As Joy returned to the bedroom, she caught a glimpse of a navy blue slack outfit in the corner of the closet, partially hidden by a jacket. Joy felt exhilarated as she tried on the blouse and closed each button. She knew this pants outfit always flattered her and the reflection in the mirror proved her right. She added a turquoise pendant and thought... I hope Billy loves the way I look tonight. She twirled around and around, singing "I Feel Pretty" until she felt dizzy. Finally she decided she'd better stop this nonsense immediately!

Now that her choice of clothing was out of the way, Joy calmed down and thought about calling Claire. She handles Mom like a professional. I think my mother hates Billy, without knowing him. Joy dialed her sister and waited.

The aide, Susan, picked up. "Hello, may I help you?"

"Hi, may I speak to Claire?"

"Sure, hold on a minute." Susan turned to Claire and told her, "Your sister is on the phone."

"I have it, thanks." Then, speaking into the phone said, "Joy, how are you, honey?"

"A little exhausted tearing apart my closet. I couldn't find a decent thing to wear."

"You could always go shopping," Claire laughed.

"I finally found something I like. The reason I'm really calling is to thank you for protecting me. You always know how to deal with Mom."

"Look, just because I had a lousy experience it doesn't mean that everyone else will! You're a different person, capable of making choices. Don't let her stop you, especially when it comes to your love life. I know she's pretty tough on you. Don't be angry with her. It's because she loves you so much, and wants you to have the best."

"Claire, imagine if I didn't follow my heart. I'd be angry with her for the rest of my life. I have to find out about Billy for myself. I'm so lucky you're my sister. Love you!"

"I feel the same. We're all fortunate to have each other."

"Are you feeling better?" Joy asked.

"I'm ready to get out of this house now!"

"Give yourself a little more time to rest."

"I need to get back to work. It's never the same when others handle my business. I'm as strong as a horse and ready for action. Joy, there's a huge commission if I close this transaction. I could use the extra money with all the hospital bills."

"Well, then, let's get on with it. Get your rest and I'll talk to you later."

Joy hung up the phone, smiling as she thought about seeing Billy.

Thoughts of Joy also clouded Billy's brain. I can't think of anything but seeing Joy tonight. Billy rushed to his locker, opened the door, and removed his overnight bag. I can't believe Donna Weintraub thought I was a doctor. He smiled, remembering. That's the best thing anyone ever said to me. As he changed out of his uniform, Penny tapped him on the shoulder.

"Fancy meeting you here?"

"Jesus! You scared me!"

"Going on a date tonight, right?"

"What are you talking about?"

"Well, you're getting all dressed up."

"Look, Penny, it's none of your damn business. Since when do I have to report to you about my personal life?"

"You don't," she answered. "For whatever it's worth, have a great time."

Billy relaxed and said, "Okay, thanks."

He waved to her, and finished changing his clothes. Okay, he thought, now off to the bathroom.

Billy washed his face and brushed his teeth. I haven't felt this good in awhile. She has to fall in love with me. I'm damn handsome, he thought, looking at himself in the mirror. He combed his blond hair back away from his face and stepped back. I look too stiff with my hair slicked back, he thought. I'm changing the look. He brushed his hair over again and combed it into a softer look, a wave on the right side. That's better, he thought, as he took another look at himself. "Holy shit, what girl in this world could resist me?

Billy felt exhilarated as he looked at his watch. It was six o'clock. One hour to go. I'm Goddamn excited about seeing her again!

Billy arrived at the diner early, while he waited for Joy with great anticipation. He looked at his watch; in five minutes his life could change. Will she like me or am I going to have to persuade her? While he fantasized Joy walked in, and he knew his mother was right. As she approached, his heart raced. Look how beautiful she is. What a body! What a face!

Oh my God! My knees feel weak, Joy thought, as she sat down. Slow down, don't make a fool of yourself, she told herself. Let him wonder for a while. Finally she looked up at him and said, "I hope you weren't waiting too long?"

He looked at her, smiled, and said, "No, maybe 10 minutes."

She's more than I hoped for, but I've been sitting here five minutes and she's not showing any emotion at all. Billy was disappointed with her lack of warmth and nervously began cracking his knuckles under the table.

They looked at each other and an awkward silence permeated.

"Well," Billy said, "Think we should check the menu and order some food?"

"Good idea."

"I know what I want," Joy said. "I always enjoy a Cobb Salad and coffee."

"Great! I think I'll order a strip steak, baked potato, and coke."

They ate, barely talking to each other. This is not what I expected, Billy thought. She doesn't talk. How am I supposed to know what she thinks? He moved around restlessly in his seat while he ate, thinking maybe he was completely wrong about her.

Joy finished her food and quickly excused herself. "I'll be right back; have to go to the restroom. When we're finished, maybe we can take a walk to the park?"

"Good idea," Billy said and watched Joy leave. He couldn't take his eyes off her as she departed. It was not a good beginning, but it seemed to be getting better.

When Joy entered the rest room, she checked to make sure it was empty. She walked to the mirror, looked at her reflection, and blurted out: "Stupid, stupid, stupid. What are you doing? Did you lose your tongue? He's going to hate the way I clammed up. I was completely overwhelmed and couldn't speak. When I get back I'll be more cordial and make him feel more comfortable."

Suddenly the door of the bathroom opened. Joy opened her purse and took out her powder, lipstick and hairbrush. She attended to herself carefully. Satisfied, she put her cosmetics back in her handbag. As she left the bathroom she felt a wave of excitement. This date means a lot to me. I must handle him right!

Billy kept his eyes peeled on the bathroom door. Jesus! When the hell is she coming out? As he turned to check the time, Joy finally walked toward the table.

"Bet you thought I fell in, right?" Joy coyly chuckled.

"Well, not really," he lied. "Let's decide where you would like to go. You mentioned the park. It's quite a way from here. Let's walk up to First Avenue."

"Fine, we can walk, talk, and get to know each other."

As Billy paid the cashier, he thought of ways he could entice Joy to become his girlfriend. What do I have to offer someone like her? She's pretty and bright, so I'll probably have to make up stories about my past.

As he planned his maneuver, Joy tapped him on the shoulder. "Hey Billy, hello..."

"Oh, I was thinking about which direction we should walk: north or south. The scenery is much nicer heading south."

"I really don't care, whatever you say."

She's easy to influence, he thought, as he pocketed his change.

"I would like to pay for my share of the meal," Joy offered.

"It's on me tonight. Maybe next time," he told her. Jesus, he caught the look she gave him. I think she really likes me. A strange feeling overcame him. I haven't felt this happy in months.

They walked out of the diner and headed toward First Avenue.

"I love this time of the year," Joy smiled. "The leaves are turning smashing shades of red and yellow. Mother Nature at her best, and we're the lucky ones who enjoy all the beauty."

"Are you a painter?"

"I love to paint and sculpt, but I've been neglecting my work lately. My job as a teacher's aide at Grover's Middle School keeps me pretty busy, but lately, my mind has been on my family. Things are starting to return to normal. My sister is finally home and completely recovered. In fact, she's going back to work tomorrow."

Billy stopped short for a second, "Wow! Maybe she could help me find an apartment?"

"I don't see why not," Joy answered.

Suddenly, without hesitation, Billy grabbed her hand and held it tightly. His gesture surprised her.

Oh my goodness, she thought, that funny feeling again. Her face flushed.

"Why are you blushing, Joy?"

"I'm not, really. Walking fast always makes me get rosy cheeks."

She made an awkward attempt to change the subject. "I told you about myself. Why don't you tell me a little about yourself?"

"Sure, you know I work as a doctor's aide at the hospital. It's temporary until I finish taking classes at Columbia. I'm gonna be a nurse eventually. The bills are incredible, but I'm getting a grant. The doctors and nurses said they would give me referrals."

"Billy, that's incredible. We're both aides in helping professions, and we're both planning to advance. We're soul mates! If I were your parents I'd be so proud of you."

"My mom is dead and I haven't seen my dad since he abandoned us. How could he be proud of me? All he ever did was criticize me and beat me when I was a kid." He shrugged it off, but the bitter memories remained.

"You seem to work so hard and deserve to get a nursing degree. Maybe one day you and your dad will have a reunion? When he discovers how productive you are, he'll certainly be proud of you." She couldn't forget Billy's sad story.

They were so engaged in talking, neither one realized they had walked twenty blocks.

"Where did the time go?" Joy uttered, surprised to see her apartment building down the block.

"We had a great time, right? I would like to see you again," he said.

"Me too, I'd love to see you again. Call me and we'll make another date. Look, I live right down the block. I must go home now!"

Billy walked her to the entrance of her apartment building, turned to her, and said,

"How about if I come up and see your paintings just for a little while?"

Joy wrinkled her nose and gave him an apologetic smile. "Not tonight, maybe next time." She looked him in the eyes and said, "Goodnight, Billy," turned away and walked into the building.

Billy couldn't believe she wouldn't invite him up. He felt a rumbling in his stomach. The tremor rose to his head, turning annoyance to a slow simmer. I thought we connected, but I guess I was wrong. I'm not giving up. I'll call her when I get home and invite her out again on Monday night. I know she likes me.

It was no use. Billy could think of nothing else but Joy as he made his way back home. The attraction was incredible. I can't get her out of my head; she's all that I need! Why wouldn't she let me go up to her apartment? We got along great, and I know she has feelings for me. I'll call her back. She could be very useful. Joy can get me referrals, and her sister could find the right apartment.

Billy was emotionally distressed after he left Joy. She affected him so completely he couldn't concentrate. Suddenly he realized he was walking in the wrong direction. This is nuts! I'm a real asshole walking north instead of south! Thinking of her made him nervous. He started cracking his knuckles, sweating, and his hands felt wet and clammy. Jesus, I better get home fast, I'm losing control. He turned and headed home.

On the west side of the avenue he noticed a liquor store. The same little place he passed a few weeks ago. Great, he thought. Why don't I buy a couple of bottles? He crossed the street, entered the store, and approached the clerk.

"Whattaya need?" the clerk asked.

He shrugged his shoulders as he answered, "Two pints of Absolut?"

The clerk looked at him curiously as he wrapped the bottles. Billy handed him a fifty-dollar bill. "Thanks! See ya," Billy said, as he picked up the brown paper bag, took his change, and walked out. I can't wait to call Joy. He pulled out his cell phone and dialed her number. He waited.

"Hello," she said.

"Hi," Billy answered excitedly. "I'd like to ask you out Monday night."

"Oh, I can't see you Monday, Billy."

His heart raced as he replied. "Why not? I thought we liked each other."

"I do like you, Billy. Something just came up. I've been invited to a welcome back party for my sister tomorrow."

"Oh. Can I come?"

"I don't know. I'll have to check with the hostess. Let me call you back, okay?"

"Great! I'm on my way home. Give me about twenty minutes. I'll be expecting your call."

As soon as Joy finished her conversation with Billy, she called Rose.

"Rose, this is Joy. I'm so happy that you're planning a party for my sister. That's real thoughtful of you. I'm definitely coming. I was wondering if I could bring my friend."

"I don't think so, Joy. This party is for the office staff. Of course you and your mother are welcome."

"Are you sure about that?"

"Yes, I can't make exceptions."

Joy ended the conversation and called Billy. As she dialed his number, she had a feeling he wouldn't be happy with Rose's refusal.

Billy ran all the way home and jumped two steps at a time up the staircase. He opened the lock to his apartment and made a dash for the ringing phone.

"I hope the answer is yes!"

"How did you know it's me, silly?"

"I knew by the sound of the ring." He smiled, waiting for her reply.

"I'm sorry. I called the office and spoke to the broker. She said no. If she let's you come, others will want to bring guests. Why don't we get together the following night?"

"Well," he answered, disappointed. "She sounds like a bitch!"

"Rose is not a bitch. She wants to be fair."

"Joy, I'll call you tomorrow."

He hung up abruptly. I feel like exploding. I'll get even with that whore one day, he promised himself. She'll be sorry she screwed me. Feelings of isolation enveloped him. Maybe a little drink will make me feel better. Rejection always had a negative effect on Billy. He hated to feel like an outsider. Rose's final refusal for him to attend the party enhanced his feelings of alienation.

I'm unable to control my feelings anymore. My body keeps shaking uncontrollably, and everything I do sucks! Maybe I'll kill myself and end my misery. No, maybe somebody else deserves to die. That's it ... that's it! He suddenly cracked his knuckles with great intensity.

"Where is that fuckin' drink? I can't stand it," he yelled. Billy grabbed the bottle of vodka and hungrily slurped half the liquid down without a stop. He walked over to the mattress on the floor, sat down on it, and guzzled the second half. The phone kept ringing, but Billy was oblivious to the noise. He collapsed on the mattress. It didn't take long for him to fall into a deep sleep and have another dream.

*

Where am I? This isn't real. Look at me! I'm 13 years old. What am I supposed to be doing here? I don't even know where the hell I am. Gosh, I remember this place. I used to come here to meet my friends. Who the heck is walking toward me?

"Hey, Billy, remember me?"

"How the heck am I supposed to know you? You look familiar. Yeah, I remember. We used to meet all the guys here and fool around."

"Look, you're still a kid. I'm Nick, the experienced guy around here. Maybe you could learn some stuff from me, or are you too dumb?" Nick faced young Billy with a cigarette dangling from his lips, circles of smoke floating around them.

"I ain't stupid."

"If you ain't a moron, why don't ya sit down with me?"

"Sure."

"Come here kid, look at these pictures."

Billy's eyebrows lifted in shock. "Jesus, those girls are all naked."

"Shut up moron, of course they're naked. How do you think you could have fun with girls unless they're undressed?"

"Gee, I never saw any girl naked."

"That's because you're a kid. When you get to be my age, you'll be an expert with the girls." Nick laughed and said, "Wait, those aren't the only pictures I have. Look at these." He took another drag of the cigarette and then showed Billy more photos. By this time cigarette smoke encompassed both, and they could hardly see each other.

"Hey Nick, what kind of pictures are you showing me? Looks like those girls are dead. What did you do to those girls?"

"I had a good time with them and then I slit their throats. It was a thrill. Once you do it, you want to do it again and again."

"Go away! I don't like what you're saying." Billy covered his ears with both hands.

"I'll go away, but you'll be back one day. You'll ask me for more."

Billy watched Nick walk away in a cloud of smoke. His dream ended, and he was beginning to wake up. He tossed and turned, still groggy with sleep. It was all coming back to him.

He ran home, shocked and furious at Nick. Who was he to have shown me such horrible, unthinkable pictures? Should I have told my mom? No way! She would have a fit, and Nick would have thought I'm a baby. He'd have said, "Look at the baby. Had to go home and tell his mommy!" Better to have left it alone.

*

In a corner of his brain, Billy thought he heard a phone ring. It continued ringing until he awoke.

"W-W-What the hell is going on?" he stuttered. He staggered to his feet holding on to the wall for support and answered the phone. Too late, the person hung up. Oh, he thought, if they want me they'll call again. He felt like a wreck after the liquor binge. Gee, I still can't walk a straight line, he thought.

Billy looked at his watch. Jeez, I slept the night away. Today's the fucking party. I'll show them for not inviting me. Little do they know the uninvited guest will be waiting outside in the shadows. Gotta call the hospital to tell them I'm sick. What the hell do I care? Important things must be taken care of first.

Even though I'm still staggering, have to get the hell out of here. He grabbed his jacket and left the apartment, anxious to pursue his plan. There must be more to the wild dreams I'm having. How the heck do I find out the rest of the story? He smiled as he thought... guess I gotta get drunk again.

*

The crisp air cleared Billy's mind as he sprinted up Second Avenue. The effect of alcohol slowly dissipated. Billy dialed the hospital and was connected to the main floor office.

Penny picked up. "May I help you?"

"Hi Penny, this is Billy. I'm sick … think I have a virus."

"Sorry to hear that. Better stay home and rest."

As Billy hung up the phone he thought, I'm not really in a hurry to get back to work. He took his time getting out of the apartment and walking to the bus stop.

The bus stopped; Billy hopped on and paid his fare. He glanced around the bus and made his way to a seat in the back. Great, he decided, I'll make a plan. It took a few seconds for Billy to nod off.

*

This hallway seemed familiar. Holy shit, Nick's here! He looks a little older, but it's him.

"Hi, Nick."

"Hey kid. You look like you aged about five years. How old are you?"

"18. Why are we in this hallway, Nick?"

"You've grown up. Not a kid anymore, huh? It's time to get a good lay."

"Is that what I'm supposed to do, get laid? Who am I supposed to do it with?"

"Don't worry, follow me down the hall. Take the second door on the left. Don't make a sound until I say so." When he reached the door, Nick knocked twice and entered. Billy waited outside.

Nick came out and grabbed Billy by the shoulders. He whispered in his ear, "She's waiting for you on the bed. Don't talk, just walk over and sit down next to her. She'll give you everything you've dreamed about and never had."

Billy did as he was told. Why am I sweating, he thought. Jesus –

Jesus. My heart's racing like a machine. Then he saw her for the first time. She was lying in a massive bed, covered only in chiffon. Her left breast was exposed to excite him … and it did. He could feel the hardness in his groin. How could I help it? He thought she was the most beautiful woman he'd ever seen. Smooth olive skin, pink cheeks, long dark hair around her flawless face and deep brown eyes. The thrill and fear of the moment enhanced his hunger and lust for her.

"Come sit next to me," she whispered.

Billy slowly sat down on the bed next to her. She smiled as her arms enveloped him and his lust for her became unbearable. As his hunger mounted, she waited for the special moment when they would become one. His inexperience in sex caused him to fail. Thoughts of fear raced through Billy's mind causing his erection to shrink. The prostitute sat up quickly, looked at him and laughed.

*

Horns--where was all that noise coming from? Billy thought he was still dreaming.

"Hey mister, this is the last stop for my bus. I don't know where you have to go, but you gotta get off now!"

"Jesus, I must have dozed off. What street is this?"

"96th Street."

"Damn, I missed my stop."

*

A short walk from where Billy hopped off the bus, Rose crossed Second Avenue and walked into the party store. She thought to herself, I can't remember feeling so happy fussing over a party Claire deserves. She quickly inspected the party merchandise, and within 10 minutes, had a shopping cart filled with balloons, paper goods, and plastic glasses. Now, on to the caterer, but first I'll call the office and check in with Rachel.

"Hi, Rachel. Any calls?"

"Yes, Tony."

"Did he say he's coming in to set up for the party?"

"Yes, at 3:00."

"Great, that's what I needed to know. If he calls again, tell him I should be back at the office by then. Who else called?"

"William Reilly. He wanted to know if you have any rental apartments to show him. He also said he's anxious to move."

"What a pain he's turning into. I never received referrals, so why would I bother showing him my listings? The next time he calls tell him to get the referrals here fast. Have to hang, see you later."

She left the party shop and continued walking up the avenue toward Joe's Caterers. Rose entered the deli with her list of guests. She approached the counter and said, "Hi, Joe, I need a cold cut platter for 12. Add all the side dishes too."

"Sure, Mrs. Field. What time and day?"

"Have the order ready tomorrow at noon."

"You'll have to pick up the food an hour before then."

"Fine, someone from my office will come."

"Thanks, Ms. Field. Have a great day."

Rose left the caterer happy that she had accomplished everything.

After making her way back to the office, Rose wondered briefly whether her decision not to invite Joy's friend was wise. She finished the remaining details for the party. The last few balloons rose to the ceiling, creating a colorful vista. Rose stood back and admired her work.

"Don't you think the office looks great, Rachel?"

"Everything looks terrific, Ms. Field. Claire will be very surprised."

Rose looked at her watch and hesitated.

"God, Tony isn't back yet. He better not ruin our plans"

"Maybe he's waiting in a long line for the food. Don't worry, he won't be late."

"Rachel, everything is ready. Ask Harry and the others to meet in the office. Claire and her family will be here in 25 minutes. We can all have drinks and get the party started."

"Great idea," the receptionist answered.

"I'm going to the rest room. Please get things going!"

Rachel this, Rachel that, she thought. I'm getting sick of Rose ordering me around. Maybe I'll leave as soon as I can find another job. I don't particularly like real estate anyway.

As Rachel pondered a career change, two phones began ringing. She picked up line one: "Field Real Estate, one moment please." She picked up line two: "Field Real Estate, how may I help you?"

"It's Tony, I'm leaving in two minutes. Tell Rose I got stuck in a long line. See you soon."

Rachel picked up line one: "May I help you?"

"This is Mr. Goldman. Rose Field, please."

"Ms. Field is not available. Would you like to leave a message?"

"Tell her to call me back immediately; it's important." He hung up.

Rose checked herself out in the bathroom mirror. I don't look too bad, considering I've been running around like a maniac all morning. My makeup looks fine. Damn, my hair is a mess. I'll comb it back with my brush... There, much better. She turned around and checked herself in a full-length mirror and laughed. My skirt is lopsided. How would that look, a real estate broker with a crooked skirt?

So many things muddled her mind. She sat down on a stool and meditated. I'm always in the middle of turmoil. If it's not one thing it's another. Joy may never talk to me again. It's not worth it. I think I'll call Joy and tell her to bring her friend. After all, it's her sister's party. She tapped in Joy's cell number and waited.

"Hi," Joy answered.

"It's Rose, honey. I thought it over and decided you can invite your friend." She fidgeted for a few seconds.

"Thanks Rose. I'm so happy. I'll call him immediately. Don't know how to thank you. See you soon."

I'm glad that was resolved, Rose thought as she heaved a sigh of relief.

Another worry, I don't know whether the Goldman deal is still intact. Nothing is working for me. Tony is another story, he and his crazy unpredictable behavior. Maybe things will change soon. She took a last look in the mirror and returned to the office.

CHAPTER 16

Joy tried calling Billy all morning without success. Where can he be? She threw her hands up and shrugged. When she checked the time and saw it was 11:15 a.m., she began fidgeting. Better call Claire, she thought. It's almost time to pick her up.

Joy dialed Claire's number.

"Hi," she answered.

"Claire, it's me. Are you almost ready?"

"Give me 10 minutes more. Are you sure you want to come with me?"

"Look, it's your first day back. I don't want you going alone. I'll feel better."

"I love you, Joy. You're always there for me."

"I wouldn't have it any other way."

Wow, Joy thought. She has no idea about the surprise party!

"I'll pick you up at 11:30. See you then." As soon as she hung up, Joy called her mother.

"Hi," Betty answered.

"Mom, it's me. I think you should meet us at the office or she'll suspect something."

"Okay, I'll make sure I arrive before noon. I don't want to ruin the surprise. How are you doing, sweetheart?"

"Everything would be perfect if I had spoken to Billy. I can't reach him."

"There's nothing else you can do. Did you leave a message on his voicemail?"

"Yes."

Betty reflected that she was so relieved Billy couldn't be reached.

She thought her daughter didn't realize she's better off without him. The only thing Betty could say was, "Maybe it's not meant to be."

"How can you say that? I found my soul mate and I'm not letting him get away! Anyway, I think he forgot his cell phone; otherwise he would have returned my calls."

Billy was so preoccupied with his racing thoughts, he didn't realize he forgot his phone. Wondering why he was having wild dreams about Nick, his confused mind tried to figure out answers to many questions. I'll get my revenge. Someone will pay dearly for excluding me!

He touched the pocket of his jacket and noticed that he didn't have his cell phone with him. Oh, who the hell cares? Who's gonna call me, anyway?

Better hurry, there's the downtown bus pulling up right now. If I pass 75th Street I'll be in trouble. I better not fall asleep again.

Billy boarded the bus and paid the fare. He found a window seat, sat down, and focused on his next move.

*

Back at the office, Rose looked at her party list and checked off every item. She turned to Rachel and asked, "Is Tony back with the food?"

"Everything is under control. Tony just returned. He's putting the food in the fridge."

"I'm sure Joy will be here promptly at 1:00 o'clock. Let's all get together now for a drink." As Rose and Rachel set up the drinks, Betty walked in.

"Am I the first one to arrive?" Betty asked, as she walked into the office.

"It's all-right to be the first. Come in and have a drink with us." Tony and Harry finally joined the group.

Tony became the official bartender. "Can I offer anyone a drink?"

Rose answered, "How about a screwdriver?" Rachel and Harry asked for the same.

"You guys are making it easy on the bartender." Tony smiled as he handed everyone their drinks.

Betty raised her glass and made a toast. "Here's to the good health of my daughter and her return to work. I'd also like to thank you all for making Claire this surprise party."

"Here, here," said Tony. "And may Claire's deal close."

"Tony!" said Rose, exasperated. "I don't think now is the proper time to talk about business. This is a social get-together."

"A toast to a large commission can't hurt," he continued, a grin on his face.

Rose's body stiffened as she gave him an icy stare and said, "Have you forgotten? This is not your deal. Or are you drunk?"

Tony walked away from the group and settled by himself at a corner desk. I'll figure out a way to get my hands on that money, somehow, he thought. Rose made an offer to me. He couldn't get his mind off the five-figure commission.

The alcoholic drinks were making everyone giddy. Tony was on his third cocktail when he stealthily approached Rachel and put his arm around her waist.

"D-did anyone ever tell you what a hot looker you are??"

He was beginning to slur his words a little, but that didn't stop him from making a pass at the receptionist.

"I guess you're telling me now, right?"

She was slightly tipsy herself, so she went along with his antics.

"Don't you think we should eat a little food so we don't get sick?" Rachel asked.

"Come with me," Tony continued. "I'll get us some cheese and crackers. How's that for a beginning?"

They filled a plate with hors d'oeuvres; then Tony guided her into Harry's office and closed the door.

"Hey, wait a minute. Why are you closing the door?"

"Okay, I'll open it. I thought a little privacy was in order."

"Hey, Tony, it's all right. I'm kidding. You can close the door." She started walking toward him with a drink in her hand. "I'm in a great mood, and so are you. Let's fool around."

"That's a great idea. Come here, girl!"

They embraced tenderly as Tony unbuttoned her blouse. Before he was able to undo her bra, she started to sober up.

"Hey, hey--slow down!"

Rose walked into the room at that moment, shocked to see Rachel's blouse open. Tony's jaw dropped, a guilty expression on his face.

"You're up to your old tricks again, aren't you Tony?"

Rachel, red-faced, hands shaking, started to button her blouse.

"I had one drink too many, and couldn't resist Rachel. Nothing happened."

"I'm not interested in what happened. I really don't care." Rose said in a cold voice. "By the way, the guest of honor should be here any minute." She returned to the other office without looking back.

As Rose made her way back to her desk, she made a fast dash to the rest room. It was the only way for her to control the rage that was building up. She locked the bathroom door, sat down on the toilet, and cried hysterically. "How could I have loved him?" she thought. "Those intimate hours we spent together, all a lie. I hate him with all my heart!"

I know it's all over. He'll never know I cried for him. She wiped her tears away, repaired her makeup, gave a last glance at the mirror, turned, and opened the door to the office.

*

While the party continued, and everyone gathered together for the special occasion, Billy wandered around outside with evil intentions.

I'll show them all, he thought. Nobody ignores me and gets away with it. He left the bus stop, walked up Second Avenue, and finally approached the building. He was looking for an elusive hiding area where he could wait and not be seen. Suddenly he heard someone call his name.

Joy had just stepped out of the cab when she saw him standing in the shadows. "Billy," she yelled. "Billy, it's me! I must go to him," she said to her sister.

"Don't worry, I'll pay the cabbie and wait for you at the door." Joy left and ran toward him.

"Billy! Are you okay? Where have you been?" she asked. I've been calling since yesterday and couldn't reach you."

Billy turned to Joy, shocked at seeing her at that moment. Suddenly his harmful thoughts disappeared. All he wanted to do was to take her in his arms and hold her close. He grabbed her and they passionately embraced in front of curious bystanders. Joy looked up and whispered, "Thought you had an accident." She smiled and added, "I'm glad you didn't."

They were still locked in an embrace when Billy said, "I was real upset about not joining you today. I had to get out of my apartment and get some fresh air. Baby I missed you and needed you bad. I was angry as hell when Rose excluded me."

Joy stepped back and said, "I tried calling you on your cell phone. Rose called me back to invite you after all."

"I forgot my cell phone. You know I would have called you back if I had gotten the message. God, what a misunderstanding! Where are you going now?"

"I picked my sister up. She's waiting for me at the building and has no idea about the party. Why don't you come up with us?"

"I'll take you up on that offer. After the party you have to promise we'll be alone."

"I promise."

They walked hand-in-hand back to the building, where Claire was waiting patiently.

Finally she saw Joy with a man walking toward her. When they were close to the entry, she ran out to greet Joy and meet her friend.

"Claire, I found Billy walking down the avenue. One minute later and I would have missed him." Joy took Billy's hand and brought him closer to meet Claire.

Claire held out her hand, "I'm Joy's sister," then stepped back with a start. Did she know him from somewhere? She knew Joy had talked about him, but she was pretty sure she had not brought him around to meet her, yet somehow it felt like she had. She couldn't shake the feeling of *déjà vu*, and it was a bit unsettling.

Nice to meet you," Billy answered. They shook hands, neither one realizing they had met before.

Joy finally said, "Why don't we go up to the office?"

Everyone was huddled together waiting breathlessly for Claire to arrive. Finally, Claire, Joy, and Billy walked in together.

"Surprise, surprise, surprise!" they all yelled as Rachel turned on the lights.

The look on Claire's face revealed that she was genuinely surprised, as she introduced Joy to everyone. As Billy watched, he recalled the dream he had about his mom. She was right about so many things, especially my relationships. He thought of Joy as the one special person in my life my mother would approve of, but the problem is, she comes with a package.

How do I deal with her relatives and friends? What do I know about things like that? All I remember is unhappiness growing up in my family. I could gain plenty if I play my cards right. Joy came along in the nick of time. Who knows what I could have done if she hadn't?

Things were a bit overwhelming for Billy, so he stepped out into the hallway to cool off. He leaned against the railing in the hallway, closed his eyes, and just when his mind started to wander, he felt a jab in his ribs. "W-w-hat's going on, he stuttered.

"Hey, Billy," Joy beamed. "The surprise worked, come with me." She grabbed his hand as they walked into the office. Everyone was talking and laughing with Claire, so Joy pushed Billy into the group. "Hi, I'd like to introduce my friend Billy Reilly."

The guests turned and smiled. Joy had hardly finished the introduction when her mother walked away, clearly ignoring him. I'll never talk to him, Betty thought. Look at those beady eyes, sneaky too. My daughter doesn't listen to my warnings. She'll learn the hard way.

Billy thought... she insulted me. One day she'll be sorry she did that. His hands felt wet and clammy as he cracked his knuckles. Jesus, Billy thought, I'm sweating and feel damn lousy. "Joy, I have to talk to you."

"What?" she answered, "Are you enjoying yourself? Come on now, I haven't introduced you to Rose and Harry. Are you getting hungry?

There's plenty of food set up on the table."

Billy looked at her, trying to explain. "Meeting all these people--it's too much for me. I want to leave now! I feel awful that your mother ignored me. Why did she walk away?"

"Billy, I have no excuse for her. She has her own opinions; it doesn't mean I agree with her. You know how I feel about you." She squeezed his hand and smiled sweetly at him. He smiled back, still feeling uncomfortable.

Harry and Rose joined them. Joy did the introductions.

"Billy," Rose said, "I'm so happy you decided to join us today. It's a very special day having Claire return to our office. Please enjoy yourself."

After Joy reassured him, Billy settled down and joined in on the conversation. "I'm happy to be here and meet you all." He held Joy's hand as he turned to Harry. "So you're the other broker."

"Yes, but no talk about work now. I always like a party, especially when there's good food and alcohol." Harry laughed.

They chatted until Joy said, "Billy, why don't we get something to eat? I'm starved." They walked to the corner of the office where all the drinks and food were set up.

"Everything looks mouth-watering," Joy exclaimed. "I'll make you a deli sandwich."

"Great," he answered. "You're right, I'm hungrier than I realized."

As Joy filled her plate with food, Claire approached, her eyes sparkling.

"Joy, I can't begin to tell you how happy I am to be back at the office. You're amazing keeping the surprise from me. I don't know how you and Mom did it. She's usually a walking telephone."

"It wasn't easy," Joy replied. "Seeing the look on your face when you walked in made it worthwhile."

Billy interrupted, "Excuse me. I'm going to the bathroom; be back in five minutes." When he left, the sisters took the opportunity to discuss their mother's rude behavior toward him.

"Your friend seems personable. I can see the attraction you two have for each other. Don't know why Mom is making a big deal over your dating him. Maybe it's her over-protective instincts."

"Oh, Claire, don't you think she should get to know him better? Only then she'll realize how much I love him. Isn't he gorgeous?"

"Yes, he's handsome – he seems familiar to me, absolutely don't have any idea why. I'll try to talk her into changing her opinion."

"Maybe you saw him around the hospital? You know he works there." Joy thought, he also reminds me of Jim.

Maybe that's it. I was so doped up on meds, I couldn't tell you if I was coming or going half the time."

While taking care of his business in the bathroom, Billy was still emotional from his encounter with Betty. He washed his hands, dried them; looked into the mirror and was ready to comb his hair when he noticed the mirror was covered with moisture. He couldn't see his reflection until he used a paper towel and wiped down the mirror. As he began to see what he thought was his reflection, he did a double take; it was Nick's face in the mirror smiling at him.

"Jesus! Nick what the hell are you doing here?" He stepped back, away from the sink in shock.

"Look Billy," Don't be scared, I came to help you. It seems you're getting yourself into one jam after another. Joy's mother is gonna make trouble for you. Stay clear of her, she's bad news. Also I know you'll never forgive the whore for laughing at you and your limp dick. That's why we have to get rid of vermin like her. Go back to the party and concentrate on Joy! She's like putty in your hands. You can do whatever you want to her. She's got no backbone, only love for you. Take advantage of her for your own needs. In the end all will work out for you. I have more plans for you. Suddenly Nick disappeared as fast as he came. "What the hell?" Billy shouted, "What was that all about? Did I see Nick or was it just my imagination?" He thought, if I don't get out of this bathroom, I'm gonna break this mirror with a chair! His body was drenched with sweat thinking about his encounter with Nick. He cracked his knuckles and decided, I'll wait here awhile until I calm down, then I'll return to the party. After ten minutes, more in control, he decided to join the others. He opened the bathroom door and left.

"Where's my sandwich?" Billy laughed, as he joined the sisters.

"Sure, take this plate of food. I'll join you both in a minute with the drinks." Joy left them engrossed in each other and walked to the bar.

Billy turned on the charm. "Claire, I'm glad to share this time with you, especially after all you've been through."

"Thanks Billy, I appreciate your being here."

He looked Claire in the eyes and smiled. "Hope Joy hurries back with the drinks."

Claire said, "I'm so happy you and Joy are here to celebrate with me. I still don't know how you all pulled this surprise party off."

"You realize how much you're appreciated?" Billy answered, smiling, trying to impress her. "Wish I had a fan club too. I wouldn't know how to start one."

"You impress me. I'll be your first fan." She smiled back at Billy.

This is getting better every minute, he thought. She wants to be in my fan club! Ha, ha. Who does she remind me of? Who knows?

"What are you two up to?" Joy laughed, balancing two soft drinks in her hands. Can't leave you guys for a minute, can I?"

They looked up at Joy and laughed. "Sure," Claire giggled, "I'm going to elope with your boyfriend if you don't watch out."

"Please hand over those drinks to two thirsty people." Billy ordered, laughing along with them.

Suddenly Joy sat on Billy's lap, kissed him and whispered in his ear, "Honey, we may not get a chance like this again. Let's get out of here and go to my apartment."

"I'm hot for you too, baby," he replied, as they embraced.

Claire watched awkwardly, and then decided to join the others. "I'll see you two later."

"I'm so rude," Joy bubbled as she continued to kiss Billy and tongue his ear.

"I'm getting a hard-on for you," Billy whispered. "Let's get to your place fast."

"Okay," Joy mumbled as she slithered up against his manhood. They pulled themselves apart and walked back to the others.

"Where are you two going?" Tony said sarcastically. This party is not hot enough for you both?"

"Don't leave yet." Rose suggested. "The celebration just began."

"Sorry, Billy and I have another important appointment to keep. *Maybe* one of you guys could give my sister a lift home?"

They left the office waving to everyone. The minutes seemed like an eternity until they would be alone. With their sexual desires burning, they moved into a dark corner of the hallway. Billy embraced her hungrily, and Joy responded passionately. His probing tongue and wet kisses made her more excited than ever. He held her up against the wall as he opened her blouse. She trembled as he removed her bra and kissed her breasts tenderly.

Joy was in ecstasy kissing him back, touching his manhood. "I love you," she whispered. "I don't think I've ever felt this way."

"I feel the same," he panted, still holding Joy close, pleasuring her as much as he could. He was lifting up her skirt, ready to continue their lovemaking. Suddenly Joy grabbed his hand and stopped him.

"What's the matter?"

"I think we're out of line, fooling around in the hallway. Let's go to my apartment." She pushed him away and closed the buttons on her blouse.

"I couldn't control myself. You got under my skin, and I couldn't wait to love you."

"Oh, Billy, I feel the same, but what if someone comes out of the office and sees us? I would be so embarrassed."

"Nobody is coming out of that party for awhile." As Billy finished his sentence, the door to the office opened and out walked Tony and Rachel.

"Shh, don't say a word," Billy whispered. "They can't see us."

"Goodbye, everyone," Rachel yelled as she and Tony left the party and walked down the steps.

"See, I told you," he said quietly, "They didn't see or hear us."

"Come on now, let's get out of here. What if someone else comes out?" she mumbled.

"Okay, okay."

Joy straightened her skirt while Billy buttoned up his pants and put on his jacket. They quietly passed the door of the office and quickly walked down the steps exiting to the front of the building.

"Thank goodness," Joy said as she grabbed Billy's hand. "Let's take a brisk walk down Second Avenue. I think we need to cool off."

Billy looked at Joy and grinned, "What would I do without you? Somehow I always knew you were the girl for me." He held on to her hand as they walked away.

Suddenly the sky darkened, and black clouds passed overhead. The wind blew stronger as heavy rain enveloped them.

"Look at the wind blowing those tree branches," Joy laughed. "Let's run out of the storm."

"You're right; it's getting worse. We're soaked." Billy shouted above the roar of the wind.

They rushed toward Joy's apartment building. The rain turned into a churning storm.

"Let's stop; it's impossible to continue," Joy said, huffing and puffing.

"Great idea. There's a café up the block," Billy answered, cold, wet, and uncomfortable.

Once in the coffee shop, the hostess brought them to a small booth in the corner, where they finally settled down and looked at each other.

Joy shivered as her wet clothing clung to her skin.

"Holy mother of Jesus," Billy laughed hysterically, "You look like a wet rag. What a poor soul, with your dripping hair matted around your face and your nipples showing through your blouse. I'd like to get you into my bed right now!"

Joy looked straight in his eyes, laughing too. "It's not my fault my nipples excite you, is it?"

Billy took Joy's hands in his and kissed them lovingly. "You know I adore you. You're my girl."

"And you are my true love, too," she cooed.

"Can I help you two?" the waitress asked, invading their private world.

"Oh, yes," Billy answered. "Two cups of coffee and a toasted corn muffin, please."

CHAPTER 17

Despite the earlier events, Rose was determined to appear completely composed, a bright smile lighting up her face. The others will never know how devastated I am, she thought. How could Tony run off with Rachel? He'll never change. Hearing the beat of Latin music, Rose began swaying. I've always loved Spanish music, she thought, especially the rumba. She remembered the good old days and smiled; she had fewer worries then. She was deep in thought when Harry walked up to her from behind and said, "Don't waste all your rhythm. Come and dance with me."

Rose turned to him, smiled, and twirled around the floor with Harry, shaking her body in tune with the music.

"You're a terrific dancer, Rose."

"Thanks, you do all right yourself."

Claire yelled from the side, clapping her hands. "Let's give them a hand."

Everyone joined in the applause. "If I had a trophy, you two would win," she laughed. As the music finally ended, Rose curtsied and answered, "Thanks a million."

Rose heard the phone ring and yelled, "Is anyone picking up?"

"I'll get it," Claire answered.

"Field Realty, may I help you?"

"Rose Field, please. This is Mr. Goldman; it's important. I called last week. Nobody called me back!"

"Mr. Goldman, this is Claire, how are you?"

"Oh Claire, I should be asking how you are doing? I heard you had an unfortunate experience, but I'm happy you're on the mend. We'll be talking to each other about our negotiation for the property you showed me, but I must speak to the broker now.

"Fine, I'm looking forward to working with you. Please hold on one minute. I'll get Ms. Field," Claire answered.

Claire put the call on hold and walked over to Rose.

"Rose, it's Mr. Goldman! He sounds upset!

Rose turned to Harry.

"I'll take the call in your office, Harry, if it's all right with you."

"Are you kidding?" Harry responded. "I'm sure you'll be able to hear much better without all this noise. See you later." He walked to the bar and ordered a Margarita.

"Thanks, Harry. I don't want to lose my dance partner. I'll return in five minutes for a repeat performance, I promise."

Rose sat down at Harry's desk and answered the phone. "Hello, Mr. Goldman. This is Rose. How are you? Is anything wrong?"

"Yes, I'm upset. My secretary told me a man has been calling my people asking us to switch from your agency to his. I would like to know whether everything is all right with your company and is our deal still okay?"

"Mr. Goldman, I'm so sorry. I'll find out who did this." Rose felt a cold sweat break out over her body. No, it couldn't be, she thought. Could Tony be the culprit?

She composed herself and said, "Do you remember the man's name and what firm he works for?"

"No, I'll ask my secretary to check her notes on that call. I'll call you back on that."

"All right," Rose continued. "The deal is going along as planned. There will be no problem! We have an agreement that Claire is the sales agent of record. I agreed to help her if necessary. Nobody else will get involved, I promise you." Her heart was racing, and a dull headache was developing. Then she thought to ask him, "Are your investors ready to go forward with our deal?"

"It's a go on the transaction as soon as we work out the final details you spoke of. Once we do that, my lawyer will draw up the contracts. As soon as Claire is available, we should meet to hammer out the details. Please call me to set up a meeting."

"Great, thanks for calling and keeping me up to date." Rose hung up the phone. She opened her pillbox and removed two Advil tablets. I'm getting too old for the stress in this business, she thought. She swallowed the pills with a cup of water.

Rose slowly stood up. Why are my knees shaking? Who else could it be but Tony? I'll fire him! But what proof do I have? The smartest thing I can do is help Claire close our deal. She took a deep breath. Okay, Rose, you've been through worse times than this. If I got through the murder of Alana, I can get through anything. I have to be strong and smart. Now, fix your lipstick and hair! Go back to the party and enjoy the rest of today.

Rose returned to the party. Nobody seemed to miss her. Tony and Rachel were back, and they were eating, drinking, and having fun.

"Where were you, Rose?" Tony asked. "God, you must have been gone more than fifteen minutes. I thought you left the party."

"I don't think it's any business of yours where I went. Besides, don't judge other people. Look at yourself first!"

"What do you mean by that?" Tony answered, surprised at her comment and accusing tone. He was still feeling tipsy when he grinned, "Let's not be so serious on this joyous day. After all, soon you and Claire will have another celebration. I wish I had a deal closing with a huge commission." He was getting sarcastic, and Rose was furious.

"Tony, we have to talk tomorrow. I don't like your insinuation. Claire worked hard for this contract and suffered because of it. You know yourself she was attacked the night she showed the property to Mr. Goldman. Don't say anything to upset Claire, especially today."

"Don't worry, why should I upset Claire? Somehow I remember you promised me part of her deal!"

"I never made any promises, and in the heat of passion, neither did you. So let's both just walk away with no apologies, okay? Thank goodness Claire is able to work the deal herself," she continued. "I made the offer under different circumstances, remember? Look, this is not the time or place to discuss this subject." Rose turned away from Tony and walked directly to Harry.

"Hi, Harry, I'm back for another spin. May I have this dance?"

"Of course," he answered, with a grin.

Claire wondered, it's almost 5 o'clock and I haven't seen my mother. She walked to the end of the office, passed Harry, and waved, "Have you seen my mom? I can't imagine where she is."

"No. Why don't you look in the rest room? By the way, do you have a lift home? If you don't, I'll be happy to oblige."

"Thank you, I thought I had a ride with my mother. I'll let you know." Harry is tipsy, she thought; I'll pass on his offer. She continued walking toward the bathroom, looking for Betty.

"All right, I'll see you later," Harry said, as he poured himself another drink. He was slightly drunk, but sober enough to look for Rose. What a dancer, he thought, as he continued drinking. Soon he began calling for her. "Where are you, Rose? Rose, Rosie, dear."

"I'm right here," she giggled. "Do you want to dance with me again?" Rose was slightly tipsy too, happy to have Harry's attention.

"Come here, woman," he said, as he walked toward her. He put his arm around her waist and said, "How about a little more rumba?"

Rose was happy to accept his invitation. Dancing was like therapy; it relaxed her completely. They swayed to the Latin beat of "Besamé Mucho." As they danced around the room, she looked out the window and watched the sun set. "Time goes fast when you're having fun," she whispered.

"You're r-right," Harry answered, slurring his words slightly.

"Harry, I want you to know I enjoyed your company immensely. I haven't had this much fun in a long time." She smiled as she gave him a hug.

"Mom, Mom, where are you?" Claire yelled, as she opened the door to the ladies' room.

"Yes, yes, I'm here," Betty answered.

"Why didn't you tell me where you were going? I was worried when I didn't see you."

"Where would I go?" Betty responded. "I was getting frustrated and decided it was almost time to leave anyway. I'm very upset about your sister."

"Why don't you come back to the office? I'd like to discuss Joy with

116

you, but not in the bathroom, please."

"I can't talk about my worries and heartache at a party. Why don't you say your goodbyes, and we'll go home. We can discuss Joy on the way back to your apartment."

"No, thank you. This is my party and I'm not ready to leave. I'll come into the rest room now, as long as nobody disturbs us. What's on your mind?"

"Well, I know you won't agree with me, but I'm concerned about Joy's relationship with Billy. I can't explain, say it's a mother's intuition about a person, but I didn't like him the first time we met. Every time I looked into his eyes, I saw two cold blue stones. It scares me. He also reminds me of that ex-boyfriend who broke Joy's heart and almost drove her to suicide. I just don't want to see a repeat of that scene. That's why I walked away from him at the start of the party."

"It's a terrible thing, walking away like that! You embarrassed him in front of Joy and all the other guests. You judged him without any proof or reason. Just because he looks like somebody else doesn't mean he's going to act the same way. I think you should apologize to both of them. You must know how Joy feels about him. You may lose her if you continue on this path. If you get to know him, you will find he's quite charming. Why aggravate Joy without a good reason, only your mother's intuition?"

"You're right," she sighed. "I'll try to do it your way. Tomorrow I'll get all those negative feelings out of my head, as though I met him for the first time. Does that make you feel better?"

"It sure does. I know Joy will be a much happier camper. I love you for trying, Mom. You'll see I'm right."

"I hope you are. Let's go home now. I'm getting very tired." Betty hesitated about her decision but didn't say another word.

Claire embraced her mother. They hugged, kissed, and went back to the party. After saying goodbye to everyone, they went home. Harry and Rose were the only ones still dancing to the Latin music.

CHAPTER 18

Billy and Joy sipped their coffee, ate the muffin they shared, and whispered words to each other only lovers knew.

The magical spell of romance ended when Joy's cell phone rang. "Okay, okay," she muttered, annoyed that anyone would interrupt their private world.

"Who is this?" Joy said.

"Why do you sound so funny?" Claire asked. "Did I take you away from your lover?" she laughed.

"Oh, sorry. We're in a coffee shop just about ready to leave. What's up?"

Billy was curious to know who was on the phone. He mouthed the words, "Who's that?" Joy kept the conversation going and didn't answer him.

"Joy, I just dropped Mom off at her place and had a great talk with her about Billy."

"Oh, did she bend your ears with negative stories?"

"Don't be so pessimistic. I think I was successful in changing her opinion. She promised she'd start all over and try to be civil to him."

Threatened by the call, Billy yelled, "Hey Joy, who are you talking to and why don't you answer me?" She won't tell me who the hell she's talking to, he thought, anger rising in him. What am I doing, he thought, as he began cracking his knuckles. She's gonna think I'm nuts, but I can't help it.

Joy put her hand over the mouthpiece of the cellphone. "Billy, what are you doing? This is personal and has nothing to do with you."

"When are you getting off the damn phone? Tell me who you're talking to!" he demanded in a menacing way.

Joy turned away from Billy and whispered into the cell, "I've got to go! He's getting upset. Talk to you later."

"You must have been talking about me!" Billy said, getting more annoyed. "I do not appreciate being ignored. The fact that you won't share the caller's name with me shows they're more important to you than me." He turned away and pouted.

"Nobody is more important to me than you! We just finished showing each other how much we care. Do you think I can change my mind so fast? Look, Billy, I can't share every single aspect of my life with you. This was a call from one of my co-workers. She needed my advice on something I discussed with her last week. Don't you know I love you with all my heart?"

Billy looked her in the eyes and finally smiled. "I feel much better knowing who you talked to. Don't you know I love you back? Anyone coming between us upsets me." He took her hands into his own, and said, "Let's get out of here."

"You're right. I think the storm weakened." They looked out the window and saw the wind had calmed down and the rain slowed to a drizzle.

"Let's go to my apartment," Joy said. "We can finish off the evening there."

But Billy couldn't stop thinking about that phone call. I got crazy jealous. If she hadn't told me who she was talking to, I would have walked out mad as hell.

Joy grabbed Billy's hand and said, "C'mon, let's get out of here and go to my place."

He grinned. Joy always had a special way about her. They left hand in hand and walked south on Second Avenue.

"I'll call Claire tomorrow and ask her to check on apartments for you."

"You read my mind. My place is too small and cluttered. Thanks for mentioning it to your sister." Jesus! He thought, what a lucky break for me, knowing Joy.

They finally arrived at the apartment building. Joy opened the front door with her key. Billy held the door open and they walked to the elevator, still clutching each other's hands.

She noticed her neighbor Peter walk into the elevator and moved aside so he could enter.

"Thanks, Joy," he said smiling, and acknowledged Billy with a polite nod.

"Are you going to the board meeting tomorrow night? Maybe we'll learn something worthwhile for a change."

"Gosh, I forgot about the meeting. Thanks for reminding me."

Peter gave them a mock salute when the elevator got to his floor. On the 10th floor they exited and headed for Joy's apartment.

"Who was that guy?" Billy hissed. "He couldn't take his eyes off you."

"Stop it!" Joy yelled. "He's a neighbor who lives in my building. Do you think I'm interested in him?"

"I'm gonna be jealous of anyone that looks at you. That's how much I love you!"

"Oh, come now, am I going to get the third degree whenever someone talks to me? I won't be able to stand that, and I'll probably die of claustrophobia." Joy pressed her hands against her temples and said, "I'm getting a bad headache and I think you should go home."

Billy looked her in the eyes and said, "You're right, maybe we're wrong for each other." He left her standing at her door and headed back to the elevator, fuming with anger. I'll show her, he thought. Nobody dumps me and gets away with it.

Joy regretted her hasty words as soon as Billy left in a huff. He's angry with me, she thought. I'll call him and apologize. Maybe I can catch him before he gets too far away and he'll come back up. She tapped in his number on her cell phone. Then she remembered that Billy didn't have his phone with him. She heard his greeting, waited for the beep and decided to leave a message anyway. "Honey," she began. "I'm so ashamed of myself yelling at you. I apologize. When you get this message, come back to me. I'll wait, all night if necessary."

Joy walked to the door of her apartment and locked the bolt. Then she headed to the bathroom for a painkiller and water, as the throbbing in her head worsened. I can't remember feeling so rotten in months.

Now I know I'm hooked on him.

As he rushed out of the lobby into the street, Billy didn't know yet where he was going, but he knew someone had to pay for Joy's action. When he reached the front of an office building, Billy hid securely in the shadows until a woman walked out. He watched carefully which direction his new victim would take. He concentrated on his next move and felt an explosive wave of energy. Billy caught a glimpse of the petite female with long dark hair passing the street lamp. He thought a small woman would be easy prey. Killing her emitted a thrill. Sweat covered his body, and he yearned for the kill. This must be what Nick meant when he told me all his secrets. Billy crunched his knuckles hard and his fingers froze for a few seconds. He licked his lips and followed his victim down Second Avenue.

Meanwhile, Billy's heart raced like a machine as he continued stalking his prey.

Look at her, she has no idea she's gonna be dead soon. He controlled the urge to laugh. His excitement increased as he watched her walk down Second Avenue. He quickened his pace and stayed far enough behind not to lose sight of his victim. Suddenly Billy was shocked when she turned toward Beth David Hospital. He slowed down and watched carefully where she was going. The aide waited in the corner of the lobby wondering who the hell he had chosen to murder. His body trembled, and he cracked his knuckles until his fingers turned white.

Billy watched every move the woman made as she talked to the receptionist. He pushed his body behind a large pole and held his breath. What if she sees me? Can't hear what she's saying. I can't fail now; I'm so close. His attention was momentarily diverted as he watched Dr. Wang pass. With a hysterical laugh, Billy thought, wonder what he would say if he saw me here tonight? Why would I give a shit, anyway?

Billy watched. I picked the perfect whore, he thought. She looks like someone in my past. Her dark skin, long hair, and brown eyes look familiar but I can't identify her. Every nerve in his body shouted for action; move out of here soon, he told himself, or I'm out of luck!

The young woman finished her conversation, turned around, and walked out back to Second Avenue. This was her unlucky night, Billy thought. As soon as she left the building, he was close behind.

It was a dark night. Billy was having a hard time keeping up with her. Incredible, he thought, she must be some kind of athlete. Once she turned on 25th Street, he knew it wouldn't be long. She continued running down the block. It was very quiet, not a person in sight. Perfect, he thought, and hurried to catch up. She suddenly sensed someone following her and jogged faster. He continued the chase, determined to catch her and fulfill the act. Faster, faster, faster he ran to keep up with this amazing athlete. He almost failed, but she slipped and fell to the ground. Billy jumped on her like a snake attacking his prey and almost let her slip through his sweaty fingers. "Help, help!" she yelled, kicking, scratching and finally tearing his shirt. "Stop, stop!"

His face a mass of perspiration, sweaty hair pasted back, Billy hissed, "Shut up!" He straddled her and grabbed her throat as he kept squeezing her neck. She fought and pulled at his hands, but he was too strong for her. He knew when he heard her neck snap, she was dead.

Grinning as though nothing had happened, Billy picked himself up, wiped his hands and face with his handkerchief, and walked away. He never looked back or noticed a card next to the body.

CHAPTER 19

Claire couldn't understand her sister's secretiveness. Why did she hang up, and why make such an issue over my conversation about Billy? She noted that her discussion with Joy seemed to trigger his anger, and wondered that her mom may not be that far off about lover-boy after all. Then she sighed and pondered, Whoa. What am I thinking? She tried to forget her annoyance with Joy.

The following morning, Claire was happy to return to the office. I certainly have enough to do at my desk, she thought. I can't find a damn thing.

Rose, recovering from too much partying, interjected, "By the way, Claire, have you spoken to Sam Goldman about your deal? He's very anxious."

"Not yet, I was going to call him after I spoke to Joy. She's certainly involved with Billy. I think she has finally found her soul mate."

"Before you get involved with finding an apartment for Billy, please connect with your client!" Rose was adamant. As they talked the phone rang.

"Hey Claire, it's me. I have a question and a favor to ask.

"Sure, Joy. What's on your mind?"

"Do you have a one-bedroom apartment available immediately?"

"Are you thinking of moving?"

"Of course not; it's for Billy. His studio is too small, and he's ready to upgrade."

"I'll look around," Claire replied.

"Don't forget to let us know as soon as possible. If you have an apartment, we would like to see it immediately. I've got to go now. Love you, Claire."

"Bye, sweetie. Now, how do you like that?" Claire mentioned casually.

"How do I like what?" Rose answered, as she fingered through some papers.

"My sister has taken Billy under her wing. She's helping him find a new apartment and I'm the one they're depending on. Now what do I do about referrals?" Claire moaned.

"She's your sister. Are you going to ask her for referrals? Don't you trust her?"

"It's not Joy I'm worried about; it's Billy. How come he didn't come up with the referrals when you requested them several times? He just never bothered to follow through."

"Don't get paranoid. Even when customers bring them in, you never know if they're legitimate. Try to think positive. Find a nice apartment for your sister's boyfriend. He seems like a charming young man. I can see why Joy fell in love."

"I guess you're right, as usual. I'll check for Billy after dealing with Mr. Goldman."

"Claire, call Mr. Goldman right now! There's a big commission if we use our brains. We have to take care of him so the contracts can be signed. Once that business is completed you can help Billy."

Claire picked up the phone and dialed her client.

"Mr. Goldman's office, may I help you?"

"Is he in? I'm Claire Smith with Field Realty.

"He just left the office. Would you like to leave a message?"

"Tell Mr. Goldman I called and will call again."

"Of course," his secretary answered.

Good, Claire thought, now I can concentrate on the apartments. "Who ever said it was easy to find one bedroom apartments in midtown Manhattan?" Claire laughed, as she turned to Rose.

"Times are changing," Rose answered. "New rental apartments come on the market daily. Keep checking the internet. Call the landlords in the listing book, or try cold canvassing. Sometimes the most creative way to get listings is to look in the reverse directory. You'll find owners' names and phone numbers. Good luck! Let me know if you hit gold."

Rose smiled and walked back to her desk.

Claire buried her head in the computer and kept clicking the mouse until her temples ached. Finally she announced, "I've had enough for one day."

My sister seemed quite anxious for me to move forward on this apartment deal, so I'll do it now! She turned to Rose and said, "I have something. As we were talking, I noticed two one-bedroom apartments on East 79th Street. The building has a part-time doorman and is located on a nice tree-lined street."

"What are they asking?" Rose asked.

"Wait, I'm checking the rent and amenities. Aha, yes, the price on second floor apartment is $1800 a month. The second apartment is on the seventh floor, at $2000. It sounds expensive; I'll speak to Billy. What do you think?"

"I think you should do what you said, call Billy and Joy. Ask them if the numbers make sense. Then you can move forward."

Rose turned back to concentrate on her cluttered desk. One day this desk will be neat as a pin and I'll know it's time to go out and have some fun, she told herself. Right now I need the money so, Rose, it's time to get back to work!

Claire called Joy, excited to tell her sister about the apartments she found.

"Hi," Joy answered.

"Hello, it's me. Just wanted you and Billy to know I found two apartments I can show you."

"I knew you would find something for us. When can we see them?"

"Come up to the office and I'll show you photos on the computer. If you both like what you see, I'll make an appointment with the rental office. After I make the call, I'll contact you. Just a thought, let's keep the paperwork in your name. Is that all right?"

"Sure, is there a problem?"

"No. Well, sort of. I'm trying to avoid unforeseen issues. Billy couldn't come up with any referrals when he applied for an apartment. If I use your name there won't be any problem."

"I don't mind helping Billy. His landlord is a real moron, never following through on broken pipes and leaky radiators. He knew he'd never be able to get a referral from him. I'll handle everything, Claire. Don't worry."

"I'm not really worried about Billy; I'm concerned about you. Are you sure you want to become his co-payer?"

"I'm okay with it. We're looking forward to this new move. It will be good for him, and I'll feel great knowing I'm helping someone I care about."

"All right, you understand you'll be responsible for paying the rent if he doesn't?"

"I'll work it out with Billy. He's coming to see me this afternoon. I can't wait to tell him the news. Thanks for all your good work, Claire. I knew I could always count on my big sister. You've always been there for me, and now you're helping Billy, too."

"I've gotta go now. Love you, Joy!"

After hanging up on her sister, Claire turned to Rose and smiled.

"How do you like that? I just made my little sister happy."

"You're a good person, Claire. What about Mr. Goldman?"

"He just left the office. I left a message and I'll follow through tomorrow. I feel as though I've been productive today. I think I can go home without a headache."

CHAPTER 20

After sleeping most of the day, Billy crawled out of bed in the late afternoon. He took a walk down Second Avenue after leaving his apartment. I haven't felt this great in weeks, he thought. Who the hell was she? Just a whore taking up space! I did a good deed ridding the city of her kind. He took a deep breath and continued walking south, hands in his pockets, not a care in the world.

He looked at his cell phone and noticed there was an unheard message. He listened to the message, surprised as he heard Joy's apologetic voice. She wants me back. Who does she think she is? A snap of her fingers and I crawl? No, Billy Reilly doesn't jump for anyone!

He glanced sideways at the window of a lingerie shop. Jesus, look at those panties and nightgowns! Joy would look hot in the red ones. Billy suddenly felt sexually aroused. He walked into the shop and approached a saleswoman.

"May I help you?" she asked.

"Yes," he said. "I want to buy the red nightgown and panty set."

"Do you know the size?'

"Well, not exactly. She looks a little thinner than you."

"I wear a medium, so maybe she's a small."

"Good, I'll buy both. Please gift wrap them."

"You made a good choice. Give me five minutes to wrap the gift."

"Sure," he answered in a cheery voice. Billy walked around the store and fingered the silky items. He couldn't get Joy out of his mind. He thought how gorgeous she was gonna look in the red nightgown. I'll call her back, he decided with a grin. We have a lot to talk about. I really need her, he admitted. Without Joy and her sister, how the hell am I gonna get a new apartment? She's opening the door to a better life for me. How many years do I have to waste working as an orderly in the hospital? The salesperson handed Billy his purchases and said, Thanks! Sorry for the delay."

"Sure," Billy answered, as he paid the saleswoman and called Joy. He heard her phone ring several times.

"Hi," she answered.

"Hey, it's me." Billy responded with excitement in his voice.

"I'm so upset about treating you so lousy. Come back tonight; I must see you!" Joy insisted.

"Fine. I'm on my way," he said with a complacent smile.

"I'll be with you in 15 minutes. Can't wait to see you, baby." He hung up the phone, picked up Joy's gift, and flagged down a Yellow Cab.

After hanging up the phone, Joy moved quickly through her apartment, organizing things. As she finished the last chore, she looked at the time and realized Billy would arrive any minute. She thought, I'll be careful not to make him angry again. Why don't I surprise him with a home cooked meal?

After removing two steaks from the freezer, Joy washed and marinated them. Then Joy considered... if Billy knew I lied when Claire called at the diner, I don't want to think about the consequences. Shaking her thoughts away, she decided to add a small salad and vegetable. She set the table with a colorful green and yellow plaid tablecloth and two place settings of her favorite beige and gold dishes. Now all I need is silverware and two water goblets. As the steaks were marinating, potatoes baking, and peas ready to cook, the doorbell rang. In her haste to open the door, she tripped over the chair. "Stupid, stupid," she yelled frustrated over her carelessness. "I'm coming," she shouted, as she ran to open the door for Billy.

"What took you so long?" he asked, holding the gift behind him.

"Billy," she laughed, "I'm such a klutz. I tripped on the leg of a chair, as only I can do."

He walked into the apartment, set the gift down on a chair, and immediately turned back to Joy and smiled. "No matter where I go or what I do, you are my inspiration," he told her. "I love you, Joy, more than you know." He took her hands in his, brought her close to his chest, and kissed her passionately.

"I missed you and couldn't wait for this moment," Joy whispered, as she looked up into his eyes.

Billy carefully nudged her forward, looked back at her, and said, "No more attacks on me?"

"I already apologized on the phone. I don't know what got into me," she answered.

"Oh," she coyly asked, as she cuddled back into his arms, "what's in the box you put on the chair?"

"You'll find out soon enough," he answered. Billy picked up the beautifully wrapped gift, took Joy's hand, and led her to the bedroom. "You'll have to remove your clothes first," he calmly said, as he began to open the buttons of her blouse.

"Oh, my goodness, it must be quite a present," she answered. "Let me guess, a new blouse?"

"You'll have to try again."

"Can I open my gift now?" she coyly asked, as her body tingled with sexual excitement.

"I'll tell you when to open your gift," he replied, as he felt chills and sweat breaking out all over his body. "Come here," he said, looking at her standing in her panties and bra.

Joy walked into his arms and they embraced passionately. He held her close, while guiding her toward the bed. He carefully nudged her down on the mattress, both still entwined in each other's arms.

The hunger never stopped as they made love over and over.

"Yes, Billy, yes!" She moaned as he entered her and the volcano erupted.

"I love you, I love you!" Joy kept repeating, as she exulted in the pleasure he brought her.

"That's what I always want to hear," he whispered, exhausted, as he rested his head on her breast.

"I'll be right back," he said. "Need to pee."

"I can't move yet. I'll be waiting for you," she murmured. My goodness, Joy thought. I'm the happiest girl alive. He's the best friend and lover in the world. She was in ecstasy, still feeling the euphoria after the climax.

"Billy," she shouted. "What's taking you so long? When am I gonna see my present?"

"I'm coming," he answered and smiled to himself, thinking about the literal meaning of what he had just said. "You'll see your gift now; you certainly earned it."

When Billy returned, he gave the box to Joy. "Here, open it and enjoy."

Joy took the beautifully wrapped present from his hands and impatiently tore the paper off. "I can't wait to see it," she said. She opened the box, removed the tissue paper, and saw the red nightgown and panties.

"Oh, my God!" she yelled. "I love them, I love them!"

"Good," he answered. "Now put them on."

She jumped off the bed and put the panties on first. Jeez, I'm getting another erection, he thought. That's what she does to me. Next, Joy put the nightgown on, looked up at Billy, and smiled.

"You like?"

"Come here," he ordered. "Get that nightgown off. I want you again!" He grabbed her, slid her panties off, and unveiled her loveliness. Locked together in an embrace, they returned to the bed and made love again. This time they dozed in each other's arms afterwards.

Suddenly Joy jumped out of bed. "Holy cow, I forgot about our dinner. Hey, you better move your butt. Guess who prepared food?"

Billy sat up, rubbed his eyes, and stretched. "Shit, I knew I felt my stomach growl. My mother always told me to hook up with a chick that loves to cook."

"Come with me," Joy proudly said, as she pulled him toward the kitchen. "Look how pretty my table looks! By the way, I spoke to Claire. She wants to show us some rental apartments. Isn't that great?"

"Your sister really moves fast. When can we see them?"

"As soon as we come in and look at the photos she can set up an appointment with the rental office."

"Swell," Billy said, thinking how lucky he got when he met Joy. A new apartment in his future sounded perfect. As they walked into the kitchen, Billy watched Joy prepare the final touches for their dinner.

"Would you like a drink before we eat?" she asked.

"Of course, I want to toast a special gal."

"I'll change into my robe and bring a bottle of red wine to the table."

"Good," he said.

While Joy was gone, Billy thought about his possessive feelings for her. My entire life is devoted to this woman. Whatever I do will be the result of my relationship with her. I can't help it. As he waited, Billy's eyes focused on a photograph of Joy and Claire, taken years earlier. Something about Claire made him feel uneasy. He started to sweat, but not for sex. What the hell is wrong with me, he wondered. Don't tell me I'm having another one of my episodes! His nerves were overactive and his heart began to palpitate. He suddenly began cracking his knuckles so hard, he cringed from the pain. Why the shit am I doing that? I just got laid with a gal I love. I must be nuts!

"Is something wrong? I heard noises," Joy said, as she walked over to Billy and sat on his lap. "What's the matter, honey? Are you ready for dinner and wine?" She was about to plant a kiss on his lips, when Billy pushed her off his lap and ran into the bedroom for his clothing.

"Billy, did I say something to upset you? Where are you going?"

Billy clumsily got dressed and walked past Joy on his way out, saying, "I have to go now. Don't even think about stopping me!"

"How could you leave, after all we've meant to each other? Are you crazy? Or am I crazy?" She paled and stood rooted to the floor. A frown appeared on her forehead and shock registered in her eyes. Oh, no, it's happening again, she thought. Don't leave me!

"Yes, I think I'm nuts. You don't want to have anything more to do with me. Get yourself another boyfriend. I'm no good for you."

He ran out the door without turning back, a lust building up inside his gut that he did not understand.

CHAPTER 21

It was a typical day at Beth David Hospital, with the staff attending to their daily routine. Dr. Roth stopped Penny on the way to his office.

"Did you see Doris today? She was scheduled to work this morning in Pediatrics." Dr. Roth, a stickler for punctuality, was annoyed at her tardiness.

"No, she didn't sign in or call," Penny responded. "When she does I'll let you know." Penny turned to Gene, who was checking his morning assignments. "Gee, it's unlike Doris to be late. She stopped in yesterday to check her messages and seemed perfectly fine."

Suddenly Dr. Roth approached Gene and spoke impatiently. "You need to replace Doris in Pediatrics right away! There's no time to waste!"

"I'm on my way, doctor," Gene answered. Jesus, he thought, where the hell is she? Since I've been working at this hospital, Doris has never missed a day of work, nor has she ever been late. I hope nothing happened to her. He felt a chill go up his spine and willed it away. I don't like premonitions; I never believed in them, he thought. He continued on toward the elevator and pressed level five. Still brooding about Doris, Gene walked toward the Pediatric section of the hospital. Once he saw the babies in the nursery, all his feelings of gloom disappeared. He approached the nurses' station and signed in. "Hi, I'm covering for Doris. Where do you want me to help?"

"Doris was supposed to assist in the recovery room for preemies. Why don't you see the head nurse at the end of the corridor? She'll give you a schedule."

"Thanks." As Gene walked down the hallway, thoughts of Doris filled his mind again. Why can't I forget her? I'm magnifying the situation without cause. He pushed the uncomfortable thoughts aside for the second time. If we don't hear from her by noon, I'll give a call to her roommate. When Gene reached his destination, he asked for his assignment.

"Hello, who are you substituting for?" asked the nurse.

"Doris Walker."

The nurse handed him a plan for the day.

"Great," Gene said. "I'll take a minute to check things out. Could you tell me which direction to take?"

"Walk straight down the hallway and make a right turn. You can't miss it."

Gene followed her directions and walked out of the swinging doors into a huge room filled with dozens of crying babies.

How am I supposed to know what to do, he wondered. Gene walked to the nurses' station and told the nurse his dilemma.

"I'm filling in for Doris Walker."

"Yes, I was told you would be helping us today. Is Doris all right? It's unusual for her not to show."

"I thought so, too. Where do I go?"

Later in the day Gene was enjoying himself in Pediatrics. What a lucky assignment! It must be great caring for these babies. I'll call Penny and ask if she's heard from Doris. She'll tell me what to do. He walked out the swinging doors into the lounge and called the supervisor.

"Nurse Gayte, may I help you?"

"Hi Penny, it's Gene. Have you heard from Doris today?"

"No, she hasn't called in yet, but I don't think we should be concerned. Do you have her roommate's phone number? Maybe she can help you."

"Hold on a minute," Gene replied. "I'm checking my address book. Her name is Lisa Brooks. I'll try to reach her." He was concerned at this point, but thought no news is good news. He dialed the number and waited. After three rings Lisa's voice mail kicked in. What a bad break missing her! He dialed the head nurse's desk again and let her know that he couldn't get through to Doris's roommate.

"Please call me if you hear anything," he requested.

"Okay," she answered, hanging up the phone.

When Penny ended her phone conversation with Gene, she was more concerned about Doris than she dared to admit. As much as she tried to concentrate on the paperwork on her desk, she was unable to.

"Shit," Penny murmured when she heard a knock on the door. She found herself facing the two NYPD detectives, as they flashed their badges and identified themselves.

"How can I help you?" she asked, trying to appear calm.

"I'm Detective Pezello and this is Detective Green. May we ask you a few questions?"

"Sure," Penny answered. "Won't you both sit down?" The cops walked toward her desk, sat down, and were just about to start questioning her, when Gene walked into the office. "Oh, Gene," Penny sighed, quite relieved.

Penny introduced Gene, and the cops began their inquiry.

"A murder was reported late last night. A resident was returning home when he discovered the body of a young woman. We were informed her name was Doris Walker, a nurse at this hospital. We're sorry to be the bearer of bad news, but could you tell us about this victim?"

Penny gasped and held her hands to her mouth. Gene's eyes revealed his disbelief. Silence permeated the room.

Penny said, "Doris worked here for three years. She was a great gal, respected, diligent, liked by everyone. Do you have any leads?"

"Sorry, we're not at liberty to release any information at this time."

Detective Green requested names of family, friends, and associates in and out of the hospital.

"I can help you." Gene hesitated. "I have her roommate's phone number. When Doris didn't report to work I tried to track her down, but her roommate wasn't home. I left a message, but she never returned my call." Gene opened his notebook and checked the roommate's name. "Lisa Brooks, 555-6324. I'll have to ask Dr. Wang about any other friends and associates."

"Thanks, we'll be in touch if we need you for anything further." Green turned to Penny. "By the way, may we have your business card?"

"Sure," Penny whispered, as she handed over her card. She was shocked by the discovery of the nurse's body and tried to control her emotions. As soon as the cops left the office, Penny turned to Gene. Her eyes filled with tears as he tried to comfort her.

CHAPTER 22

Why did he walk out on me? It must be my fault! I never knew how to hold a man close and keep him happy. I thought my bad luck in love was gone. Tears trickled down Joy's cheeks as she realized the truth. I have to talk to someone. Who do I call? I can't talk to my mother. She's too one-sided against Billy. She'll only say, "I told you so, didn't I say he was no damn good?" Joy tapped in Claire's number.

"Hi," Claire said.

"It's me," Joy murmured, in her tiniest voice.

"Something's wrong, I can tell."

"Claire, you won't believe what just happened!"

"If you don't tell me, I won't know."

"You're making fun of me," she answered, and the tears started again.

"Oh God, you're crying. I'm sorry. I didn't realize it was that serious."

She held her head and sobbed. "Billy walked out after we made love. He told me how much he adored me and gave me the most gorgeous lingerie set. Wait until you see his gift! I don't understand it. It's just like when Jim dumped me, remember? Maybe I'm not lovable." She lowered her head and whimpered.

"Come on, Joy, something else must have triggered it. Think hard and try to remember."

"Everything was perfect until I went out for five minutes. I thought a bottle of wine would add a romantic touch to my dinner."

"Look, maybe he's got a problem and hasn't shared it with you yet. What can I do?"

"Could you come over and keep me company for awhile? I made

this terrific food, but now I'm alone and miserable. He told me to forget him and find someone else."

"Of course I'll come. Who could resist a dinner my little sister cooked? Promise me you'll dry your tears. No man is worth crying over."

"Claire, you know I adore you. You're the only human being I've ever been able to confide in."

"You are so worth it. Look, I have to finish some work. I should be at your place about 6:00. Is that all right?"

"Sure, I'm going to wash my face and comb my hair."

"That's great, can't wait to see you … love you!"

Joy thought about the happiness she had experienced with Billy, and wondered. Why did he turn on me? What did I do to trigger his wrath? It seems every time I get close to a man, something happens. I thought Jim had feelings for me, but one day without any hint, he stopped calling. I never heard from him again and never knew why.

As she thought about her bad luck, her head throbbed. I can't stand it. Why am I so miserable? What do I have to live for, now that Billy left me? I wanted to share my life with him.

I know what I need! Joy ran to the bathroom, opened the medicine chest, and fingered through the items. Yes, I knew I had a bottle of sleeping pills. That's the answer. She grabbed the bottle, and hurried into the kitchen for a glass of water. Joy started with two, then swallowed half the remaining pills in the bottle and downed them with water. This is the best decision I made in my entire life, she told herself. No more broken heart for me.

Joy was frantic when she dropped the half-empty bottle and ran into her bedroom, where she collapsed on the bed. Slowly the pills took effect.

"What have I done? Oh shit, who cares? I'm so tired of everything. Why am I so worthless? I just want to die. I don't deserve to die … I don't want to die … I don't want to die!

An eerie silence filled the room.

Right on time, Claire stepped out of a cab in front of Joy's apartment building at 6 p.m., and opened the lobby door with her spare set of keys.

She hurried into the elevator, pressed 14, and finally walked down the hallway toward Joy's apartment. Claire rang the doorbell, but her sister didn't answer. Without wasting time, she used the spare keys.

"Joy, I'm here!" she yelled. No answer. Claire walked into the kitchen first, and saw the pill bottle on the floor. Her heart raced. She ran into the bedroom and saw her sister sprawled out on the bed.

"Joy, Joy, Joy, what have you done?" She turned Joy around and took her pulse … very low. She listened to her breathing. It was shallow. Claire ran to a phone and dialed 911.

"What is your emergency, and what is the address?" a voice on the phone asked.

In a shaky whisper, Claire answered, "An overdose of sleeping pills. The address is 800 East 74th Street, Apartment 14D." She hung up the phone and returned to Joy.

Claire was in a state of shock but knew enough to try and awaken her sister. She put a cold compress on Joy's head and kept changing it. Then she tried to call Billy, but he wasn't home. As she put the receiver down, she heard the doorbell ring.

Two cops entered the apartment. One officer asked, "What's the problem here?"

The shock of finding Joy at death's door was too much for Claire.

The officer said, "Please, Miss, try to calm down; can you tell us what happened?"

"Go into the bedroom!" Claire murmured, as she tried hard to brace herself. The paramedics arrived soon after and joined the cops, who were checking Joy's limp body. The medics examined her as Claire watched.

"Her vital signs are fine, but the pulse seems to be weak. He turned to Claire, "Are you a member of her family?"

"Yes."

"Do you know whether she was on medication?"

"I found this bottle on the floor," Claire answered, handing it to the medic.

"Joe, let's get her on the stretcher." He sounded worried, as he turned to Claire and said, "We're taking her to Beth David Hospital."

Claire watched as though she were in a dream. Somebody shake me and say this isn't happening! Oh God! I have to call my mother! She rubbed her wet clammy hands in desperation.

Her thoughts were interrupted when she heard the paramedic say, "You can meet the patient in the emergency room."

"Y-yes." Her voice quivered.

As soon as the paramedics and cops left Joy's apartment, Claire found the energy to call her mother. I have to be in control, she told herself. Nervously, she dialed Betty's number and waited. On the third ring she picked up.

"Hi."

"Mom?" she began. "I'm at Joy's apartment. She had an accident. She's okay! I need you to meet me at Beth David Hospital. Go to the emergency room! I'll tell you more when we meet."

"I'm on my way," Betty replied, as she grabbed her jacket and hurried out, thinking there's never a dull moment in this family.

Claire dashed out of Joy's apartment, down the steps, and out the front door. She hailed a cab and was at the emergency room in fifteen minutes. As Claire scanned the waiting room looking for Betty, she saw Dr. Roth walking toward her. She took advantage of the moment, approached the doctor, and smiled.

"Doctor Roth, I'm so glad you are attending to my sister, Joy Smith. I don't know if you remember me, but you practically saved my life. Is she going to be all right?"

"Of course I remember you, Claire. She's a lucky lady. When the doctors remove the drugs from her stomach, she'll be fine."

Claire scanned the waiting room, looking for Betty. She saw her mother sitting in the corner, a worried look in her eyes. She quickly walked toward Betty and greeted her with outstretched arms. "Thank goodness Joy is going to be all right!"

Betty, exhausted and emotionally drained, answered, "You never explained exactly what happened to Joy. Please tell me everything!"

Betty took Claire's arm and guided her toward two empty chairs in a secluded part of the waiting room. "Let's sit here where it's quiet; nobody has to hear our conversation." By this time Betty had calmed down, waiting for answers.

"Mom, forgive me. I don't seem to be in control since I discovered Joy unconscious. I feel as though I'm walking in a dream."

"Look, Claire, I'm confused. All you do is talk in circles. I'm her mother, and I still don't know what happened. Can you pull yourself together and tell me why Joy is in this hospital?"

Claire calmed down and finally said, "I think Joy was depressed."

"Why? A beautiful young woman should be happy!"

"All I know is she sounded sad, so I agreed to have dinner with her and talk. When I arrived, she didn't answer the door. I opened the door with an extra key Joy made for me, and found her limp body on the bed. I thought she was dead, so I dialed 911. The cops and paramedics came and here we are."

"You still didn't say what made her pass out. Tell me the truth!" Betty yelled. "You're not telling me something important!"

"Please lower your voice; It's embarrassing," Claire said. "There are people all around us!" Claire put her hands over her eyes and cringed. She was hesitant to tell her mother about Joy's overdose.

"Okay," Claire braced herself. "She passed out from an overdose of pills." She turned her head away from Betty. "I wish I could have gotten there sooner; maybe I could have stopped her!" Claire moaned, feeling responsible for Joy's dilemma.

"Claire, it's not your fault. I have a feeling she may have had an argument with Billy. If she did, I guarantee it upset her."

While Betty talked, Claire thought for a moment about Rose. I wonder what happened to her?

Her mother's loud voice startled Claire.

"Where are you? In Never-Never Land?'

"Mom, I'm sorry, I'm sorry! My mind is so muddled."

"Let me ask you something," Betty said, her eyes turning to ice. "Have you spoken to Billy?"

"No."

"Why haven't you called him? This is probably his fault!"

Claire stiffened as she faced her mother. "There you go, blaming Billy for everything. When will you stop?" Without knowing what had caused Billy to storm out of Joy's apartment, Claire was reluctant to pass judgment. As she turned toward the door, Betty grabbed her arm and pulled her back.

"Please don't leave me, dear," she said nervously, "Why don't we go see Joy together?" Claire pulled away from Betty and rushed out of the waiting room. She never looked back.

Betty raised her hands to her head in frustration, "I can't get normal answers from a stubborn daughter—can't find the doctor!" Tears filled her eyes as she yelled, "How much suffering must I go through because of my children? First Claire was attacked, now Joy's overdose. When will it stop?" Betty slumped down on a chair in the back of the waiting room, drained and weak. There's nothing I can do but wait for the doctor or Claire for information.

CHAPTER 23

The following morning, the office was busier than ever. Rose had several ads in the *New York Times* and *The Voice*. The staff couldn't keep up with the ringing phones.

"Jesus," Rose said. "Too bad Claire isn't in yet to help."

"Where is she?" Tony asked, in between calls.

"I don't know. Perhaps she had to help her sister with something."

"Shouldn't personal matters be resolved after office hours?"

"Sometimes problems raise their ugly head at inconvenient times. How do we know?"

Rose's phone rang and she answered. "Field Realty, may I help you?"

"Hello, Rose. Goldman here. I have some good news for you."

"I'm always happy to hear those words," she laughed.

"I met with my investors and I think they've come up with some additional terms we can all live with. When can we meet with you and Claire to go over them?"

"I'll call you back after I make arrangements with Claire. Thank you for working with us. As soon as I get an agreeable date I'll contact you." Rose tried her best to sound calm as she hung up the phone.

It was no use. Rose was so excited, she had to tell someone. "Oh, thank goodness," she said.

"What's going on?" Tony asked, as he covered the phone.

"Well, you're gonna find out sooner or later anyway," she continued.

Tony excused himself to the customer, and wrote down his new client's number. He hung up the phone, turned to Rose, and said, "Okay, what's happening?"

"Claire's deal looks very good," she answered, suddenly regretting she told him.

"What do you mean, very good?" he said sarcastically. "Is it a deal or isn't it?"

Rose thought, I'm excited for Claire and the firm, but Tony is going to give me trouble. She had to answer him, "Well, not yet. Mr. Goldman is ready to work out the final terms. I'm keeping my fingers crossed."

"I seem to remember you offered me part of the commission if the deal goes through. I hope you're a woman of your word. I'll be around the office all week waiting with bated breath for the outcome of this business venture." He smirked, turned away from Rose, and walked back to his desk. The phone rang and as he answered he felt the rage building up inside. I'll deal with her later, he thought.

Rose made a mental note to find out from Mr. Goldman who had contacted him from an outside firm, when her phone rang again.

"Field Realty, may I help you?"

"Rose, it's me." Claire answered.

"Dear, you're just the person I need," Rose said cheerfully. "I have some promising news for you."

"Well, I'm glad you have good news; I have bad news. Joy was just taken to the hospital last night. I'm so afraid for her."

"Oh my God, what happened?"

"I really don't know. I found pills."

Rose felt a compulsion to help. She said, "Claire, I'm coming to the hospital!"

When Claire hung up, she realized she never gave Rose a chance to tell her the good news. I could sure use some happiness and cheer, she thought.

Rose couldn't comprehend Joy's unfortunate accident. I must go to the hospital and support the family, she thought. She straightened her desk, put her jacket on, and hurried out of the office. Tony watched her leave and wondered where she was going in such a hurry. His curiosity got the best of him, so he decided to follow her. Before leaving, Tony asked Rachel to take his calls. As he walked to the door he said, "I'm not sure when I'm returning."

"Don't worry, I'll take your messages," she assured him. "Where did Rose rush off to without a word?"

Tony turned to Rachel and said, "What a coincidence, I was just wondering the same thing. That's what I'm going to find out!" Tony waved and sprinted down the steps two at a time. Hey, maybe it's Claire's deal, he thought. Perhaps I can persuade her to join forces with me. Why shouldn't we both get the commission? After all, Claire is overwhelmed with so many distractions; she's incapable of handling everything. I'll convince Rose to agree with me.

As he walked out the door and scanned the street, another idea entered his mind. We were lovers; maybe I can entice her again and get her on my side. A little lovemaking and sweet talk will do it. He was so excited with his new plan, that he almost missed seeing Rose get into a cab. She turned her head and saw him run toward the taxi. "Tony," she yelled. "Where are you going?"

"Rose, would you mind sharing your cab with me?" he answered, huffing and puffing, as he slowed down.

"Look," she said. I'm in a real hurry."

"Where are you off to?"

"Just get in the cab and don't hold me up."

Obediently, he got in and slid next to her. "Now tell me what the big secret is? You ran out of the office without a word."

"Wait," she held up her hand as she spoke to the cab driver. "Cabbie, please drop me off at Beth David Hospital."

"Are you all right? Tony asked. "Why are you going to the hospital?"

"Claire's sister had an accident, and she asked me to join her."

"An accident! Is she badly hurt?"

"I don't know."

"Oh, I'm sorry to hear that. Look, Rose, I've been thinking about us lately. I really miss the times we used to spend together." He moved closer and said, "How about coming to my apartment for awhile. What do you think?" He winked.

"Are you serious? Why now, after all that you did?"

"Don't you still have any feelings for me at all?" he asked, as he touched her hand and held it tightly.

When his body brushed hers, she felt a familiar tingle. What am I thinking? He still has feelings for me. "What about Joy?" she whispered.

"You can visit her and the family a little later, after they've had some private time," he suggested. "I miss you and need you." He waited for her answer.

She hesitated. Here he was, sitting next to her, offering to fulfill her dashed hopes. "Yes, I'll come to your place for awhile, and I'll go to the hospital later."

What am I getting myself into, she thought. The warning signals didn't stop her from responding to Tony's advances in the cab. I know, she thought, I'll pay heavily tomorrow for what I do today. Who cares, I'm yearning for him now.

Although Tony's arms were wrapped around Rose in the cab, his mind was filled with plans to betray Claire. When I get Rose into my bed, she'll do anything I ask, like putty in my hands. Look at her. She thinks I adore her. Huh! Sure, I'll make believe I care for her, like I've done before with many other women. Even my stupid ex-wife thought she was the one and only. She learned fast enough there are many fish in the ocean.

Rose was in denial of Tony's dark side and continued to fantasize over his love for her.

Tony slid closer. He kissed her cheek as he put his arm around her shoulder. She couldn't stop thinking selfishly about her desire for him as she embraced him and sighed.

"Just wait, baby, we'll be at my place soon. I'll give you something wonderful to remember." He kissed her on the lips, oblivious to the cabbie and his occasional sneaky peeks into the rear view mirror.

Rose felt her body shiver as thoughts of sex entered her mind. Whatever happens, I'm going to enjoy tonight.

A moment later she was dozing peacefully in his arms.

Suddenly Tony's voice startled her. "We're in front of my place."

"Yes," she answered lazily. I was daydreaming about you and me." Rose sat up and straightened her blouse.

He paid the cabbie as Rose stepped out the door.

"Okay," Tony said, as he took Rose's arm in his. "Let's go." He opened the front door with his key.

"It's only two flights up. Good exercise for your thighs." He laughed.

They walked up the steps until Tony approached the door of his apartment. "Here we are," he said, as he turned the key, opened the door, and walked in.

Although his mind was plotting betrayal, the sexual impulse in his groin led him in a different direction. He locked the door and turned to Rose. Their fiery eyes met as they embraced in each other's arms.

CHAPTER 24

Billy was unaware of Joy's hospitalization as he was sleeping through the day. In his deep sleep, he had another flashback dream about his father.

"Hey dad, it's me, Billy. What are you doing here?"

"You'll wish I wasn't here by the time I finish with you--you bum!"

"What did I ever do to you, Dad?"

"That's the trouble, you never did nothin'!"

"But you never showed me nothing."

"So what, your sisters did things by themselves. Why couldn't you?"

"It's different with girls. My bad luck is I met Nick. He showed me things. See, if you showed me stuff I never would have listened to Nick."

Suddenly Billy jumped up in his bed. The ringing of the phone interrupted his dream. "Where am I? Where's my father? Jeez, I must have been dreaming. My old man never cared about me. All he did was shout and curse. Well, I don't give a damn about him!"

Billy heard the phone but let it ring several times since he was still shaky recalling the dream. Who the hell is calling me? He lifted the receiver and said, "Yeah?"

"It's Claire. I've been trying to reach you all afternoon. Where were you?"'

"Do I have to report to you? I was out! What's going on?"

"It's about Joy."

"What about Joy?" Billy's body tensed up, as he sensed something foreboding in her voice.

"Joy was taken to the hospital, Beth David. I found her unconscious in the apartment and thought you should know."

"Oh God," he shouted. "What happened?"

"We don't know yet."

"I'll be there as fast as I can." He hung up and grabbed his head, pressing his temples so hard that his head began to hurt. This is my fault. Joy is suffering because of me. He began cracking his knuckles until the fingers were swollen. Why the hell did I run out on her? I'm no damn good. Gotta make things better. Have to see her and find out what she did to herself.

Billy left the bedroom, went into the bathroom, and took care of his needs. The cold water energized him as he washed his face and brushed his teeth. When he combed his blond hair, he looked at his reflection in the mirror. Suddenly, he saw the image of Nick shaking his head in disapproval. Then Nick's image was replaced with that of his father, also shaking his head in disapproval. As these images flashed, he heard inaudible voices. The voices turned to laughter, as the image in the mirror was that of the woman who laughed at him when he was unable to perform.

He grabbed his head and screamed, "Noooooo!" Then there was silence as his own reflection reappeared in the mirror. He thought... I better get the hell out of here fast! He walked out of the apartment, rushed down the steps and out to the curb, where he was lucky to hail a cab. "Get me to Beth David Hospital as fast as you can."

CHAPTER 25

The hospital corridors buzzed with activities. At 4:00 p.m. orderlies and nurses wheeled patients along the hallways. Some were returning to their respective rooms after surgery. Joy, finished with her tests, was alert but clearly exhausted. Gene escorted her back to the room. She remembered both Gene and Rena from Claire's hospital stay.

"How are you feeling?" he asked, as he pushed the gurney.

"Miserable," she answered.

Trying to comfort her, he said, "I'm sorry, I'll get you into a comfortable bed." Gene moved quickly around the corner of the hallway. They arrived at Joy's room as Rena and one of the aides were making up her bed.

"I'm ready to help you transfer the patient," Rena said.

"One, two, three, let's do it!" Gene and Rena helped Joy slide on to the bed.

Joy tried to stay calm, but to no avail. "My stomach hurts and I feel nauseous. Can I have something for the pain?" Her eyes filled with tears as she began to lose control. "Please, help me! I feel so sick."

"You've had your stomach pumped, and it's normal to feel queasy after a procedure. I'll bring a cup of tea to help settle your stomach." Rena continued to straighten the blanket and soothe the patient.

Joy asked, "Why did they take so many tests? It seemed like a waste of time."

Gene said, "The doctors always take lots of tests to safeguard you. They must be certain that your entire body hasn't been affected by the drug. Don't worry, you'll probably be fine and out of the hospital by tomorrow."

"I hope you're right," Joy replied in a whisper, feeling a little more relaxed. She closed her eyes and fell asleep.

The two nurses left the room and discussed Doris's murder on Second Avenue. "Have you heard any news, Gene?" Rena asked.

"It's all very vague. The cops haven't called us yet, so we have no idea what happened to Doris. Even if they do have evidence, they won't tell us."

As they walked back to their stations, Dr. Roth approached them.

"I was looking for you both."

"Is something wrong?" Gene asked.

"Well, I have one very interesting test result for Miss Smith," Dr. Roth continued.

Rena and Gene asked together, "For which test?"

He answered, "Our lovely patient is pregnant."

Rena and Gene looked at each other in amazement.

*

Betty's attempt to clear the air with Claire had the opposite effect.

Claire came back into the waiting room, as Betty attempted to make amends with her daughter. It seemed useless as in an annoying tone Claire snapped, "You know how upset I get when you keep blaming Billy for everything!" Betty hung her head with a sullen, apologetic look. Claire's expression softened and the two women embraced. "I can't stay angry at you, Mom, but I do get frustrated. Of course I'll join you and we'll visit Joy. I think by now the doctors must know something. Promise me you'll try to control your anger at Billy, especially in front of Joy."

Betty stepped back, looked at Claire, and said, "I'm going to try real hard to keep my mouth shut tight. I can't help feeling that since Billy and Joy are together bad luck is at our door."

"Mom, you're doing it again. I'm going to leave you if you keep it up!"

"Oh, no, no, darling. I promise, I promise. How can I wait in this hospital alone? I love you, Claire. Please stay here with me and be supportive."

"Let's get out of here now. I'm anxious to see Joy. If she's awake she'll wonder where we are."

They left the waiting area and made their way to the reception desk. "What room is Joy Smith in, please?" Claire asked.

"Third floor, Room 304A," the receptionist answered.

As they entered the elevator, Claire wondered where Rose was. Even though Rose and I just work together, I've come to regard her as a friend. Something must have happened. It's unusual for her not to call.

Suddenly she felt Betty's hand on her shoulder. "Let's get off, we're on our floor. Hurry!" She raised her voice. "What's wrong, are you dreaming?"

"All right, Mom, I'm sorry. I was thinking about Rose. She usually keeps her word. I expected her to meet us at the hospital."

"You know dear, you can always count on family; I don't know about someone like Rose." She grimaced as she gave her opinion.

"Now you're saying something about Rose, who was so good to me. You forgot she gave me a party when I came back to work and kept my real estate deal going. How can you be so negative?"

"I'm sorry, dear. I mean well, but everything I say makes you angry." Betty knew that she made another blunder.

"Look, I bet Rose will call you soon. Let's get going down the hall. I think this is the 300 line." Anxiety was something Betty was learning to live with. As they walked down the hallway, they saw Dr. Roth.

"Thank goodness, a lucky break for us," Betty murmured. They continued walking.

The doctor approached and turned to Betty, a serious look on his face. "I'm so glad we met. It will be easier to talk to you about your daughter."

"How is she?" Betty blurted out. "Will she be all right?"

"The doctor answered, "She's fine. Joy gave her consent to discuss her case with you both."

The doctor smiled as he opened Joy's report.

"Your daughter will be well enough to leave the hospital tomorrow. The procedure went well and we are pleased with her other reports. She's in very good health. As far as her pregnancy, she'll have to visit an obstetrician as soon as possible."

"DID YOU SAY PREGNANCY?" Betty and Claire screamed in unison.

"My God! Pregnancy! What next?" Betty moaned. Claire held her close, understanding her mother's emotional outburst.

At that point, Dr. Roth realized he spoke to soon to Joy's family.

"Ladies, I want to help you both, but my advice is to accept the truth. Please go into your daughter's room and try to be civil. You are her family, aren't you? Who else can she turn to?"

"Yes, yes, doctor. We'll do what you say." Betty murmured weakly.

"Thank you for giving us all the information," Claire added. They left Dr. Roth and walked to Joy's room.

CHAPTER 26

Billy arrived at the hospital and put on his ID badge. He approached the receptionist and asked, "What room is Joy Smith in?"

"Room 304A."

As he walked toward the elevator, Billy tried to control his emotions but couldn't stop his racing heart.

The aide walked quietly into Joy's room and found her fast asleep. As he sat next to her, he thought... I'll be the first person she sees when her eyes open. I never loved no one, but I love Joy. I would kill anyone who tried to hurt her!

Billy watched her sleep. Every once in awhile she would toss and turn, make funny noises, then turn on her side and sleep quietly again. She loves me so damn much she tried to kill herself, he thought. If Joy knew who I really was, she would dump me. She and I were planning so much together, that nobody could ever come between us!

My mother knew we were meant for each other. Isn't that what she said in my dream? "Billy," she repeated two times, "Don't lose Joy, she's the best thing that ever came into your miserable life!" Anything I did to hurt Joy I'm sorry! Maybe together we could figure out what makes me get crazy!

Billy took Joy's hand in his. He sat this way for a half hour, and then she looked up. Her eyes fluttered as she tried to keep them open. She finally awakened and noticed him holding her hand, so gently. With much effort she sat up and gave him her other hand. They looked at each other and embraced lovingly.

"I know you're hurting, and for that I apologize. I never wanted to harm you. You, who are the one human being I care for. Why did you try to kill yourself?"

Murmuring in his ear, she answered. "It was an accident. I was in pain and thought you hated me. I took too many pills, trying to make the ache in my heart go away."

"I'm here now, baby. Don't worry about a single thing. We'll get you well and out of this place. We have lots to make up. How are you feeling?"

"Except for stomach cramps, I think the nap made me feel better. The nurse said she would bring me some tea. That should help. I'm so happy you were sitting next to my bed when I woke up. Please never leave me again. I love you so much!"

They embraced again, whispering loving words to each other. Suddenly they realized they were not alone.

Betty's jaw dropped when she saw Billy sitting next to Joy's bed. She was ready to attack him verbally, but Claire grabbed her wrists, held them tight, and whispered, "You'll be sorry! The doctors will kick you out of this room. What would you accomplish? Mom, you don't seem to get it! Why can't we walk in and tell Joy how happy we are? He may become your son-in-law, so calm down."

They walked into the room and walked to Joy's bedside. She embraced her mother and sister, then turned to Billy and smiled.

"Mom, Billy was at my side when I woke up."

They looked at each other and beamed. Billy smiled at Betty and Claire, but evil thoughts filled his mind. What shitty luck to have her family here. Who the hell needs them? I'm all she needs.

While Billy was immersed in his thoughts, Betty and Claire had many questions for Joy.

Claire asked, "How are you feeling?"

"The doctor said I would be going home tomorrow. I'm much better, but still nauseous. The nurse promised to bring some ginger tea to settle my stomach."

Betty moved closer to the bed, kissed Joy's forehead, and whispered, "Darling, is there anything we can do to help? You know we're here for you. It was a shock to hear about the pregnancy, but..."

"Pregnancy? What do you mean?"

"Dr. Roth told us."

"He never told me!" Joy exclaimed, sitting up in bed.

"I thought he did," Betty said. "Don't worry, it'll be okay."

Billy couldn't believe his ears. How was this possible? He raised his voice.

"Joy, pregnant!" He looked up at Joy and asked in a shaky voice, "Is it mine?"

Joy looked at him, tears filling her eyes and in a soft voice said, "Of course it's yours!"

Billy jumped up, suddenly nervous and jittery. His hands were clammy and he felt ill. He rubbed them together and cracked his knuckles so loud, all three women turned toward him. Without warning, he suddenly ran out of the room. Claire, Joy, and Betty looked at each other in amazement, not knowing what to do next. Betty murmured, "There he goes again."

Joy turned desperately to her family and yelled, "Why did he walk out on me?

Please, tell me the truth. What's wrong with me?"

Claire and Betty looked at each other, hugged Joy, and tried to console her.

"There's nothing wrong with you," Betty answered. "It's Billy causing all your problems. We'll try to help you!"

Joy asked, "Should I have an abortion?"

"It's obvious lover-boy isn't happy about your pregnancy," Betty said. "He can't seem to handle any major dilemma. For him it's easier to run away than face the truth." She looked into Joy's eyes and spoke to her in a soft, loving tone. "Let's not talk abortion yet."

"I didn't think about a baby in my mixed up life. Now that I know the truth, I realize why I've been so nauseous since I've been in the hospital. I thought it was from the procedure they performed."

Joy was more in control as she tried to cope. "Mom, I must be in my second month. I missed one period, but didn't think anything of it."

Suddenly a thought entered Claire's mind. I hope Mom doesn't lose it. I could anticipate an outburst condemning Billy in front of my sister. If she does this, I'll ask her to leave the hospital room. She's going to explode soon!

Claire sat quietly next to Joy, and suddenly thoughts of Rose entered her mind. What happened to her? I was always able to rely on her kindness. See, in an emergency you know who your true friends are. Hmm, that's not true; didn't she come through for me after my accident? Maybe something happened. Perhaps I should call her and make sure she's all right. Claire felt someone pull at her wrist.

"Where were you for the last five minutes?" Betty jolted her daughter back to reality.

"Sorry, I can't seem to get Rose out of my mind. I'm disappointed she's not here."

"It's fine to wonder about Rose, but with all due respect, we have a major issue here, and we need your support. Joy is thinking about an abortion. You know I'm against it. The baby should be born and given up for adoption. What do you suggest?"

"I haven't given it enough thought. Joy, what do you want to do?"

"I'm too confused to make a decision now. Why don't we give it a little more time? Maybe Billy will have a change of heart and come back to me. I know he has problems, but I love him. I have to do everything in my power to help him, no matter what happens."

Betty couldn't control herself. She grabbed the bar of the hospital bed, shook it, and shrieked, "How can you say that, now that you know what kind of horrible human being he is! He walked out on you and wouldn't admit the baby was his! How can you love a man like him?"

Claire had predicted this outburst. She jumped up from her chair, ran to her mother and guided her out of the room into the hallway. "I told you not to yell at Joy. She can't help loving him. How could you say all those horrible things? She's so vulnerable; Now go back and apologize!"

Betty turned to Claire, her face tomato red, and said, "I tried so hard not to lose my temper, but when she kept saying she loved Billy, I couldn't stand it. Yes, I'll go back, I'm always unhappy after I mess up. I apologize to you too."

"It's all right; let's go back together." Arm in arm they walked into the room. Joy sat in her bed, the saddest look on her face.

"Joy, Mom has something to tell you." Claire nudged her mother next to the bed.

"Honey, I'm sorry I opened my big mouth again. Somehow I can never learn to keep it shut. Can you forgive me?"

"I'm not angry at you, and you're probably right about Billy. He can be such a pain in the ass, so unpredictable. But I can't help it, I melt when I'm with him. If that's not love, then I don't know what is. Come here, sit next to me."

As the morning hours crept in, Betty did as she was told. Joy continued figuring out what she should do.

"Let's not fight any more. I don't know if I'll ever see him again. Maybe he's so scared he'll run far away. I have to solve my own problems! Mom, you and Claire will help me. When I leave the hospital tomorrow, I'll think things over and make decisions. I'm so disappointed in Dr. Roth. Why didn't he tell me I was pregnant? That took me completely off guard."

Betty and Claire listened to Joy's complaint, and as Claire got ready to respond, Dr. Roth walked into the room with Joy's chart, a big smile on his face.

"How is my favorite patient feeling today?"

"Doctor," Joy blurted out. "I can't believe you told my family about my pregnancy before you told me! I'm disappointed."

"Miss Smith," he answered. I didn't tell them; I suggested you see an obstetrician. Then I realized they didn't know. I'm sorry if I upset you, but who is closer than a mother? I thought it wise to inform her first so she could help you."

Joy looked at Betty, Claire, and Dr. Roth. "Well, I guess you thought you were doing the right thing. Please give me the results of all my tests, so I can prepare to leave tomorrow."

"All your tests except the pregnancy test were negative, and you, young lady, are in excellent health. You can check out of the hospital tomorrow morning. Get a good doctor to care for you. If you don't know any, I'll recommend someone I know." He turned to Betty and Claire, said his goodbyes, and left the room.

CHAPTER 27

Billy weakened as he relived the hospital scene with Joy's family. He cracked his knuckles so often, his fingers turned white. Jeez, I felt my entire body react to every accusation. What the hell am I supposed to do now? How do I know the kid is mine? Too many questions, I hate her family, especially her mother. Someone is going to pay for making me miserable. Betty is the one to deal with. If I get rid of her, she won't be around to manipulate Joy any more.

Billy ran up Second Avenue and released his pent-up energy, while trying to figure out a way to trap Betty. I need a few shots of booze to help me think. Billy kept running until he approached a liquor store. I'll buy one bottle, just to calm me down. He went into the shop, bought the vodka, paid, and left quickly.

His fingers quivered as he pulled the cap from the bottle and took a swig. Good, now I'll find a good spot to hide and enjoy a few minutes alone with my booze. He slowed down and checked out several places. Okay, he thought, behind the tree near the wall is the best spot. He slid behind the tree, completely hidden, and sat down on the pavement.

"Wonderful," Billy murmured, as he unscrewed the cap, leaned against the wall, and began slurping the booze. Oh, this is great. I'm gonna strangle that bitch. Maybe I'll slice her up. He laughed, just thinking about it, then fell into a stupor, bottle on his lap.

A crack of thunder, bolt of lightning, and heavy rain began to fall. Billy didn't feel a thing. He was out of his body, hovering overhead. Suddenly he saw a figure standing next to him. "Holy cow! Nick, what the hell are you doing here?"

"I figured you need me around a little. You seem to be messing up your life again. I know what you're thinking, kid. You gotta have a good plan. If you're planning to kill her, do it right!"

"What do you mean, right?"

"Your idea of revenge is good. The mother suspects you, but does she have proof? Who's the one that was supposed to better your life? She was supposed to help you find a new place, give you all the good things in life you wanted."

"I don't know what you're talking about, Nick. Why should I change my plan?"

"Kill Joy! She's the troublemaker in your life. Now she's pregnant; who needs that? You have no proof the baby is yours, and even if it is, who cares?" Nick pulled the old photos out of his pants pocket. "Look at these pictures again; they'll give you ideas on how to do it."

Billy looked at the horrible photographs of dead women with their throats slashed. "Jesus, Nick, do you think I could go all the way with Joy?"

"Sure," he answered, smirking. "You'll feel so much better after the deed and you'll have your revenge."

Suddenly Nick disappeared, and Billy's heart thumped faster and faster. Yes, he thought, Nick was right; it's Joy who's causing all my trouble. I've got to get rid of her and start all over. When she's gone things will surely get better. The hell with Betty; it's Joy I want!

Heart racing, body in motion, Billy kept running south on Second Avenue. I feel terrific, he thought, like I could conquer the world. Nick came to me at just the right time. His words were true; Joy is giving me too much trouble; I've gotta get rid of her! She served her purpose; now I'm moving on. Some inner strength made him run faster and faster. Beads of sweat trickled down his body. Huffing and puffing, he muttered, "When I get home I'll plan my next move."

It was daylight by the time Billy reached his apartment building, and he was ready to collapse. He quickly ran up the steps two at a time and opened the door. Jesus, I feel like a fish swimming against the current. I need a shower bad; that's the first thing I'll do. He let himself into the apartment. Yeah, it feels good to be home by myself. After I get cleaned up, I'll sit down and make a plan. Wouldn't it be great if I killed her mother too? I can't stand the bitch! No, Nick said I should do Joy, not her mother.

Suddenly the phone rang and disturbed Billy's thought process.

Who wants to talk to anyone now? I have too much on my mind. The phone kept ringing. Reluctantly he picked it up. "Who's this?" he asked brusquely.

"Billy, it's Joy. I didn't know if you were home. I miss you. Why don't you come back to see me? You know I have feelings for you. Remember all our plans? I thought you cared for me."

Shit, he thought, shouldn't have picked up this call. What do I say to her? Yes, I know what to say. I know very well what to say.

He got so excited he could hardly hold the phone in his hand.

"Billy, are you there? I know you picked up."

"I'm here," he answered, a devilish smile on his face.

"Why did you run?"

"I couldn't stand everyone accusing me. It was easier that way."

"Don't you realize how much I need you?"

"Yes, I know. To make it up to you, I'll come and see you tonight. How would you like that?"

"Oh Billy, I can't wait. Nobody will be here if you come after visiting hours. Wait until late this evening. We can have time alone with each other. Maybe we could talk about our plans. Don't worry about my pregnancy. I'm trying to figure out what to do. I need more time to decide."

"I'll do whatever you want. Expect me to visit late tonight. It'll be easy to sneak past the nurses on duty. They'll never see me. I'm good at being invisible."

"Don't be mad at me, I'll never be angry at you. See you later; love you." With her last words, Joy hung up the phone.

Billy dropped the phone on the floor as he laughed hysterically. He laughed so much he had to hold his stomach as tears dribbled down his cheeks. "What a stupid whore she is. She gave me the perfect opportunity I need to do her in." He looked up, raised his arms, and shouted, "Nick you're gonna get your wish tonight!"

Now I don't need any plan, he told himself. She wants me there. After my shower I'll figure out the details. Nick said I should slash her throat. I need the right knife to complete the act. Things couldn't be better for me, he thought. The stage is set.

Billy laughed. What luck! I'll slit her throat; she'll never know what hit her! The icing on the cake, my life gets better. No more accusations, no more involvement! I don't need her; she's a means to an end. Just because my mother liked the idea of me and Joy, doesn't mean a thing to me. I make the decisions from now on. Nick is smart. He's the one I look to for direction. What a brain, don't kill the mother, kill the daughter! Why the hell didn't I think of it?

His body was drenched with sweat; the shirt stuck to his body.

He smelled under his armpits and made a face. "Jeez, I stink."

I need a shower. He walked into the shower, turned the faucet on, waited for the water to heat up, and yelled, "Tomorrow Joy will be a memory. She triggered my sexual appetite, but there's always another broad around. I've got a job to do, and it's going to be done tonight!"

He finally relaxed as the powerful hot currents of water hit his body. This is why I was born, to clean up a dirty city. As he lathered his body he rationalized, Joy is just like all the other whores. She must be eliminated!

He dried his body and applied some lotion thoroughly, obsessively rubbing so hard his skin turned pink. He checked his armpits and sniffed. Good, nice smell! After he brushed his teeth and combed his hair, he smiled. "Not bad, don't you think?" he said to the reflection in the mirror. He left the bathroom thinking of the new idea.

Nick was right when he showed me pictures of girls he cut. Now I'll start doing the same thing -- keep a diary and take photos of all my work. He took a camera from the closet and checked for film. I'm getting excited! Maybe after I take a picture, I'll take a trophy too, an earring, a ring? I'm not sure. His heart raced, hands shook, as his anxiety triggered him to crack his knuckles. The sheer joy of his scheme made him feel euphoric.

I have to think smart tonight. It won't be easy sneaking past those nurses. I need to relax and have a glass of vodka. That'll calm me down. He put his clothes on, grabbed his coat, and left the apartment.

CHAPTER 28

After hours of pure pleasure, Tony and Rose were exhausted. Rose started out for the hospital, but hit a detour and ended up spending the night at Tony's.

"All I feel like doing right now is lying here, with you in my arms," Tony murmured.

"I feel the same, tired and contented," Rose sighed, and kissed him on the cheek.

"Look," he said, suddenly more awake. "We have some things to talk about."

Rose suddenly remembered, "Claire--Oh my goodness, I forgot! I said I would meet her at the hospital."

"Not yet," Tony answered. "Now we talk commission."

"I can't do that! Do you think Claire is stupid? She would sue us. Then we would be in big trouble!"

"By the time she figures it all out, we would have cashed our commission checks and that would end it all."

"I'm not doing that," she insisted. Why should I do that to Claire?" She looked him straight in the eyes."

"You have to - I love you," Tony responded. "And because I know you love me!" Besides, you promised! He was adamant, and returned her stare. Then he grabbed her in his arms again.

"So that's what this was all about," Rose responded, humiliated, she pushed him away and shouted, "Don't you ever use that word again. You don't know the meaning of love, just lust! And I was fool enough to believe you." She jumped up and grabbed her clothes. "I should never have let you talk me out of going to the hospital," Rose told him in parting. "And tomorrow at work, you are to act as though nothing has ever happened between us. Do you understand?"

*

After she stormed out of Tony's apartment, Rose went home, got cleaned up and left for the office with a heavy heart. I'm so Goddamn depressed, she thought. I have never felt this guilty. Why did I allow myself to be manipulated by Tony? When will I grow up? How can I run a business, sell real estate, be a psychiatrist, and have a love life all at the same time? What about Claire? I promised her I would visit Joy in the hospital. She tapped in Claire's number and waited. Having spent the night in the hospital, Claire was in Joy's room with Betty when the phone rang.

"Hi," Claire answered.

"Yes, it's Rose checking in. How are Joy and your mom?"

"Fine, where are you? I thought you promised to join me at the hospital last night." Claire responded in a brusque, disappointed tone.

"You have no idea how busy it's been at the office and most of the excitement is about you."

"What do you mean?" Claire answered.

"I didn't get a chance to tell you about your deal. Mr. Goldman and his investors want to meet with us as soon as possible to go over final details."

Claire clapped her hand to her forehead and blurted out, "It's about time!" She ran her fingers through her hair and grinned from ear to ear. Betty and Joy couldn't imagine the reason for Claire's excited behavior.

Betty's curiosity won out. She said, "What's going on?"

Claire put her finger up to her mouth to quiet her mother and whispered, "Wait a minute."

Betty and Joy backed down as Claire continued her conversation.

"Claire," Rose continued, "We need to set a date to go over the final details of the contract. The investors have their own list of demands and we have to make sure everyone is satisfied."

"Okay, I'm going to go home and get a few hours sleep, then I'll come to the office as soon as I can."

"Good. Try to get here early. I'm leaving at 5:00, and we have important things to discuss. See you soon; love to the family." As Rose put down the receiver, she thought, I'll talk to Mr. Goldman about Tony's involvement later.

Claire hung up beaming and turned to Betty and Joy. "Guess what? It looks like my deal is going to happen."

"What are you talking about? What deal is this?" Betty wanted an explanation.

"Yes, my deal is happening, and if it comes through, I'm getting a very large commission, enough to take care of us all." A big smile appeared. "This is my first big sale; I'm so excited!" Claire was elated as she hugged them both.

Joy smiled. "I knew you would make it in real estate."

"Honey," Betty exclaimed; "That sounds wonderful, but be careful. It hasn't happened yet."

"I know, I know. Real estate takes time. There are the final details to work out, then a contract signing and a closing. I'll get my share at the closing, and then we'll celebrate." She looked at her watch, "I've got to run. Rose is waiting for me at the office. Mom, why don't you go get some breakfast and let Joy rest? I'll call you later." She kissed them both, grabbed her purse, and left the room humming a song.

"Trouble breeds trouble," Betty exclaimed. "But aren't we the lucky ones? In the midst of all our misery I see a little sunshine. I hope she's not getting excited over nothing!"

"What do you mean? Aren't you happy Claire is finally making it? Knowing my sister, she'll share her good fortune with us."

"Of course, but the deal is far from being settled. You never know. I'm truly happy for her success, and hope it happens. Maybe if this unexpected money comes through, it will help you make a decision about your pregnancy. Since your father left us, I was never able to get ahead financially; otherwise, you can be assured I would help pay all your expenses, especially the hospital bills."

"I always knew you would help me, but it's not the money. Everything is moving too fast. I need to think."

"Take all the time you need, but try to make the right choice."

"Mom, I'm suddenly so exhausted."

"Now, dear, you need to rest. I'm going down to the coffee shop." Betty kissed Joy on the cheek and left.

As Betty walked down the hospital hall, she couldn't help thinking about all the decisions they had to make. Claire's forthcoming money would help, but then we have Billy wandering around. We don't know where he is or what he's up to. Why does he always run away from problems? Why did he walk out on Joy? She's lucky to be alive. The problem is I have no proof he's trouble. Maybe I can alert the nurses on Joy's floor. There's always been something about him I disliked; he reminds me of that other fellow who walked out on Joy after getting what he wanted. How can I convince my daughters that he's not the man they think he is? Every time I bring up the subject of Billy, Claire attacks me. Of course Joy is in love; she'll never see his failings. I hope I'm wrong about him.

Upset and distracted, Betty almost missed the nurse's station. Gene and Rena were on call. When they saw Betty walking toward them, Gene waved and said, "Hi, you look a little worried. Is everything all right?'

"I'm more than a little worried. Do both of you have a few minutes for me?"

Rena looked at Gene and answered, "We have all the time you need."

Gene nodded his head in agreement. "What's the problem?"

"I'm concerned about Joy."

"Does it have anything to do with her pregnancy?" Rena asked.

"No."

"She's doing well, so if that's not the question, what is?"

"I'm suspicious of her boyfriend. He makes me nervous. I have no proof, but I really believe he's unstable."

"What makes you worried?" Gene continued.

"My daughter is in this hospital because of him. She's lucky to be alive.

When he found out about the baby he got crazy. He refused to admit the child was his and ran out of the room, never looking back. You could imagine how upset Joy was."

"We hear you loud and clear, but none of the things you say means he's going to harm your daughter." Gene was adamant.

"Okay, I understand, but please keep your eyes and ears open. I hope I'm wrong, but every instinct in me says he's up to no good."

Gene turned to Betty and said, "Remember, we aren't the police, but we'll keep an extra watch on your daughter. By the way, who is this boyfriend? What does he do?"

"Well, he works at this hospital as an aide."

"If he works here, we must know him. What's his name?"

"I think its Billy Reilly."

"Billy Reilly? The name is familiar," Gene exclaimed. "I think he helped me with my patients a few times. I thought he was a great help. The patients liked him too, but come to think of it, there were a few times I caught him sneaking around the hospital rooms. It seemed as though he was looking for someone. I'm probably off base." He smiled at Rena and Betty. "Hey, why don't you relax for a change? We don't know for sure anything happened. Maybe it's all unfounded."

"Oh, I caught him sneaking around the halls, but I reprimanded him," Rena recalled. I think I shocked him with my presence."

"Please keep an extra eye on my daughter," Betty requested.

"We promised you we would," Gene answered, as he and Rena excused themselves. Betty left the nurses' station with an uneasy feeling and headed for the café.

As she sat with her breakfast, Betty couldn't seem to get rid of that jittery feeling. I can't concentrate on how to protect Joy. I'm miserable thinking she may not be safe. Maybe I'm imagining too many things. I wish Claire was here. She has a way of calming me down.

Betty's insecurity caused her much stress. "I'm so confused! If I call the police they probably won't do anything. Enough of feeling sorry for myself; I'm not going to cry. She wiped a few tears from her eyes and took a deep breath.

As Betty left the café, she placed the tray on the automatic dish rack and went back to see her daughter. Betty walked quickly through the hallways toward the elevator. While she waited she thought, after I check on Joy I'll go home and get some sleep. I'm so tired. She stretched her arms and yawned. Since Dr. Roth mentioned she might come home tomorrow, I'll have to prepare food and set up the guest room.

Betty finally entered the elevator and pressed the button for the third floor. When Betty left the elevator she walked briskly past the nurses' station and waved to Gene and Rena without saying a word. I've talked myself to death, she thought, and I don't think they give a damn.

"Mrs. Smith," Gene called.

Betty turned around and caught his eyes. "Yes," she answered, unable to hide the annoyed look on her face.

"Did you have some breakfast? They say food has a way of comforting the heart."

"How can I be comforted? The food was horrible, and I'm just concerned for my daughter. I couldn't wait to get out of there."

"We want you to know we're keeping an extra eye on her." Rena nodded in agreement.

"Thank you. I'm sorry if I'm being rude. I can't control the way I feel. I know something bad is going to happen." She grabbed the desk's edge to help support her.

Rena admonished Betty and said, "You can't walk into her room with a negative attitude. The smartest thing to do is smile and tell her everything is going to be all right. Go back to your apartment and rest. You'll need all your energy to make your daughter comfortable when she comes home."

Betty listened to Rena's suggestion. "I think you're right. If my daughter Claire was here, she'd give me the same advice. Thank you both for caring. I'm going to see Joy, then head home."

"Just to let you know," Gene interjected. "I checked on her about 20 minutes ago. She was resting and reading a magazine."

Betty waved at the nurses, walked into Joy's room, and caught a glimpse of her daughter hanging up the phone.

"Oh, Mom," Joy said, as she reclined into a more comfortable position and smiled. "Did you have a nice breakfast?"

Without hesitating, Betty asked, "Who were you talking to?"

"Oh, nobody you know, just a girlfriend of mine." She doesn't have to know I called Billy, Joy thought. Jesus, I feel guilty lying about the call. She fidgeted as her mother approached the bed.

"Is something bothering you?" Betty asked. "You look tired and uncomfortable."

"No, I'm fine. What's wrong with you, Mom? You look as though you have something to tell me. Better tell me now; what have I done?"

"Why would I complain to you? Haven't you got your own troubles? The problem is your troubles are mine. Is there anything I can do for you?"

"No thanks. The nurses are great. They make sure I take my pills and eat my meals. It's nice having you here, Mom. I'm lonely stuck in this bed and can't wait to go home."

"Dr. Roth said if all goes well you can leave tomorrow. I'll bring you to my place. You'll have a chance to rest for a few days."

"That sounds nice. I wish this entire incident had never happened."

Betty sighed and said, "One time many years ago I felt the same passion for your father. I was so much in love, but he betrayed me. I found out he was having an affair with my friend. I had to leave him, even though he begged me to stay. How could I, after knowing he slept with another woman? Maybe if I had forgiven him it would have been easier for you and Claire. He never helped us financially, and that created problems. There was never enough money. I did the best I could to make a life for us."

"Did we ever complain to you? Claire and I knew we had to work and help out, and we did."

As they talked, Betty realized Joy was beginning to doze. She kissed her sleeping daughter, and was just about to leave when she had second thoughts. There's no hurry, I'll sit at her side for 10 minutes. She watched her daughter sleep and stroked her hair.

It didn't take long for Betty to fall asleep. Rena passed by the room and saw them sleeping. The nurse shook Betty gently and whispered, "Mrs. Smith."

"What, w-what?" Betty stuttered.

"You promised to go home."

"I was too concerned; I couldn't do it."

"Gene and I said we would keep an eye out. You must leave!"

"Okay," Betty whispered, since she didn't want to awaken Joy. She stood up, took her jacket, and finally left.

Once she stepped outside the building Betty inhaled deeply, as though to get the extra energy she needed to sustain her. Why can't I shake this gloom I feel? She looked up to the sky and prayed, "Please protect my family at this difficult time."

A woman tapped her on the shoulder and asked, "Are you all right?"

"Oh, yes, I'm sorry," Betty responded nervously. She straightened her jacket and continued on her way. How embarrassing, she thought, as she approached the curb and flagged down a cab. As she entered, she said, "Seventy-first and Second." I have to calm down, she thought, so many chores to complete.

The taxi arrived faster than she realized. She paid the cabbie and walked to her building. I feel better, she thought. When I return to my apartment, I'll prepare the guest-room for Joy. I'm happy my daughter is coming home. Things could have turned out different; we're so lucky. I pray Joy wakes up to the truth. It's so obvious Billy casts a dark shadow on all of us. How can I be the only one that suspects him? One day he'll be caught and then I'll say, "I told you so."

When Betty arrived at her place, she kicked her shoes off, put on her slippers, and prepared a snack. The tea and almond cookies tasted delicious and helped her relax. She decided to make up the guest room bed and bring soap and towels to the bathroom. After tucking in the corner of the sheet, and tossing the blanket over the foot of the bed, she figured on getting a few hours sleep before going back to the hospital. Betty was so exhausted sleep came to her at once.

Suddenly the phone rang and she jumped out of bed. She grabbed the phone, worried that something had happened to Joy.

"Who is it?" she asked.

"Mom, it's me, Claire."

"Is something wrong?" Betty moaned.

"Mom, I just had a terrible dream. I had to call you. Who else would I call?"

"What kind of horrible dream did you have?"

"It was so real. I'm shaking all over. I saw the man who stabbed me, and got a glimpse of his face."

"Who was it?"

"It was hazy; I couldn't see him completely. He had light hair; that's all I recall."

"Claire, that's great, but you have to remember more than that. Do you think you can call the police with such trivial information?"

"No, I'm frightened remembering even that small slot of time. I'm really sorry I called you."

"Claire, now I have to help you relax. It's important for you to try and get some rest. Forget everything. Go back to sleep."

"Oh, I can't. I have to get to the office."

"Claire, this dream could be an important breakthrough. Let's talk later about getting you some professional help. I love you."

CHAPTER 29

Rose was happy after her earlier conversation with Claire. I'm glad I resolved some issues with her, she thought. When she gets to the office we'll discuss the Goldman deal and work out some scenarios and also a fair commission split. Since Tony is not part of the transaction, he's not part of the deal. I hope he doesn't give her a hard time. This was a good month; can't believe I have three contracts in the works. If Claire's deal closes, her commission will put me up in the high numbers. As Rose fantasized about how to spend the money, Tony approached her desk, an angry look in his eyes.

"I'm expecting you to come through with my share," he asserted. Rose lifted her eyes and met his cold angry stare. How did I get myself involved with him? He's a snake, and that's the truth.

"You did nothing to earn it," she said. "And if you decide to press the matter, you may find yourself in hot water." She pursed her lips into a mysterious smile, as if to suggest she knew something about him.

The phone rang and interrupted her showdown for the moment.

"Hi, what's up?"

Rachel whispered so low, Rose had to strain to hear. "Two detectives are standing in front of my desk, and they want to see you now. What should I say?"

Rose was surprised; first Tony, now the police. Why do they want to see me? "Rachel, send them in." She hung up the phone, took a deep breath, and sat back in her chair, waiting for them to enter.

She recognized them immediately as they flashed their badges. Pezello and Green were the detectives on Alana Stone's murder case, as well as Claire's assault. She looked at their identification and asked, "How can I help you?"

"Our precinct is in the middle of a murder investigation." As Pezello spoke, he placed an evidence bag with a business card inside on Rose's desk. He took a cigarette out, was about to light it, but asked, "Is it all right if I smoke?"

"Sure, smoke doesn't bother me," she answered.

He exhaled his cigarette, as billows of pale blue smoke rolled and tumbled together.

Rose looked at the card and recognized it immediately. "Yes, this is my company card. What does it mean?"

"We found it at the side of a murder victim. Do you recognize the name on the card?"

"Yes, she's one of my sales agents, Claire Smith."

"We would like to talk to her. Is she available?"

"I'm expecting her shortly."

"Don't concern yourself with us. We'll wait for her in the outer waiting room. Thanks for your help."

The detectives walked out of Rose's office, leaving her in a state of anxiety.

What's going on here? Now I'm getting in the middle of a murder investigation! Her head throbbed and her body felt limp. All she could do was put her head down on her desk and sigh.

Claire had just stepped out of a cab in front of the office. As she opened the front door and stepped down, she almost tripped on the curb as she checked the time.

She couldn't believe her deal was going ahead. I have to stay calm and not seem over-anxious when I meet with the Goldman group. I'm glad Rose will be there to give me some guidance. It's about time something good happened in my life. The last few months have been awful. It seems I just recovered from my attack; now Joy is going through hell.

As she entered the office Claire noticed two men sitting in the corner. They looked familiar to her but she couldn't immediately recall where she knew them.

"Hey, Rachel, how are you? Are there any new messages for me?" She felt the men still watching as she asked, "Is Rose here? She's expecting me."

"Yes, Rose is in her office. No messages."

"What's going on?"

Rachel shrugged. "Wish I knew. Maybe you'll find out."

Claire walked into Rose's office.

"Hi Rose, you look awful. What's wrong?"

"Claire, there are so many things to discuss, I don't know where to begin. Do you want the good or bad news first?"

"All I want is good news about the Goldman deal. We need to set a time and date to discuss the next step."

"Why don't we do it now, while it's quiet." Rose continued, "I'll call Mr. Goldman and set a time to meet with his lawyers. Is your schedule pretty clear?" She held her hand up to let Claire know she needed to speak to Mr. Goldman on the phone. When she finished her call, she had a date for the meeting.

Rose told Claire the date for the meeting and she started to leave.

"Hold it Claire, don't leave yet."

Claire stopped in her tracks and said, "Oh, yes, I forgot to ask for the bad news."

"Don't be sarcastic. This is serious. There are two detectives waiting for you."

"Detectives---What do they want with me?" Suddenly her hands become wet and clammy. "What's this all about?"

"I don't know. I'll go get them. Use my office for some privacy and I'll be outside if you need me."

As Rose stepped out, Claire sat down, crossed her legs, and nervously waited for the detectives to enter. Could this have anything to do with the attack on me? No, nothing that awful has happened in my personal life since that incident. What about my sister? Maybe something happened to Joy!

As Claire tried to figure out why she was of special interest to the police, the door opened and two detectives walked in. Guess I'll find out soon enough, she thought.

"Hello Claire. I don't know if you remember us. I'm Detective Pezello and this is Detective Green," one of the men said. "We'd like to ask you some questions."

Claire answered, "Yes, I think we met at a past inquiry. Have I done anything wrong?"

"No, absolutely not," Pezello replied. "We were hoping you could give us the information we need to solve a current case."

Claire felt weak with relief. "Are you telling me I'm involved in some police case?"

"No, but you may have some pertinent facts for us." Green took a cigarette out of his pocket and asked, "Is it all right to smoke?"

"Sure, it's not my office."

"All I'm at liberty to say is it's a murder investigation." He blew a puff of smoke into the air. It took the shape of a circle.

"I'm involved in a murder case?" Claire questioned.

"Don't get nervous, Miss!" Pezello took out the evidence bag with the business card inside, and handed it to Claire. "Do you recognize this?"

Claire held up the bag, inspecting the card, and replied, "Yes, this is our company card. I have many exactly like it." She was getting more confused than ever.

"Look," the detective said, "we found a card with your name next to the victim. Maybe you can recall who you gave it to?"

Claire laughed as she replied, "Do you know how many people I give my cards to? I couldn't even imagine where to begin." She suddenly broke into a light sweat. "Please, detectives, I'm feeling weak and uncomfortable."

"Oh, we didn't want to upset you. I'll get you a glass of water. That should make you feel better." Green ran to the water fountain, and returned with a cup of water.

"Thanks, but I don't think I can help you." Claire looked at the officers with a worried expression on her face.

"You don't have to answer this minute. Just think about our problem. Why don't you check your client list and see if you remember something?" Pezello handed Claire his card.

"All we're trying to do is gather some leads. Contact me if anything comes to mind."

As the detectives left, Green looked at his partner and said, "My money says that Claire Smith was assaulted by the same person who murdered Doris Walker!"

Claire was sitting on the chair, agitated, when Rose walked back in.

"You look upset. What the heck happened?" she asked.

"Rose, it's all about murder, and I may be able to help the cops. God help me."

"Claire, take it easy! What do they want?"

"It seems my business card was found next to one of the victims. How do I know who I gave that particular card to? It's like a jigsaw puzzle, or finding a needle in the haystack. What should I do?"

"Now I know why the detective asked me for one of our business cards. I'll help you. We'll get your client list and go through each profile; you'll remember eventually. Now I know you must be tired, nervous, and hungry. Let's get some Chinese takeout for lunch, and we'll go over the Goldman deal in the conference room. I think both of us could use something to eat."

"It's a great idea, Rose!" Claire answered, as Rose pulled out her menus from a drawer.

CHAPTER 30

As Billy eagerly jogged toward the hospital, he thought about Nick's idea. He was right, why couldn't I see it coming? End of story! Joy brought me bad luck, accusing me of knocking her up! Gray clouds gathered, and a chill in the evening autumn air made him tremble. So many things had happened in such a short time. I can't believe I'm finally confronting the reason for my existence.

If it weren't for my friend Nick, I would have gone after the wrong bitch. He is God! No one else! Nick taught me from the beginning that there are whores everywhere that must be eliminated. He accomplished that end; now I'm his disciple. I'll clean up the mess around this city. The more he thought about Nick, the more excited he got about killing Joy! He kept running, hoping the activity would stop the anxiety building up.

If I could only see Nick one more time, maybe he could show me those photos again to remind me how he killed those sluts. Who helped me when my hormones were going crazy? Nick! He always rescued me from myself. Now the time has come for me to pay him back. When I see him I'll explain how easy it was to slit Joy's throat!

She actually called and invited me up to her hospital room, then told me how much she loved me. Billy slowed down and laughed aloud. "Come see me, darling," she had said. Wait until she sees the present I have for her! He touched his right pocket and felt the outline of a knife. Nick, if you were only here to watch me in action, you would be so proud. Didn't I honor you by strangling all the whores in the past? They were only the seeds for future cleansing. But tonight is going to be my masterpiece; she loves me too much to suspect anything.

Billy calmed down, stopped running, and began walking quickly toward the hospital. As he reached 18th Street, he noticed a bar on the east side of the street. It can't hurt to stop for 10 minutes and recharge myself, he thought. I need a little booze to help me get through this night. Billy walked in and scanned the saloon. Seeing nothing or no one of interest, he walked directly to the bar.

"Anyone serving drinks here?" he hollered.

"Hold ya horses!" the bartender hissed. "What's ya big hurry, anyway?"

"I'm gonna do something very important, so I have a good reason to hurry."

"Okay, okay, give me a break. No one comes in here yellin' they want a drink! What do you think I am, a soda machine? Anyway, what are you having?"

"That's more like it. Gimme an Absolut, straight up. Make it two, one for good measure."

The bartender said nothing. He left Billy and returned with two drinks. "Well, what's so important?"

"I'm not in the mood to tell anyone my private business. Let me enjoy my drinks." Billy looked away and gulped down his first glass. "Wow," he said, "This is better than ever."

The bartender turned to Billy and said, "I made you a good drink, yes?"

"Sure," Billy answered.

As soon as he swallows his second, he'll spill his guts to me, the bartender laughed to himself. He waited while Billy began working on his second drink. He was getting tipsy and was in a talkative mood.

"Hey b-bartender," Billy said, slurring his words.

"Yeah, are you ready to tell me your life's story, and spill the beans?" he asked, wiping down the bar counter. They all get drunk and talk to me, he thought. Helps make the night go faster.

"S-spill the b-beans? What d-do ya mean by that?" Billy was getting drunk.

"I'm all ears," the bartender said sarcastically.

"I'm g-gonna clean up this city!" Billy roared.

"Should I give you a pail and mop?" the bartender laughed.

"A p-pail and m-mop? No way, man! I'm g-gonna kill all the whores in t-this city!"

"Sure," the bartender howled. "All by yourself? Do you want me to help ya?"

"I d-don't need no-one to h-help me." Billy stuttered. Didn't you read about the nurse that was killed? It was in the p-paper the other day. Th-that was me, I strangled her! And tonight I'm gonna k-kill m-my girlfriend!"

"What are you gonna do?"

"I'm gonna k-kill m-my girlfriend tonight!"

"What are you talking about?" The bartender thought these were the words of a drunken man who didn't know what he was talking about, but then again, why is he saying things like cleaning up the city and killing his girlfriend and a nurse? The bartender left the bar to replenish the liquor. He returned with several bottles of Scotch. He thought, I should call the cops, but maybe he's just talking through his ass. I better ask him some more questions.

Billy put money on the bar counter, got up, and trudged his way out of the bar. He was no longer sitting at the bar by the time the bartender returned. Where the hell did he go? I better do the right thing, he decided, as he dialed the police. If those murders really happened, then he could be the killer! When he explained the situation to the desk officer, he was transferred to Detective Pezello.

"Yeah, I'm a bartender at Charlie's Bar."

"What's your name and phone number?"

"Kevin Blue, 555-1234."

"Okay, what's the problem?" Pezello asked.

"I'm not sure. Something happened just a little while ago at the bar, and I can't figure it out."

"Do you want to tell me what happened, or would you rather come in?"

"First I'll tell you about the freak that came in for a drink. He looked innocent enough at first, but once he had a few drinks in his gut he spilled the beans."

"What do you mean, he spilled the beans?" Pezello was getting impatient, listening to the voice. He began fidgeting with the paper clips as he continued listening.

"He said he was going to clean up the city and kill his girlfriend."

Pezello blurted out, "Kill his girlfriend? Maybe the liquor got to him."

"Yes, but by the time I got back to the bar to ask him more questions, he was gone. Am I stupid for calling the cops?"

"No, no, you did the right thing. Did he say where he was going?"

"No, but our bar is on Twenty-first and Second. I don't know, he never said anything."

"Look, Mr. Blue. Thanks for calling us. We'll get back to you if we need anything further."

Detective Pezello put the phone back on the cradle, placed all the clips back in the box, and put on his thinking cap. Well, he thought, this call could mean nothing, but it could be a connection to the lover's quarrel--and the bar is near the hospital. I don't know yet. Better talk to Green; maybe two heads are better than one.

Pezello left his desk and walked over to another section of the station. On one side of the room all the suspects were lined up. On the other side, several desks were occupied by police officers, clerks, and detectives.

Pezello walked over to Green and said, "Do you have a minute?"

Green looked up, put his cigarette down, and answered, "Sure, what's up?"

The detective said, "A bartender just called with some information. A guy stopped in for a drink, and after a few shots bragged he was going to kill his girlfriend. Does that sound familiar?"

Green scratched his head, looked up at Pezello, and said, "It's a lead, isn't it?"

Pezello continued, "He said the guy didn't say where he was going, but the bar is on Second Avenue, and the hospital is a few blocks down. We should probably check into it."

"We definitely have a nut job walking around the city. I'll stop over and get a statement from the bartender," Green offered.

Green arrived at Charlie's Bar and got a description of the customer from Kevin Blue, the bartender. He then walked over to the hospital, where he was met by Pezello. As the two detectives entered the lobby, they just missed Claire and Betty, who were leaving from their visit with Joy. The two detectives made their way up to the third floor, where they approached Gene and Rena at the nurse's station.

"Good evening, my name is Detective Pezello and this is Detective Green." They flashed their badges as Pezello reached over the counter and shook Gene's hand.

"Yes," the nurse said. "May we help you?"

"Sure," Green replied. "We'd like to ask you both some questions."

Rena fidgeted in her chair and looked directly at the men.

"Are you always at this station?" Pezello asked.

"We're reassigned periodically, but, I would say yes, this is our station until further notice."

"Have either of you seen anything unusual?"

"Look," Gene said, "What's unusual? Lots of things happen here at the hospital. I think you need to tell us more information."

"The only thing I can tell you is we're working on a murder case. You would be helping the family of the victim if you could remember something." Pezello reached into the pocket of his raincoat and pulled out a card with his name and phone number.

"Is this about the nurse who worked at this hospital? Rena asked.

"Right," the detective answered.

"Doris Walker."

"Please try to remember everything you can about the victim. Every bit of information will help us catch the perpetrator. Keep my card and call us any time."

Suddenly Gene stood up and put the chart he was working with on the counter. "Rena and I know information that may have nothing to do with that murder, but since you are here, I should mention it."

"Let's hear what you've got." Pezello said.

"I feel stupid saying anything, but it's about a mother of one of our patients, who is extremely worried about her daughter's safety."

"Don't feel stupid; you never can tell. Mothers have good instincts. Could you tell us more specific details?" Green asked.

"It's really dumb. All about lovers fighting and the mother thinks the boyfriend is going to harm her daughter. I don't know anything else, except she asked both of us to keep an extra watch tonight. That's how worried she is. The girl is supposed to go home tomorrow."

Pezello asked, "What's the patient's name and room number? We'll look into it."

Gene answered, "Joy Smith; her room number is 304A. I don't know anything else, officers, but if I find anything out, I'll call." The detective wrote the information down in a notebook.

Gene looked at the card in his hand, then up at Rena. "There's never a dull moment at this hospital, is there?" They watched as both detectives turned away and walked toward the elevators.

There was an aura of serenity in the hospital as visiting hours ended. Nurses and aides helped patients retire for the night. Rena adjusted Joy's pillows for her comfort, "Is there anything else I can do for you?" she asked.

"No, thanks," she answered. "I'm hoping everything goes well so I can go home."

"If you have any questions, I'll be happy to help in any way possible."

"No, I'm fine."

"Now, are you sure you don't want tea?" Rena asked.

"No tea tonight, cold water is fine. Thanks anyway. You and Gene are wonderful. I'll always remember your thoughtfulness." Suddenly Joy thought of Billy and had a tense moment. She smiled at Rena and asked, "Could you bring me an extra pillow tonight? I'm a little stuffy."

"Sure," Rena answered, as she turned to leave the room.

Oh, will he come tonight? Joy grabbed the sides of the bed and squeezed hard. I hope I'm not sleeping when he gets here. I miss him so much! He can't help the way he is. It's my fault. I have no coping skills. Why did I overdose? WHY?

I had a bad relationship in the past with Jim. Maybe I need a shrink. That's it. I'm the one that needs help, not Billy, she told herself. At that moment the nurse brought a pillow. Joy said, "Thank you." She clicked on the television and watched the news.

"Sleep tight," Rena said, as she turned off the lights and left.

The hospital halls were quiet, and the lights were lowered for the night. Rena walked back to the nurses' station where Gene was attending to clerical work. He hardly noticed her returning. "How's everything going?"

"I just set Joy Smith up for the night." Rena looked at her watch and said, "So far, so good. Let's hope it stays that way. Maybe Mrs. Smith was overreacting. I'll feel more comfortable tomorrow when her daughter is discharged." Rena turned to all the paperwork on her desk and started to go through the stack.

The phone rang. Rena blurted out, "I'll get it."

"Hello, third floor west, may I help you?"

"Detective Green here. "Is Nurse Rena Schmidt around?"

"I'm Rena Schmidt. May I help you?"

"My partner and I decided to hang out at the hospital tonight. We got a tip from a reliable source that there could be an incident. We wanted to forewarn you to keep your eyes and ears open for anything unusual. Call us on our cell phone if there's trouble. Write our number down, 555-321-4040. We're not going anywhere."

As Rena wrote the number on her pad, Gene scratched his head, wondering what the long conversation was about. "Clue me in. What's going on?"

"Gene, the cops suspect trouble here tonight. I don't know the details, but we have to be alert and call them if something happens. They said an informer called them."

"Okay, but it's not like we didn't suspect something. Maybe Mrs. Smith was on the money. We'll know sooner or later."

*

While all the precautions were being taken inside the hospital, the subject of their suspicions was regaining his consciousness just a couple of blocks away. Billy's twisted body was wracked with pain, as he awoke on the cold concrete ground. He sat up and grabbed his legs. "Ouch!" he yelled. Suddenly he puked on the pavement and muttered, "The liquor did me in! How the hell did I get here?" Billy checked out the dark, dirty hiding place. What am I doing in this freaken place? This ain't her hospital room. Nick wouldn't have slept on the job! Hey, I gotta pull myself together!

Billy stood up, leaned against the wall for support, and slowly checked himself out. Okay, I'm not bad; the legs don't hurt so much now. Good, nobody could see me behind this tree. He pushed back his hair with both hands and straightened his shirt and pants. Billy grabbed his right pants pocket and felt the outline of his knife. The weapon was still there. "Great," he muttered, "I have what I need to do the job. Now I have to clean myself up."

He walked out of hiding, crossed Second Avenue, and shot a side-glance ahead at a coffee shop. A cup of java would hit the spot along with a good piss. Billy walked into the diner, went directly to the bathroom, used the toilet, and washed up. He looked at himself in the mirror, grinned, and said, "Get ready, Nick, just a little longer. You're gonna be proud of Billy."

Someone entered the rest room, surprising the aide. He stumbled as he glanced at the mirror and saw the reflection of a tall gray-haired man. A feeling of panic gripped him as he rushed to leave. Could he be a cop? I don't want to know why the guy is here, and I'm not waiting around to find out, he thought. He cracked his knuckles as he rushed out of the bathroom in a sweat. As Billy reached the serving counter and sat down, he yawned, exhausted, and ordered a cup of black coffee. The caffeine recharged his body and renewed his energy.

Billy left the restaurant and made his way to the hospital. He reached into his pocket and realized that he forgot his ID Badge. Shit! I can just slip in without anyone seeing me. He walked into the lobby and headed toward the elevator, stealthily walking along the walls so as not to draw attention. The aide wiped beads of perspiration from his forehead as he entered the elevator going up to the third floor.

So far, so good, he thought. If my good luck continues, it shouldn't take long to complete my job. As he neared the third floor, Billy felt his heart race. He clenched his hands and felt the tension build up. As the tingling started again throughout his body, he cracked his knuckles for relief.

Billy left the elevator and checked up and down the hall for the nurses on duty. I don't want them interfering with my plans, he thought. The halls were empty and quiet. The nurses were on the other side of the hall, busy changing shifts. Because of the detective's warning, Rena and Gene made arrangements with Dr. Roth to stay on the late shift.

Billy tried his best to be invisible. He slowly worked his way toward Joy's room, stepped into the darkened room, and saw Joy on her side fast asleep. He smiled, thinking how easy it was to fool everyone. No one saw me. I could slit her throat any time. Knowing the moment of truth was seconds away, he felt a strong sensation throughout his body, a feeling of euphoria. Nick always told me I could do the deed and one day I would.

As he walked toward Joy's bed and removed the knife, Billy laughed as he thought, this is the time and day. He couldn't control the shaking when he lifted his right arm, knife in hand, and removed the blanket with the other, intending to commit the act. "This is for Nick!" he uttered. As he was ready to thrust the blade into Joy's neck, he heard someone walk into the room. He couldn't complete the deed. The person's presence triggered Billy to draw the curtain around the bed. He hid and watched through the opening as the woman went into the bathroom for a trash pick-up. Joy stirred in her sleep; Billy's heart skipped a beat. He waited quietly. When the cleaning woman came out to check the trash near the bed, he grabbed her from behind and whispered in her ear, "This is what you get for interrupting me!"

The maid gasped for air and to his surprise, struggled like a tiger, grabbing his hands with hers, scratching him with her nails. She started to scream, but Billy covered her mouth with his left hand; then with his right hand he slit her throat. The woman lay sprawled out on the tile floor face sideways, bulging eyes still open, blood spurting everywhere. He whirled her around with bloody hands, eager to see her face and the results of his handiwork. Billy looked at her and shouted, "Nick, I did a good job! Wherever you are I know you're proud of me. Who was she anyway, just another whore?" He suddenly emitted a maniacal laugh as he kicked the corpse and wiped the knife on the victim's shirt. "Need to keep this weapon clean, just in case," he mumbled softly to himself.

After the murder he turned to Joy, knife still in his hand, ready to finish the job. As soon as he approached her bed, preparing for the deadly act, he heard a commotion in the hallway. Joy jumped up and saw Billy covered with blood, running out of the room. Shocked and terrified, she pushed the hospital alarm and screamed for help.

The commotion triggered Nurse Rena Schmidt to call Detective Green. Hunkered in nearby, the cops moved fast. They intercepted Billy as he ran down the hall. He looked straight ahead in a daze as he was captured without a struggle and handcuffed. "I failed you, Nick, I failed you. Please forgive me!" Head lowered, tears trickling down his cheeks, limp as a rag doll, Billy listened while Detective Pezello read him his Miranda rights. The detective turned to the noisy crowd of patients and staff and raised his voice: "Everyone clear the halls!"

While the cops attended to Billy, Gene and Rena tried to calm Joy.

"No! No! No!!" shrieked Joy as she suddenly realized what had happened. "He couldn't do that, No! No!" She grabbed her face in both hands and cried hysterically. Rena soothed Joy and waited patiently for her to recover, as Gene talked to hospital security.

CHAPTER 31

Betty obsessively cleaned and shopped, while she prepared for Joy's return home. I must have forgotten something!

Now Joy's pregnancy is something else we'll have to attend to. What is she going to do with a baby? It's ridiculous! She'll have to give it up for adoption. If she hadn't gotten involved with Billy, she wouldn't be in this mess! Betty yawned from exhaustion as her brain tried to sort things out. She put the teapot on the range, just as the phone rang.

"Hello," she said, as she sat down on the love seat and slipped off her shoes.

"This is Rena Schmidt. I'm the nurse attending to Joy at Beth David Hospital."

"Nurse? Hospital?" Betty asked, her voice rising with anxiety as she wondered why she had been called.

"It's about your daughter. She's fine; please calm down."

Betty's body stiffened, her brow wrinkled with worry, "Oh, my God! What happened?"

"Your daughter is fine, but there was an incident at the hospital. She's asking for you."

Lowering her voice, Betty replied, "Thank you, I'll be right there." She hung up the phone, grabbed her jacket, and left.

*

Claire sighed; Joy's illness distracted me. I forgot about my attack, but now the nightmare is returning. I won't rest until I see his face. She put her hands up to her head and pressed her temples to make the pain disappear.

Claire worked herself into a state of anxiety and zipped through her apartment, cleaning everything in sight. I have to do something to reduce the stress, she thought, as she scrubbed the floors and did her laundry.

My office woes are another concern for me. Will I ever close my deal? As Claire folded her clothes she wondered why Tony keeps following Rose around, asking her about the Goldman deal. There must be something going on between them. But I don't give a damn about them. I'm getting myself all worked up over this deal. I need time to think things through. I have to concentrate on my family. Joy's health comes first. She stopped a moment to relax and took a deep breath. Ah, that's better, she thought. Just then the phone rang.

"It's me."

"What's up Mom? You sound upset."

"I'm on my way to the hospital. The nurse called about an incident, but Joy is all right. I don't know the details, but she's frightened and needs us. I'll find out more information later. Meet me in her room as fast as you can."

"Okay." Claire hung up the phone, put her sweater on, and left for the hospital.

Betty stepped out of her apartment and hailed a cab. On the way she reviewed her problems. A mother's intuition is always right. No one would listen to me. I know who's causing the mess! It has to be HIM! I'm sick – sick -- of all the weeks I tried to warn everyone.

In the hospital, Betty hurried along to her daughter's room, anxious to find out what was going on. The halls were quiet. The earlier commotion had subsided since the cops had escorted Billy down to the police station, where he would be fingerprinted and booked on charges. The cops secured the crime scene and called the forensic team to examine the evidence. In order for this to take place, Joy was temporarily moved to another room.

When Betty arrived a the hospital room, a uniformed cop blocking the front door stopped her. "Could you tell me what's going on? I came to see my daughter, Joy Smith." The whole scene was frightening.

The officer said, "She was moved to Room 310. No one is allowed in this room until further notice."

"Thank you," Betty answered. She started to leave, then remembered Claire would be arriving soon. She turned to the officer and said, "My daughter, Claire Smith, will be here soon. Would you please tell her I'm in Room 310?"

"Sure," he answered.

Betty quickly found her way to Joy's new room. She saw the nurses standing along Joy's bed, while Dr. Roth examined her chest with a stethoscope. The doctor shot a sideways glance at the nurses as he scribbled on Joy's chart. "She has a slight temperature. "Give her Tylenol and 5 mg of Valium." He covered Joy with a blanket, and turned to Betty. "She's going to be okay, but don't plan on taking her home tomorrow. We can't discharge her while she has a fever."

Joy was still whimpering as Betty walked toward the bed and hugged her. "Honey, what happened that upset you so much?" Betty held her daughter close, stroking her head.

Joy didn't answer; she couldn't control the sobbing. "Mom, Mom, I didn't know, I didn't know." She began to cry hysterically again.

"What's going on in this hospital? Why is my daughter so terrified?" She looked at the doctor for an answer, as the two nurses stood by listening at the far end of the room. Betty turned to Dr. Roth, her body trembling and raised her voice, "Could someone please tell me what happened here?"

Dr. Roth answered, "Of course you should know. An intruder entered your daughter's room, intent on hurting her, but turned his rage on to someone else. Your daughter was spared!"

"What? Someone tried to kill my daughter!" Betty shouted.

"We had cops on standby, and they were able to arrest the killer. Your daughter is safe now," he told her.

"How can such a horrible thing happen in this hospital? Look at my child," she said, pointing to Joy. "She can't stop crying; she's in shock."

"Mrs. Smith, she'll be fine. It's over now; she's out of danger. I gave her a tranquilizer. She'll fall asleep, and when she awakens she'll feel better."

At this point Claire walked into the room and was surprised by the commotion.

"What's going on?" Claire rushed over to Joy and embraced her.

Claire whispered, "Hush, hush. I'm here, Joy." Then she turned to her mother expectantly, waiting for an answer.

Betty cried out, "There was a murder in Joy's room and she saw the killer! They think Joy was the intended victim.

Claire was shocked at her mother's words, "A murder!"

"I'm not finished," Betty hissed. "We're going to find out who caused this whole mess!" She turned to Dr. Roth for answers.

"We don't know yet," the doctor said. "You'll have to talk to the detectives about that."

Betty and Claire sat with Joy for a while, then went to the café while Joy rested. Betty turned her attention to Claire.

"I've been worried about you ever since you called me about that dream. How are you feeling?"

"Not good, the dream set me off. I feel as though I must know who my attacker is. I'm also anxious over my real estate deal. If I don't handle this right, it might fall through."

"It's no wonder you're upset. I suggest you visit a doctor who can hypnotize you. I just read an article about some victims getting their memory back through hypnosis. Maybe that will help."

"It's a great idea," she said, "but I'm scared. I guess not knowing is worse than seeing him again in my mind."

"I'll ask my doctor for a referral."

CHAPTER 32

Billy thought, my life was not supposed to end in the back seat of a lousy police car. All I wanted was to become Nick's messenger. So close, so close. If that bitch hadn't interrupted me, Joy would be dead.

If his hands weren't cuffed, Billy would have cracked his knuckles as he reflected on what could have been. Suddenly he emitted a piercing scream. The detective turned and covered his ears.

"Shut the fuck up, you lunatic," the officer yelled back and turned away, completely ignoring him.

When they arrived at the police station, it took both cops to pull Billy out of the car and lead him up the steps.

Green pushed the suspect forward. "Walk to that desk now!" he ordered. Billy didn't answer as he moved slowly toward the main desk.

"Stop here! This is where you're gonna be officially booked. Tell the officer your name, address, and which relative to call."

They were greeted by a sullen silence. Billy looked as though he were in a trance.

The officer held an ID card in front of Billy's face and demanded, "Is this you? Are you William Reilly?"

Green said, "Hey, answer him!" Complete silence.

Green said, "I don't get it. This nut screams like a lunatic in the car; and now he won't say a freaken word."

The admitting officer answered, "Don't worry. I'll get the information later from his personal effects. Why don't you get a sample of his DNA, take his fingerprints and mug shot? You read him his rights?"

"Yes," Green answered, as he guided Billy into another room. "What the hell happened to this loser? Not one word out of his mouth since we brought him in. He probably thinks that by pleading the fifth we can't get the goods on him."

"Maybe he's insane?" Pezello smiled. "Let's get him set up so I can interrogate him. He's entitled to a lawyer. Since he's not talking I'll call a public defender."

"Hey, you! Stand against the wall! You gotta have your picture taken." He guided Billy back, where his photo was finally taken. The suspect didn't say a word."

"Jeez, that's enough of the silent treatment, you bastard. Get the hell over there so we can take your fingerprints." Green was fuming.

"Get over here and gimme both hands!" Green grabbed both sets of fingers and pressed one finger at a time, down on to the inkpad. He finally got Billy's fingerprints for the record. "Now, get him to the lab for a DNA sample. I never arrested anyone as moronic as this asshole." Green turned away while Pezello led Billy to the lab and then into the interrogation room.

Green yawned. "It's gonna be a long night for Pezello. It'll take time to break him!" He looked at his watch, felt an urge for java, and decided to walk to the coffee machine. The detective sipped the coffee and bit down on a chocolate chip cookie. Good, hopefully the caffeine will wake me up, he thought. He surmised this was the calm before the storm. Oh, what a storm this dude is gonna create, based on his recent outburst. While I'm waiting around, may as well start writing up his report. I'll fill in the blanks later.

While he was thinking about the suspect, two women entered the lobby, walked to the reception desk, and spoke to the officer on duty. While Detective Green enjoyed his coffee, he wondered what the two ladies were up to. Hmm, they look like mother and daughter. He continued drinking. When he finished, he turned and observed the two women again.

Claire asked the desk sergeant, "My mother and I were told to come to this precinct in reference to an incident at Beth David Hospital. Could you direct us to someone?"

"I'll call Detective Green. He was one of the detectives in charge."

Betty and Claire waited and shot a sideways glance at Detective Green as he approached them. Betty spoke to the desk officer, "Thanks for your help."

"Hello, Detective Green." Claire shook his hand. "I don't believe you met my mother, Betty Smith."

"No. Hello Mrs. Smith.

"The officer on duty said you could help us."

"How can I help you?"

"There was an incident at Beth David Hospital tonight. The victim was attacked in my sister, Joy's room. The nurses told us you arrested him. Who is he? It's very important to us."

"Yes, we booked him. My partner is interrogating him now."

"What's his name?"

"We're not at liberty to disclose that yet."

"Did he say anything?"

"The guy stopped talking. He refused to give us any information. I think he actually couldn't. He looked like he was in a daze. I'll know more when my partner calls."

"Do you mind if we wait here with you?" Claire asked, hoping he would agree.

"I don't know how long the meeting will last. It could take all night. I suggest that you go home and relax. But you can wait awhile, if you choose."

"Thanks," Claire responded. "We'll wait. We appreciate your time and information."

Claire and Betty sat down in the waiting area. Both were satisfied their questions would soon be answered. Betty was exhausted, so Claire took charge of ordering food. Claire turned to her mother and said, "Don't worry, we'll know everything soon. Have patience!"

Green felt apprehensive as he waited for Pezello's call. He decided to return to the interrogation room where he could at least observe what was happening through a two-way mirror. He thought about having the mother and daughter identify their suspect, but decided to deal with that later.

As he looked through the mirror, he thought, I don't like what I see. It looks like it's gonna be a long night for all of us.

Billy sat in the chair staring at the cop, eyes glazed, not a sound uttered.

"When the hell are you gonna give me answers -- where you live and work?" Pezello's blood pressure was hitting a high point.

This is easier than I expected, Billy thought, I can fool them all. He sat frozen, his brain on overload. If I deceive the cops and they think I'm nuts, I won't go to prison. They'll put me in the nuthouse. If only I can convince them I'm crazy, they'll keep me locked up for awhile. Then I'll finish my job for Nick. Yes, no matter where she is, I'll find the whore and kill her. I gotta do it for Nick and prove to him I could do the job. I can't stand living with failure.

Pezello scratched his head in disbelief, looked at Billy, and said, "All right, just your name. Nothing else!"

Still no response: just stone cold blue eyes staring straight ahead.

"Stubborn bastard!" Pezello yelled.

Pezello decided to call for assistance when he realized he couldn't get information. "Look, stay here with him until I return. I think we've got a problem."

The detective turned to look at Billy. He was still staring into space. Pezello left the room and headed toward the lobby area where he knew Green would be waiting. He didn't have to walk too far, since Green was just outside the two-way mirror, peering in.

"I'm not getting anywhere with this guy."

"What did you expect? We knew he was nuts when he screamed in the car. Who the hell knows what's going on with him? -- Oh, this is Kevin Blue, manager of Charlie's Bar. He's going to identify the subject... Well Mr. Blue, do you recognize our suspect?"

The bartender took a closer look through the two-way mirror, turned to the detectives and said, "Yes, he's the guy I saw. I heard him brag about killing his girlfriend."

"Thanks, Mr. Blue...You could leave now!"

After the bartender left, Green said, "We have the right guy, but we can't do anything yet."

Pezello answered, "Okay. Just put him in a holding cell for 24 hours to cool off. Let's not waste valuable time. The only ID he carries is a social security card with the name William Reilly."

"Good, that gives us something to work with," Green said, as he blew a puff of smoke and watched the small circles scatter.

After waiting at the police station for a couple of hours, Claire turned to her mother and said, "I think we should leave. Tomorrow we'll visit Joy and bring her home."

Betty agreed, but worried, "We'll miss something important if we leave." She held her head and massaged her pounding temples. "This headache is driving me crazy. Do you have some Tylenol in your purse?"

"Just a sec. Yes, I do," Claire replied. She removed two tablets and gave them to her mother.

"I'll be back in a minute, dear. I need some water."

Betty went to the water cooler, returned, and downed the tablets with her cup of water.

"Mom, before we go home why don't we find the detectives and ask them for an update?" Claire outlined fresh color on her lips.

"Now I feel a little better." She looked at her mother for a signal.

Betty replied, "Let's do it. I can't stand being non-productive." Claire grabbed Betty's hand and they started to walk through the corridor. They were immediately stopped and questioned by a uniformed cop.

"Just where are you ladies going?"

"We want to see Detectives Green and Pezello," Claire answered.

"They're indisposed."

"But we've been waiting so long!"

"Can I help you?"

"Sorry, they know us and have the information we want."

"Leave a number and they'll call you."

"Thanks, let us be the judge," Claire said, as she and Betty began walking through the hallway, hoping to meet up with both detectives.

"There they are," Claire said, pointing to Green and Pezello walking toward them. Claire greeted Detective Green.

"I'm so glad we caught up with you. Maybe you know enough now to give us some information?"

"I'm sorry," he answered. "But we can't give out any information pertaining to this case. We're currently in the process of gathering evidence. I suggest you both go home." Pezello fidgeted next to Green and nodded his head in agreement.

Betty and Claire showed their disappointment. In a sarcastic tone, Claire said, "Thank you both. At least we know as much as we did five minutes ago. How do we find out more about this case? After all, my sister was involved and was almost the victim."

"I understand, but there's nothing we can do to help you. If information gets out before all the evidence is in, the suspect may destroy the evidence or alter his story." Pezello and Green said their goodbyes, turned, and headed back to their offices.

Claire and Betty hailed a cab, slid into the seats, and settled themselves. "Mom, I can't remember ever going through such a horrible experience. When is this all going to end? Imagine leaving the police station without any information about the murder.

"You're the one always thinking positive. Why change at this late date? Let's go home and get some sleep. Anyway, I don't think the doctor is going to discharge Joy tomorrow. She must be stable first. I'll call Dr. Roth in the morning."

Betty said, "Driver, please let me out at Third Avenue and 70th Street." She turned to Claire, "Do you want to sleep in my apartment tonight?"

I can't. I really need to stop at the office. Rose has been so patient. I have to get ready for the Goldman meeting. I can't drop the ball on this deal. Don't worry; I'll try to see Joy before she goes home. See you tomorrow, Mom. Love you."

"I love you too, honey. I'm going to see your sister early tomorrow, too."

As Betty left the cab, Claire said, "Please, my stop is Second Avenue and 75th Street."

"Sure," the driver answered. Claire's frustration peaked as the cab crawled along in the heavy traffic, to the accompaniment of honking horns. She closed her eyes and contemplated, I have so many decisions to make about family and business. I hope I have the energy to move forward and make the right choices. Of course, my first worry is Joy's good health and quick recovery. It was horrible for a murder to take place in her room. I hope the cops will solve the crime.

Still meditating, Claire turned her thoughts to the Goldman deal. If it comes through, we'll all be better off, she thought. I hope nothing happens to ruin it.

"Hey, lady, is this your stop?" The cabbie turned around to awaken Claire from her reverie.

"I'm sorry. Yes, it is. Thanks!" She paid the driver and stepped out of the cab. A light rain was falling as she walked toward her building. She entered the lobby, walked to the elevator, and wondered … Damn it! Who needs this? She reflected; there's so much I have to deal with: Joy, the Goldman deal, the baby, and the murder. The more she thought about everything, the more anxious she got.

She went into the elevator, rode up to the apartment, opened her door, and flopped down on the sofa.

After the two ladies left, Green pondered a bit. "You know Pezello, those two got the wrong idea. Why should we give them any info?" He lit a cigarette and dragged the smoke deep into his lungs. As he exhaled, Green watched circles of smoke move across the office.

"The daughter was a target. They weren't around when the murder took place, but it took place in her hospital room. I think they had a right to ask questions," Pezello continued. "But you're right; we can't tell them anything when we haven't completed our investigation. Look, Green, why don't you start checking the suspect's social security number? His whole life might open for us when we start a search. I'll keep trying to contact Jerry Colin, the public defender. So far he hasn't called back."

"Great idea; I'll talk to ya later. While you're working on him, I'll begin checking for evidence. Her blood was all over him, so it shouldn't be hard to put the pieces together. That proof alone could put him away. While I'm at the hospital, I'll question the intended victim. She saw him when he tried to escape."

Pezello scratched his head as he replied, "You never know, she could have freaked out, so she couldn't see or remember a thing. I would question her anyway; she might have gotten a good look at him. Look, I've gotta go now. Call and let me know what happens." He turned away from his buddy and walked back to his desk.

"I'll talk to ya later," Green raised his voice, as he buttoned his raincoat and walked toward the exit. He threw the cigarette butt on the floor, stepped on it, and wondered what to do first. Finally they had a suspect! They just might solve this and other killings. Well, I'll start with the lab like I planned.

Green walked quickly toward the medical lab in the police station. The faster I get to the lab, the quicker I'll know whether the blood work was completed. Maybe I should have called first. Oh, well, too late now. I'll make a bet with myself; no results yet. Hope I'm wrong. He kept walking until he finally entered the lab through large swinging doors. Jeez, what a smell! I don't see anyone. He looked around the room and yelled, "Is anyone here?"

A technician came around the side of the lab and answered, "Yes. How may I help you?"

Green flashed his badge. "I'm Detective Green, assigned to the William Reilly case. Is the blood work completed?"

"I work on so many cases. Gotta go back to my office and check my records."

The detective said, "Okay, why don't you do what you have to do? I have several other details I could attend to. When should I return?"

"Give me at least an hour."

"Great," Green responded, as he left. Just enough time to interview a couple of nurses at the hospital. On the way there, he received a call from his partner.

"You were right about checking out our suspect's social. He works at Beth David Hospital!"

"What great timing! I'm on my way there now to interview witnesses. Now I can get the goods on Reilly. Thanks, partner!"

When he arrived, Green approached the receptionist, flashed his badge, and said, "Could you give me some information?"

"Yes," she replied.

"I need to speak to whoever is supervisor of your employee William Reilly."

"That would be Penny Gayte. She's in the office down the hallway on your left."

He smiled and said, "Thanks for your help," then walked toward the office, knocked on the door, and walked in.

"How can I help you?" Penny asked.

"I'm Detective Green. I remember you from my last visit," he said.

"Yes, you questioned me about one of our nurses who went missing and was later found dead. Was that case ever solved?"

"Not yet, we're working on it. But I'm not here concerning the nurse. This is about someone who works at this hospital. What do you know about someone named William Reilly?"

"Billy is an orderly in this hospital. I give him his daily assignments. He hasn't worked for a few days. Did something happen to him?"

"No, I'm just trying to fit some information together. Anything out of the ordinary you could tell me?"

"Well, he's worked here for about five years. He's generally well liked, but he's not too reliable. He's often late, and lately, he's been calling in sick a lot.

"Has he ever been reprimanded or placed on probation?"

"No, he generally keeps to himself, but he can be rude or disrespectful, nothing major. He really gave me a hard time once when I asked him if he was getting dressed up to go out on a date."

"Okay, thanks. This is helpful. Who else can I talk to about this Billy Reilly?"

"Rena Schmidt, you'll find her at the nursing station on the third floor, right in the middle of the hallway. She's usually teamed up with a nurse named Gene. And he works a lot with Dr. Wang. That's all I know."

"Thanks, I'll find my way up there after I take care of some other business I have." Green left the office, looking at his watch. Damn, he thought, I just have time to get back to the lab.

CHAPTER 33

The murder was too much for Joy to bear. She was in a state of shock from the incident, shaking and crying simultaneously. The nurses did all they could to comfort her.

"Gene, I've tried everything; I told her the police arrested the guy, but nothing helps. We need Dr. Roth."

"Please!" Joy screamed. "I saw the man, but I can't get his angry face out of my mind. What did he do? Why?" She grabbed her head and squeezed tightly. "I need a pain-killer. PLEASE!" Joy trembled, cried, and finally put her head down on the pillow.

Gene called Dr. Roth. "We need to give Joy Smith a sedative. She's hysterical."

"Okay," the doctor answered. "Give her 5 mg of valium IM."

Rena covered Joy with a blanket and straightened the pillows.

Gene added, "Just relax. You'll feel better when you wake up." He gave Joy an injection, and she finally fell asleep.

Dr. Roth arrived and checked Joy's vitals, "Keep an eye on her," he said. "She's been through a trying experience. Call me when she wakes up."

Rena said, "Do you think I should call her family?"

"No," the doctor answered. "This should quiet her." They watched Joy for a moment; satisfied she was resting and calm. Dr. Roth turned toward the elevator and went back to his office. As he left, he turned to the nurses and said, "A patient in Room 300 needs your attention. Please look in on her."

"Sure," Gene answered. They left Joy's room and continued on to Room 300. When they checked the patient, she was asleep. Everything seemed fine, so they continued on to their station.

199

"Boy!" Gene said, "I don't think this is over yet. You'll see. The Smith family is not finished with this mess."

"You're probably right."

"I wouldn't be surprised to see the patient's family walk down the hallway. They're really overprotective and controlling. I hope they let her have a good night's rest."

"Don't be critical. They are very caring."

It wasn't Joy's family making their way down the hall, but a man.

"It's after visiting hours; her family wouldn't come at this hour." Rena said.

As the man approached, Rena recognized him as Detective Green. She smiled, "Hello Detective Green. How can we help you?"

"I need information. Do you know Billy Reilly?"

"He works at the hospital, and is sometimes assigned to this hallway," Rena answered.

Gene added, "I sometimes see him bring patients up to their rooms. Actually, there were some nights that I'd catch him sneaking around the hallways, as though he were looking for someone. Never really caught him doing anything I should report."

"That information could be helpful. Is there anything more you can remember?"

Rena added, "I don't know if it's related, but one of our patients is in major trauma because of the attack in her room. Do you think he was involved? Maybe she could tell you something."

"Can I speak to the patient now?"

"No, she's sleeping. I'll call when she wakes up."

"Okay, I'll check with you later." The detective waved, left the nursing station, headed for the cafeteria, and phoned in to his partner.

"Pezello, it's Green. I just spoke to the nurses here. I think Joy Smith may know something about Reilly. She was in the room and there's a good chance she can identify him as the killer. She's under sedation now, but I'm gonna stick around and get to her as soon as she's awake."

After Pezello hung up, he thought about the possibility of his partner's success. If Green comes up with evidence, it won't matter if this guy never talks. He considered that and smiled, as he headed back to question the suspect. Hell, he thought, a little tuning up can't hurt. We'll see if I can't get him to open up. Pezello entered the interrogation room, where a cop stood guard near Billy, in the same position as the day before.

"Did he say anything today?" Pezello asked.

"No sir. He's just sitting in the chair, same expression on his face."

"Okay, you can leave. If I need you, I'll call on the intercom."

As the cop left, Pezello approached Billy and stared into his ice blue, expressionless eyes.

"Why were you in the hospital room, and why did you murder that woman?"

Once again there was no reply from Billy. He didn't move a muscle. Pezello was frustrated. He walked up to Billy and kicked the chair. "Answer me, you bastard! You're not gonna get away with murder, not while I'm in charge!"

Billy didn't know what hit him, as he fell backwards onto the floor. What the shit? He can torture me; I won't give in!

The detective grabbed Billy by his shirt collar. "Talk, you son-of-a-bitch, speak!" His face turned beet-red as he screamed. The suspect didn't budge an inch.

This shithead thinks he's gonna ruin my life? He's got another guess coming. He's getting nothing from me. If I control myself, I'll get what I want, the nuthouse. Do whatever you want, Mr. Cop. I'll never answer you or anyone else.

While Pezello was grabbing Billy's collar and threatening him, the door opened and another detective walked in, intervened, and quickly stopped the abuse. The cop turned to Pezello and said, "Hey, calm down. You can't knock him around like that. Let's go out in the hall and talk."

As they walked out of the room, Pezello shook his head. "I guarantee there's nothing wrong with him. He thinks if he stonewalls me he's off the hook. All he understands is strength and power. If you treat him like a pussy you'll get nothing."

"Yeah, but there's a limit to the shoving around and ill-treatment you can do."

"Look, if you wanna work on him, it's all right with me. I can't stand looking at his puss anyway. When my partner returns, we should have more evidence. We already have plenty of DNA evidence that the lab is working on." The detective scratched his head as he replied,

"There's gotta be a better way to handle this lowlife." He looked through the two-way mirror at Billy sitting in the chair expressionless. "You have a lousy job on your hands; just don't kill him. I'm going. You can continue, your way."

Pezello looked up as the cop left and muttered, "I'll be damned." He walked back into the interrogation room, looked straight at Billy and yelled, "Get ready. We're getting the goods on you! You'll go to prison for the rest of your life." He stepped away and called for an escort to take the suspect back to the holding cell.

The detective watched the guard direct Billy from the room. On the way out, the suspect stared into the detective's eyes and smirked.

Jesus, those eyes gave me the chills. "Something's gotta give soon," he muttered. Pezello left the room and headed toward the coffee machine.

CHAPTER 34

At the hospital, Detective Green asked Nurse Schmidt about Joy's status, and then decided, "I'll wait around for the patient to wake up. She must've seen something that could be crucial to our investigation." Jesus, this could be the lead I've waited for. Better call the lab and tell the technician I may be late. The girl's story and the lab report could put the suspect away for life. He picked up the phone and made the call.

The detective walked to the coffee machine, put coins in, and pressed the coffee and cream button. As he sipped, he murmured, "I'll buy some cake, too. The caffeine and chocolate will keep me alert." He put more coins into the machine, pressed the button, then walked to a table with his snacks, sat down, and savored the food.

This new information has my attention. So far we haven't got a Goddamned lead anyway. As he bit down on the cake and drank his coffee, he decided to call Pezello. The phone rang several times before Pezello picked up.

"Pezello here."

"It's me, Green."

"What's up?"

"Any results yet?"

"No, have you?"

"Not yet. She's still sleeping."

"Stay with it. She may be a vital witness. I have nothing to report about the interrogation. He doesn't talk or move a muscle--made of iron. Nothing seems to trigger him to talk."

"Well, let's hope the lab report helps. If it does and the girl's report stands up, we'll have enough evidence to put him away."

"Okay," Pezello answered. "Reilly is back in the holding cell. I finally talked to the D.A. He's reviewing the case; then he'll advise us. Reilly is scheduled for arraignment tomorrow. We're off to a good start. Keep in touch."

"Sure, sounds like things are headed in the right direction. I'll let you know if something turns up." Green hung up and thought about what he could possibly learn from the patient. He thought again about the credit he and Pezello would get if they solved this case. Suddenly, Nurse Schmidt approached him. She spoke rapidly, in a subdued voice.

"Detective Green, the patient you're waiting for just woke up. If you want to question her, do it now. She's very edgy after her ordeal; we don't know how she'll react. The sooner you question her, the better chance you have to get straight answers. Go to Room 310A."

"Thank you," Green said, as he followed the nurse through the hallways. He heaved a sigh and thought, I'm grateful to Sweet Jesus for getting me to this patient's room. Now I have to pray she doesn't fall apart when I talk to her. She must have gone through hell!

The nurse stopped the detective before he entered Joy's room. "Please remember that the patient is in a very delicate condition; she's pregnant. I'll wait at the nurse's station until you complete your questioning." As the nurse left the room, Green looked at Joy propped up in bed with two large pillows behind her head. What a beautiful young woman, so young to be in a hospital and to have witnessed a murder.

He approached Joy's bed, flashing his police badge, "I'm Detective Green. Pleased to meet you, Miss."

"Yes?" Joy uttered in a small voice.

"I don't want to upset you, but the nurse told me what you've been through. It must have been a horrible scene. Can you remember any part of that night? It would be very helpful for our investigation."

"I don't remember very much because I was in such a deep sleep. I didn't see anyone do anything. By the time I woke up, it was over. I was so scared. I don't remember the murderer's face. All I saw was blood. I'm so sorry I can't help you more."

"Are you sure you didn't see his face?"

"I was too frightened to look. All I did was scream!"

"I thought you saw the murderer's face and hands covered with blood?"

"No I didn't, no I didn't, no I didn't. NO I DIDN"T!" Joy began to get hysterical. "I don't want to talk to you anymore."

The nurse came running when she heard Joy's shouts. "It's over, Detective. I was afraid the questions could trigger this reaction."

Tears began to trickle down Joy's cheeks. "I tried, really I tried, but I can't remember anything about that terrible night." She wiped her face with a tissue, but she couldn't stop crying. "Could you please--I want to go home!"

The nurse tried to calm Joy. "Try to rest, I'll tell the doctor to call your family. Maybe that's what you need, family around you." She turned to Green.

"Detective, please leave. Hopefully you were able to get some answers. She may be going home tomorrow, so I don't know if you'll have another chance."

"I'm sorry I upset her. I couldn't get any information. Seems she was too shocked to remember anything. I'll leave now. Thanks for trying to help."

Green left the room disappointed with Joy's interview. Too bad she was so damn upset and didn't remember a thing. Her testimony could have helped our case. We'll manage without her, he thought. Well, maybe I can still get to the medical lab before it closes.

He arrived at the medical lab, hoping he was not late for his appointment. Maybe I'll get lucky.

"Hey," Green greeted the technician. "Is the report ready?"

"Yes," he answered. "I'll be back in a minute."

"Fine," the detective answered, pacing back and forth, hands in his pockets. The detective pulled out some papers and the evidence bag, when the real estate card fell from the bag to the floor. He bent down, picked up the card, and saw Claire's name. Then it clicked. Why hadn't he put this together sooner! Claire and Joy Smith are sisters! What are the odds? He put it back in his pocket, another piece of evidence to investigate. His concentration was interrupted when the technician returned. He handed Green a pen and clipboard, before giving him the package and said, "Sign here."

"Of course," the detective replied. "Thanks for your help."

The cop found a chair in the waiting room where he would not be disturbed. After reading a few pages of the report, the detective tapped his forehead with the binder and stated, "Holy Shit! The DNA of the blood taken from the hospital floor is an exact match with the blood found on the aide. According to the lab report, Reilly's DNA also matched skin found under the nails of Doris Walker, a nurse killed a few weeks ago. The real estate card was found next to her body. It all fits in like a puzzle. His DNA also matches the evidence found on the Alana Stone victim. If that wasn't enough, the hair sample found on the Lilly Moro victim also matches Reilly! Jesus! William Reilly is a serial killer! I wouldn't be surprised if there are more victims out there. "Wow, this is a bonanza! With this technical proof we can put him away for good."

"Man, I can't wait to tell Pezello the good news!"

CHAPTER 35

Claire was unable to stay asleep for more than a few minutes at a time. I saw the outline of my attacker's head, but not his face or the weapon. When will I be rid of those visions? Now the thought of Joy as a witness to a murder! I can't imagine her panic at the time. Then the police interrogation! When will it end?

As she awoke to the shrill sound of the alarm clock, Claire's body quivered as she reacted to the noise. She yelled, "Ouch," as a spasm in her left leg triggered a sharp pain. Stretching the muscle and exercising her leg a few minutes relieved the discomfort.

Okay, she decided, time to take a shower and get ready for a busy day. She moved quickly while deciding what to wear, walked to the closet, and checked her wardrobe. "The black slack outfit and white blouse will be fine." She dressed quickly and began applying her makeup. After she applied mascara to her lashes, she looked at herself in the mirror and murmured, "Not bad, considering what I've been through." This whole mess is taking a toll, she thought. I don't know how my mother is surviving this ordeal. Every time I think about Joy, my heart aches. Claire shook her head. "Who would believe my family is involved in a murder case? But now I have to hurry." She knew Rose would be in the office early, preparing for the Goldman meeting, so she dialed her...

"Hi, Rose. It's Claire."

"Hi, Claire, where are you? You sound terrible."

"Rose, you can't imagine what happened since I spoke to you last." She coughed and sounded tired.

"Don't make me hold my breath."

"I'm sorry. I didn't mean to do that. Last night there was a murder in Joy's hospital room!"

"You're serious--a murder? Is Joy all right?" Rose shouted.

"Can you believe such a horrific thing like that? We're all in shock, especially my sister. We spent most of the night at the hospital and police station."

"First of all, I'm so sorry you and your family are going through this tragedy. God, it wasn't long ago we visited you in the hospital, now it's Joy. Did they catch the killer?"

"Yes, but we don't know who it is. The detectives aren't releasing any information yet."

"Claire, is there anything I can do to help?"

"No. Everything is under control. I'm still a bit shaken, but I'll be coming in for the meeting."

"Okay. You take your time and I'll see you soon."

Rose hung up, shocked and shaken by the bad news she had just heard. She tapped on the desk with a pencil and thought about Claire. She looked up and saw Tony walking across the room. I have mixed emotions about Tony and regret the day I met him. What should I do? He's a great sales person, an incredible lover, and has brought in many deals, but he's a traitor and one day he'll destroy me and my business. The best thing to do is confront him! Claire is right, why the hell should he get a piece of her commission? He didn't do a damn thing to deserve it.

"Tony, how are you?" Rose asked sweetly.

"You know!" he answered coldly, placing both hands on her desk.

"You are not cutting in on the Goldman deal," Rose told him firmly. "And I don't appreciate your unethical conduct. I suggest you drop the matter."

"I don't give up so easily," he said. "You promised, and I intend to keep you to your promise."

"I did no such thing," she said. "May I remind you that if there is nothing in writing, it didn't happen? May I also remind you about your ethical duties as a realtor? Not to mention that I am the boss who makes all final decisions."

Tony turned red, started to say something, then just stormed out of the office.

Rose picked up the phone and dialed Claire. "Claire, I know I told you to take your time, but how quickly can you get in?"

Claire replied, "Rose, you sound upset. What happened?"

"I'll tell you when you get here."

"I'm on my way."

Claire picked a black leather purse, placed a black and white paisley scarf around her neck, and left the apartment. As she got outside, her cell phone rang.

"Claire, it's Mom."

"Hi Mom, is everything okay?"

"Yes. I just want to tell you that I just got a referral for a doctor who specializes in hypnotherapy. I was able to get you an appointment for 4:00 this afternoon. Is that okay?"

"Yes. But I'm in a rush right now. I've got to get the office and prepare with Rose for the Goldman deal. Can you phone me at the office in an hour with the information?"

"Sure. So you can make it at 4:00?"

"Yes. Call me in an hour."

"Okay. Maybe we can meet for dinner after your appointment and go to the hospital together"

"Sure."

Claire hung up and hailed a cab to the office.

Rose greeted Claire with warmth and affection when she returned to the office. "Anything new on your sister?"

"She could be better. I don't know how long it will take Joy to recover. She'll never be the same and now that she's pregnant, we're all on edge. Rose, I don't know what to do. My mother is a wreck. I hope she doesn't give herself a heart attack. With everything going wrong, it's amazing that my deal is going right. We could use the money; Joy's hospitalization is costing a fortune."

As Claire headed back to her desk, Tony entered the office. When he saw Claire, he walked toward her with ice-cold eyes blazing. Rose watched from the sidelines as she carried a mug of tea from the kitchen, waiting for the volcano to erupt.

"Well," Tony said. "You finally remembered to show up at the office. Everyone knows you have a job here, but maybe you forgot?"

"Tony, I don't answer to you. You have no right to speak to me like that."

"For your information," Tony smirked, "When your deal closes I get a percentage of your commission. There's nothing you can do about it. Ask Rose, she'll tell you I helped out with your deal while you were in the hospital." He stood at attention, hands on his hips, and looked her straight in the eyes.

"I don't think so. You won't get one red cent of my money. And if you do anything funny to try to collect it, I'll take you to court, and you'll lose your real estate license. It's against the law to accept a commission you never earned."

"You wouldn't have the guts to hire a lawyer!" Tony shouted, as the office staff listened.

"Just wait and see!" Claire yelled as she ran past him and left.

He turned to Rose and said, "What about that promise you made to me? And those discussions we had while Claire was in the hospital?"

"I told you over and over again. I never made you any promises, and your name is not on the listing contract. Having a discussion about a deal is not the same as working on it, and neither is trying to steal the deal away from this office. It won't take much for a judge to confiscate your license. I don't think you want to lose your job, do you?"

"Rose, you disappoint me. I thought you were on my side. We could celebrate with all that money."

"Look, I don't want to be with you anytime, anyplace. Lying for you puts me in jeopardy and makes you look pretty petty. Now leave me alone! Get back to work and don't cause any more trouble in this office! On second thought, don't return to work; you're fired!"

Tony was in shock and couldn't even respond. He left the office defeated, wondering what he should do next. I'm not getting involved with any lawyers, he thought. Screw her money! I can live without it! What bitches, both of them! Now I have to start over finding a new job! At least I still have my license.

With Tony out of the picture, Rose and Claire settled in as the

Goldman's arrived with their team. They were agreeable to all of the suggestions presented, but then added a list of their own demands. All of these concessions would be costly! Rose suggested a swap of sorts.

"I'll tell you what, we can reduce the commission by two percent if you drop the interior painting." The Goldman's lawyer whispered with his clients and then counter offered.

"How about splitting the cost of the painting?"

"How about reducing the commission by one percent?"

At this point, Mr. Goldman cut in:

"We're arguing over trifles. Let's be honest. We want the property, and you want to make the sale. Out of our list of concessions, why don't we each pick the three most important ones and drop the rest. No more haggling!"

This put the negotiations on a different footing, and three hours later, the parties had a list of agreed-upon terms and a tentative date to sign the contract.

After Goldman and his team left, Rose and Claire sat and reflected on their successful efforts.

Claire looked at her watch and realized she had her scheduled appointment with Dr. Gorden, the hypnotherapist.

"Sorry, I can't stay and celebrate, Rose. But I've got to run."

"I understand. With everything going on, you go ahead. Call me and let me know how your sister is doing."

Claire picked up the information her mother gave on the doctor and jumped in a cab.

*

She arrived at the office and walked into a waiting room filled with patients. Darn! How long will I have to wait in such a crowded room? Now I'll get to the office late, and there are so many things I have to discuss with Rose. As Claire considered all these questions, she heard her name called.

"I'm here!" she said, standing up. She followed the nurse to a back consultation room.

"Ms. Smith, the doctor will be in to see you shortly." The nurse smiled as she left the room; Claire waited.

Why am I feeling so jittery? This isn't the first time I've seen a doctor, but it is the first time I'm visiting a shrink. Quiet down, maybe something good will happen.

"Good afternoon," the doctor said, as he entered the room.

"Good afternoon," she greeted him. She shook his hand and smiled.

"From the brief outline you completed, it appears that you are trying to remember something in your past?"

"Yes, I was attacked a few months ago, and I can't remember the attacker's face. I guess I locked away what actually happened that night. If there's a way you can help, I would appreciate it."

"I'll try hypnosis. This treatment has been successful in releasing hidden thoughts, but it works only if the patient cooperates. Sometimes my clients fight my attempt to help them. In that case it's impossible for me to succeed."

"Doctor, I'll do my best to help. Then I can go forward in my life. Can I begin today?

"Yes, please move to the chaise in the corner."

Claire did as she was told. She sat down and faced Dr. Gorden, waiting for instructions.

The doctor sat on a chair next to Claire and started the session. "Lie down on the sofa and let your body relax completely. Remove all negative thoughts from your mind."

"I'm feeling a little tired."

"That's fine. Please don't talk; just listen to my voice. Focus on the palm of my left hand and I will talk you into a hypnotic state. When we finish this session, I'll clap my hands three times, and that will signal you to wake up. He spoke quietly in a monotone voice. Do you understand what I'm saying?"

"Yes, I do." She focused on the palm of his hand and closed her eyes.

"You are very tired, so tired you cannot open your eyes. You are slowly sinking into the first phase of a hypnotic state. Breathe deeply –

sink into the sofa. Now I'll ask you a few questions. You just finished your dinner back on that fateful night. Do you remember where you were?"

"I showed my client a loft building and decided to have dinner in town." Claire fidgeted as she reclined on the sofa, her eyes closed.

"Good, look around the restaurant. Did you see anyone watching you?"

"Yes, I noticed a man. It made me nervous."

"And when you finished dinner?'

"I paid the check for my food and started home."

"What direction did you choose?"

"I walked downtown toward the subway. The wind was blowing hard and all the leaves were flying in different directions. It was very dark and I felt cold. I couldn't wait to get to the train."

"Are you at the steps of the station yet?" The doctor watched Claire closely, since he noticed her body tense up. He thought how well the patient was doing and waited for her response.

"I was freezing," Claire shivered. "Why didn't I wear some warmer clothes, or at least have a shawl? I saw the steps of the station. Thank goodness I was almost there."

Now will she be strong enough to remember the moment he attacked her? As the doctor pondered the question, Claire almost sat up on the couch and in a loud voice said, "I was walking down the steps of the train station and heard lots of noise from the trains coming and going. I was almost at the bottom. Oh, oh. I realized I forgot to call my boss and let her know how things went. Hello, Rose? OH- OH--God! Who are you? What are you doing? Get away from me! Get away from me! Help! Help! Anyone, please help me!"

The doctor knew it was time to wake her up. She was going through the assault at that moment. He clapped his hands three times.

"Claire, wake up! Remember I told you to wake up when I clapped my hands three times?"

"Yes, doctor, I'm up, I'm up! She sat up, rubbed her eyes and looked at the doctor, her body trembling.

"Well, did you see his face?" He sat, apprehensive, hoping she had.

"No. I saw a man but I couldn't see a clear face." She tried to compose herself.

"Claire, we'll need another session. We've come a long way, but it's only the first time. Come here again in a few days. Stop at the desk and make an appointment."

Claire asked, "Is it possible I can come in tomorrow?"

Dr. Gorden hesitated a moment, then responded, "Actually, that'll be okay. I'll see you then."

Claire made a new appointment for the next day at 11:00 a.m., and left the office, hopeful that the next visit would be a success. She waved down a cab and headed to the Garden Café to meet her mother for dinner.

CHAPTER 36

Still emotional from the intensity of hypnosis, Claire pondered, what if I had stayed under a little longer? Maybe I would have seen him. She made a decision, one more office visit. Claire looked at the time and realized she was meeting her mother in 15 minutes. She continued walking up Second Avenue and arrived at the Garden Café. She knew her mother would be anxious to know the result of her session.

Betty arrived, and after the waitress took their dinner order, Claire first talked about the success of the Goldman deal closing, and then discussed her visit with the hypnotherapist.

"Mom, I'm glad you referred me to Dr. Gorden. He helped me review the night of my attack. I came close to seeing his face. One more time should do it."

"That's good news. The faster you learn the truth, the sooner a burden will be lifted."

They ate quickly. Claire paid the check, left the restaurant and hopped in a cab to the hospital.

Joy was still whimpering when Betty and Claire arrived at the hospital. They understood the magnitude of what Joy went through and tried to calm her down with loving words of encouragement.

"We understand it will take time to put the memory of what you saw behind you. Claire and I will help you through it," Betty sighed, as she stroked her daughter's hair.

Joy grabbed her head and squeezed hard, "I'll never forget the blood splattered all over him – no, no no!"

She almost lost control again and Claire tried to help her sister forget.

She said, "When you're feeling better, I have so much to tell you."

Joy looked up at her sister and said, "You know how I love to hear your stories. Especially the ones about your real estate successes."

She was feeling better and nodded for Claire to continue.

"Well, my deal is closing, and we're going to celebrate when you come home. Dr. Roth said as soon as your fever is normal, he will discharge you. It could happen tomorrow."

"I'll keep my fingers crossed," Joy said, "I want to go home."

Betty softly said, "Rest, my darling, and you'll be home before you know it. We have so much to be thankful for. Your being safe is most important, and of course, Claire's deal closing. Last, but not least, when the final verdict of guilty is rendered, and the suspect is put away in prison, we'll all feel much safer."

Joy turned to Claire and said, "Didn't you have more news for me?"

"Yes," Claire answered, "I went to a hypnotist, and he's helping me figure out who assaulted me. One more visit should bring positive results. Now I think you should get some rest. Mom and I will go home."

Betty and Claire said their goodbyes, kissed Joy and left for the night.

*

After a good night's sleep, Claire felt prepared for her session with Dr. Gorden. She dressed quickly, ate her breakfast, and left the apartment. When she arrived at the doctor's office, Claire sat down, picked up a Good Housekeeping magazine, and flipped through it while waiting for her name to be called.

"Claire Smith," the receptionist said. Claire stood up and walked to the nurse waiting at the door.

"Please follow me into the consultation room. The doctor will be with you shortly."

Claire sat down on a chair and waited patiently.

"So good to see you again, Ms. Smith," the doctor said, as he shook her hand. "Please follow me to the chaise in the corner. Lie back and make yourself comfortable." She did as he suggested and waited for further instructions. She knew from the last session, to relax completely and wait.

In a monotone voice, the doctor said, "Let your body rest, think positive thoughts, and stare into the palm of my left hand. Listen to my voice and let yourself sink into a deep sleep." The doctor counted to five and waited for Claire to go under. Assured she was hypnotized he said, "When I clap my hands three times you will wake up. Do you hear me?"

"Yes, I will get up when I hear you clap three times."

"Sleep, you are in a deep sleep. Go back to the night you were attacked. You were finished with dinner when you noticed a man watching you in the restaurant. He made you feel uneasy, so you paid for your meal and left."

"Yes, I remember walking toward the train station, anxious to get home." She was in a deep sleep, but heard everything the doctor said. "If only I had worn my coat; I'm so cold. Look at all the leaves flying around. Who's walking there? Just a young couple. Not much further to the station. I should be there in a minute or two."

Dr. Gorden knew that it wouldn't be long before the stabbing. I hope she sees her attacker this time!

Claire continued, "I'm walking down the steps of the train station. I should call Rose; I promised to call. Someone is rushing down the steps. There's a man with a knife in his right hand coming toward me!" She screamed, "Billy!!"

When Dr. Gorden heard her cry out, he clapped his hands three times. "Wake up, Claire!"

"I'm up! I'm up," the patient responded.

When Claire settled down the doctor gave her a glass of water and asked, "Did you see the perpetrator? You mentioned the name Billy."

"Yes, I did. I can't believe it. I saw his face. I know who attacked me!" She began to cry. "Billy! It's Billy," she moaned. "I know him. He's my sister's boyfriend," she said. "Doctor, you can't imagine what you've accomplished. I finally know the truth and now I can help answer many questions about a very sick man."

Dr. Gorden was pleased with the result of this session, happy to help another patient. Claire left the office, relieved that the hypnosis was successful. It was Billy all the time, she thought. My poor sister!

Claire went right to the police station to inform the detectives of this new revelation. When she arrived, she was informed that both detectives were unavailable. She left a message with the desk sergeant for one of them to phone her and then left the station.

*

After an exhausting night, Detective Pezello stared at Billy in frustration. The interrogation throughout the night yielded no results. *Will I have to beat the shit out of him before he utters a word? I didn't think he would last this long without breaking. Just look at him cracking his knuckles. I caught him doing it at least ten times; I'm accomplishing nothing. He may as well go back to his cell before we bring him before the judge. After the arraignment, he'll be transferred anyway, and I'll be finished with him.*

Pezello picked up the intercom and asked the guard to escort Billy back. The break would give him a chance to grab a sandwich and coffee.

The detective walked down to the lobby and stood in front of the vending machines. He laughed; *which machine would give me a steak and fries? Sure, sure, I'll settle for peanut butter and jelly on rye and a large cup of coffee.* Pezello sat down on the nearest chair and devoured his food. He was thinking about his partner when his cell phone rang.

"Pezello here."

"It's me."

"Jeez, I was just thinking about you, waiting to hear what happened."

"Hey, I did good. I have the lab report. It proves Reilly is a serial killer. A sample of the DNA from the blood on his hands matched the aide he murdered. His DNA also connects him the three other murders. This evidence could put him away for years. I'm damn exhausted now."

"Great news, let's put it all together so the DA can have it for the arraignment.

CHAPTER 37

Gene answered an emergency call from Joy's room.

"What's the problem?" Gene asked. The aide shouted, "STAT, I found the patient lying on the floor unconscious!"

Rena and Gene raced to the room and saw Joy lying on the floor in a pool of blood.

Gene turned Joy over. "Good God, what happened to her?"

"Call Dr. Roth, too much bleeding; I think she's losing the baby!"

Rena checked her vitals as Gene paged the doctor.

"I'm on my way," Dr. Roth answered.

The nurses cleaned the patient and made her comfortable. They worked fast and prepared Joy for the procedure.

Dr. Roth examined her thoroughly. "She's having a miscarriage! Get her on the gurney; they're waiting for us in the O.R. What happened?"

The aide said, "She pressed the buzzer, and when I arrived she was on the floor. She must have tried to get off the bed and slipped!"

Dr. Roth continued, "One of you call her family and let them know what happened. She's going to be fine. Tell them not to worry."

The nurses switched Joy on to the gurney. Gene said, "I'll get her to the O.R.; you call her family." As Gene wheeled her to the O.R., he whispered tenderly, "May your guardian angel look after you and keep you safe. I'll be saying a prayer for you too, baby." That was all he cared to admit of the attachment he was beginning to feel for this patient.

The nurse called Betty and told her what had happened.

All Betty could answer was, "Yes, yes, I'm coming!" Her nerves on edge, she hung up and called Claire. "I just got a call from the hospital. Joy had an accident!" Claire heard muffled cries.

"An accident, what happened?"

219

"Sh-she wouldn't tell me the details, just that she'll be fine and we should get there immediately." Upset and overwrought, Betty sobbed.

"Mom, calm down! I'll meet you in twenty minutes."

"Don't worry, I'll be fine." Betty dried her tears and left for the hospital.

They arrived at the nurses' station at about the same time. Claire hugged her mother.

"Nurse Schmidt?' Claire asked at the desk.

"Yes," the nurse answered."

"What happened?"

"Your sister tried to get off the bed and fell. She lost the baby. I'm so sorry. She'll be fine after the procedure."

"She's having a procedure?" Betty gasped and grabbed a chair to steady herself. "Why wasn't I told?"

Rena explained, "There was no time. She was bleeding too much, but I did call you immediately. Why don't I take you both to the waiting area? Mrs. Smith, I'll keep you updated and let you know when the procedure is completed."

Claire embraced her mother tenderly. "Don't worry, Mom. Joy is a survivor. Now she can start her life over."

"Good luck to you and your family." Rena said. "Hope everything works out well for everyone." She turned away and left them.

Claire looked at her mother and said, "You'll see, Joy will be fine and all she's been through will be like a dream."

"I hope you're right. It will be a new beginning for us all. I can't wait to see her."

Betty looked at Claire and said, "While we're waiting, why don't you tell me the truth? You've been putting me off long enough.

"I don't know all the answers yet, but when I'm certain, I'll tell you everything. You're anxious, and so am I. That's why I want to talk to the cops. After I discuss what I found out and they do their job, I'll tell you everything. I promise."

They sat, holding hands, both in deep thought, when a nurse came to tell them that Joy was out of surgery and they could see her.

CHAPTER 38

Billy's arraignment resulted in his being charged with four counts of first-degree murder. He was transferred to the municipal jail, without bail while he awaited his trial.

The guard opened the cell door to check on him. The suspect pointed to the toilet.

"So you have to take a leak, do ya? I'll wait out in the hall while you do your business, then I'll check the cell. Don't take a year!"

Billy relieved himself and smiled. Jesus, I almost peed in my pants. Funny, that damn guard looked familiar, as though I knew him in my past. How could I have known someone like him? He laughed at the thought.

Reilly spent the rest of the day in his cell, getting familiar with his new surroundings. He heard a siren screech, signaling that dinner was served. When the cellblock was unlocked, Billy followed the guards and other prisoners to the dining hall. As he stood in line filling his plate, he noticed a man who looked like Nick. His heart skipped a beat, and he blinked to make sure it was him. No, he thought, I must be seeing things. Billy calmed down and felt less threatened. He continued taking food, then walked to a seat and commenced eating.

After dinner all prisoners were required to shower. The guards escorted a group of men back to the bath area. Billy stepped into the shower and put his towel on a rod. He was not aware that he was being watched by Manny, a huge bald-headed prisoner with a round puffy face, and tattooed body. Manny's muscles showed off years of weight lifting. He smiled, thinking of Billy, as he stalked his prey. The guys were right when they pointed him out, knowing that he liked slim men with blond hair and light eyes. He thought about what it would be like to have his way with him. The image made his body shiver and sexual desire explode, as he stealthily made his way to the shower next to Billy.

Damn, Billy thought, as he removed his clothes and turned on the hot water. As the water splashed down on him, he couldn't help thinking about disappointing Nick. If I ever get out of this mess I'll find Joy and kill her! He was so angry he began cracking his knuckles, then grabbed his head with both hands and squeezed tight. The water felt good running down his body.

A guard yelled over to the prisoners, "Awright, let's get moving. Five more minutes." He then stepped out of the shower room, as the prisoners started filing out.

Billy finished, turned off the faucet, and was getting ready to leave, when Manny suddenly pounced on his victim, pinning him against the back of the shower wall. He was so turned on, moaning in ecstasy, as he pressed against Billy. Suddenly, Billy swung around and threw a knee into his attacker's groin. The other prisoners on their way, stopped to watch the spectacle, as the guards charged back in.

The fat man fell to the ground in agony as the guards stepped between the two prisoners. As Manny was being dragged away, he yelled, "Your ass is mine, punk!"

Billy couldn't stop shaking as he thought of the man trying to take sexual advantage of him. For the first time he thought, "I know ... I know the truth. Nick put him up to the assault. How else could the fat man find me? Nick wants to murder me! He's never forgiven me for not finishing the job. He sent that monster!" Billy slumped down against the wall sweating, trembling, and cracking his knuckles. Slowly he forced himself up, dried his body, and began dressing. He couldn't get the incident out of his mind. Images of the fat man's face appeared.

"Hey, are you ever coming out?" the guard yelled. He walked back again. This time he saw Billy putting his shirt on.

"What's with you?" the escort asked.

Billy knew how to keep his mouth shut.

"Well let's get a move on, back in line with the others."

The prisoners returned to their cells.

CHAPTER 39

As the orderly and nurse transferred Joy from the gurney to her bed, Betty and Claire walked into the room. The patient slowly opened her eyes, smiled, and gazed at her family.

"Hi, honey," Claire said as she hugged her sister. "You're going to have a quick recovery."

"Don't worry, my darling, we're here," Betty said. She kept her feelings in check, since she knew Claire wouldn't approve of an emotional outburst. Joy closed her eyes again and fell asleep.

Claire's cell phone rang and she stepped out to the hall to answer. "Hello," she murmured.

"This is Detective Green. I'm returning your call."

"I can't talk here. I'll come down to the station."

"Good," he answered.

Green hung up, turned to Pezello and said, "Claire Smith is coming in."

"Okay," Pezello answered, "but what could she offer us that would be compelling to a jury? We already have DNA evidence without her testimony."

"When she comes in we'll find out."

Claire turned to her mother and said, "Mom, I have to leave you and Joy now."

"Where are you going?" Betty asked curiously.

"I left a message at the police station for the detectives. One of the cops called back and I'm going to the station."

"Do you think I should come too?"

"No, you stay with Joy. She needs somebody with her.

"Joy seems awake now. Pamper her. I'll be back soon." She left the room.

At the police station Claire met with Detective Green.

"Come in," Green said.

She walked into the room, went straight to Green's desk, smiled, and shook hands. "Thanks for your time."

"Please sit down and tell me what you know."

"I was having nightmares after my attack. My mother suggested I see a psychiatrist to help solve my problem. I took her advice. When I began the treatment, he put me under deep hypnosis. I saw who my attacker was!"

"Yes, continue, please."

"I saw Billy Reilly as clear as I see your face. There's no doubt about it."

"That's very interesting, but how does it relate to all the murders?"

"I don't know. Maybe you and your partner can figure out the connection. He was my sister's boyfriend. Doesn't that tell you something?" She heaved a sigh of relief, having given him the facts.

"Thanks for the info. We'll call if we need you." Green stood up, said "Goodbye," and waited for Claire to leave. He was anxious to share the news with his partner.

As soon as Claire left, Green hurried to Pezello's office. He wondered what this new fact would mean in light of the evidence stored away.

"What's up?" Pezello asked, as he turned toward Green entering the room.

"Got five minutes?"

"Fire away," the detective answered.

"You won't believe the lady's information. She's Joy Smith's sister, who survived her own stabbing a few months ago. The killer's face vanished into her unconscious. When she went for treatment to a hypnotist, she actually saw her attacker--who turned out to be William Reilly, our main suspect. What do you think?"

"Wow! She actually saw William Reilly under hypnosis! I don't think the jury will take hypnosis seriously and it will probably be thrown out as evidence, but I wouldn't worry about it. We have plenty of proof that will stand up in court. Don't say a word to the lady. I doubt we could use her information. It just points another finger at the guy we're holding. We have to be patient and wait for his day in court."

"You're probably right. I wish we could finally close the book on him. He certainly is a strange one. Has gotta be the weirdest suspect you ever tried to interrogate."

"I'm calling it quits for today. Why don't you go home and get some rest too? Maybe tomorrow will be a better day."

CHAPTER 40

Ever since the shower incident, Billy couldn't forget the fat man. He tried to distract himself by reading and exercising, but nothing resolved his fears. He finally flopped down on his bed, trying to forget. Why me? How do I know that fat pig won't attack me again?

He slept the afternoon away, dreaming of Nick.

Billy yelled, "Nick! Is it time to punish me? Nick in the dining hall, sending the fat man to kill me. What else? My nerves are shot. How can I continue this daily routine, live every day like this? I need my day in court; I need to end it all!" He sat up in bed, his body shaking; then he cracked his knuckles until the guard banged on the cell bars and hollered, "Don't ya hear the siren? Get going; you're holding up the works! Get ready for chow."

Billy just stared blankly as he slowly stood up from his bed. He washed his hands, and left the cell with the guard at his side. He joined all the others on their way to the dining hall. The jailers followed, ready for any confrontation. As he turned and looked toward the other side of the hall, he thought he saw Nick again. Then he turned the other way and saw Manny walking toward a table a few feet away.

Reilly walked toward the food line, heart pounding as he spotted the fat man, staring at him with a grin on his face. He knew Manny was up to something and that he'd better watch his back. His body stiffened with fear as he prepared himself for the worst. There was lots of noise around him. His paranoia deepened as he realized he was right out in the open where he could be attacked from any direction. His eyes blinked, as he looked everywhere.

He filled his plate and walked slowly to a table where he joined some other prisoners. They ate without saying a word, since Billy never went out of his way to become friendly with anyone. Billy looked up from his plate and saw the fat man smiling at him, and drawing his finger across his throat, as a threatening signal. Suddenly, a commotion erupted across the room, as two prisoners were fighting. As the guards rushed over to intervene, the other prisoners stood up and started throwing plates, cups, and utensils, as a riot ensued. Billy was frantic, as additional guards came quickly to surround the troublemakers, clubs in hand, whistles blowing, and sirens blaring. In an attempt to stop the upheaval, the guards used their clubs, striking the men involved.

Panic struck Billy and paralyzed him with fear. He didn't know where to turn. He knew he had to get out of there and started to head toward the exit. As he weaved past other prisoners running in all directions, he suddenly found himself face to face with Manny. Without hesitation, the fat man thrust a knife into Billy's gut and lifted it up, as he smiled. As Billy dropped to the ground, Manny disappeared among the other rioting prisoners.

Someone yelled, "Man down!"

The hall quieted down as a guard fired a shot toward the ceiling. With their weapons in hands, the guards surrounded Billy, as he uttered his last words, "Nick, I know I disappointed you. I should have killed her. Please, give me another chance. Forgive me for not finishing the job!" A rattle in his chest, blood dribbled from his mouth and seeped from his body; his limbs began to jerk uncontrollably. Then nothing!

"What's he saying, what's he saying?" someone asked. The guard who was leaning over, answered, "I don't know what he's talking about. He called me Nick. My name ain't Nick. The guy's nuts."

Later at the police station, Detective Green walked over to Pezello's desk, and said to his partner, "You're not gonna believe this."

"What happened?" Pezello replied.

I just got a call from the jail. Someone stabbed Reilly in the mess hall. No one knows why."

Pezello said, "The Smiths will be relieved to know William Reilly is dead. Case closed! Hope they can rest better now. But now I'm so damn tired. I'm going home to sleep it off.

CHAPTER 41

"Finally a great day," Betty said happily, as she brushed her hair. Joy is coming home. We can celebrate her homecoming, along with Claire's big deal. I'll bring dinner, pepperoni pizza, and Joy's favorite, chocolate fudge cake for dessert.

The ring of the phone interrupted her reverie.

"Hi, Mom," Claire said. "You'll never guess the amount of the check: $30,000, when it comes through. I can't believe it; we can celebrate big time!"

"Oh, my goodness," Betty yelled.

"And guess what else! Rose finally fired Tony. No more skunks in the office," she continued breathlessly, "and Rose introduced me to a new client."

Betty silently issued a prayer and said, "Claire, I'm so happy for you. Now I must go to the hospital to bring Joy home. Call me later."

"Sure, sure, but in the meantime I have to return a call from Detective Green."

The secretive nature of the inquiry annoyed Claire. She brushed her hand through her hair as she realized, we've been left out of the loop. I hope the cops are finally willing to share information with us. As she relaxed in her apartment, she realized the investigation could affect her health. Why do I feel fluttering in my chest lately? I noticed it ever since I started going to Dr. Gorden for hypnosis.

I'm going to relax, she told herself. She stepped into the shower and let the hot water run down her body. How good it feels! She finished, stepped out on to a floor mat, and dried herself. Claire thought about her appointment the following morning with Detective Green.

I think it's about time my mother comes along. She's been through an emotional merry-go-round too. After I exercise I'll call her and then get in touch with Rose. She's been an angel, not badgering me about coming to the office. I must also reconfirm the closing date. She calmed down a little, thinking it was all worth waiting for. She thought about her share of the commission, and all the bills on her desk waiting to be paid.

Claire called her mother---no answer. She must have gone to the hospital, Claire thought. Then she tapped in her office number.

"Field Realty," Rose answered.

"Hi, it's Claire."

"I've been thinking about you and your family."

"Joy is coming home from the hospital today. She's recuperating nicely. Rose, I called to thank you for being so patient with me. The police are close to solving the case. We'll know more details tomorrow."

"Hopefully your problems will be resolved. You and your family deserve to resume your lives."

"Thanks for your good wishes. Is everything all right at the office?"

"Things are a little quiet these days without Tony. Thank goodness he's out of our hair."

"It's a good thing he saw the handwriting on the wall and backed down."

Claire smiled to herself at the idea of Tony's defeat.

"Good talking to you; keep in touch."

"Same here, I'll let you know what's going on. I can't wait to return to work. It's the best medicine for me. Goodbye."

Claire decided to take a long walk to the police station. She jogged up Second Avenue and finally approached the building. As she entered the reception area, she pondered, I hope the cops have enough evidence to put that bastard away for a long time!

She asked a cop on duty, "Detective Green, please. I have an appointment."

Green met Claire and walked her to his office.

"Won't you please sit down? You'll need to be seated when we talk."

"What are you trying to tell me, detective?"

"There was an incident in the cafeteria of the prison. William Reilly was stabbed to death. That's pure and simple. He's dead! No trial, no jury, no nothing! We're closing the case. That's why I called you. It's over!"

"I don't believe what you're saying!" Claire grabbed the edge of the desk for support. "Wh-what happened? Who killed him? Why?"

"The information we got was that one of the inmates at the prison stabbed him. That's all we know. You and your family will be able to live in peace from now on. Go home and tell your family the killer was punished and it's over."

"I guess it's really over for all of us. I should feel happy, but I don't. There was no real justice; no trial, jury, or verdict. One thing though, justice did prevail in a different way. He got what he deserved! I'm going home to tell my family this sick story."

She got up from her chair and left Green's office. All she had on her mind was going home.

As Claire sat in the cab reviewing the discussion with Detective Green, she couldn't believe it was true. I must concentrate on the positive things in my life. Thank goodness the Goldman deal came through. Depositing the check in the bank is something I can look forward to. I feel as though the success I am having in the real estate field helped my family and me. The commission I earned will pay our bills and give us a good life. It's all a blessing, especially Joy's coming home from the hospital, so we can all be together again!

Made in the USA
Lexington, KY
18 April 2015